PRAISE FOR

THE WAR OUTSIDE

A *Publishers Weekly* Best Book of 2018

A 2018 BCCB *Bulletin* Blue Ribbon Title

A 2019 YALSA Best Fiction for Young Adults Pick

A 2019 Notable Social Studies Trade Book for Young People

A 2019 Notable Book for a Global Society

"Once again, Monica Hesse delivers an incredibly compelling and beautifully researched novel. *The War Outside* vividly brings readers into an underrepresented and dark period of American history. A must-read for fans of historical fiction." —Ruta Sepetys, #1 *New York Times* bestselling author

"Monica Hesse...takes a setting we think we understand and shifts it in an important way....A tightly plotted exploration of the consequences of fear." —*The New York Times Book Review*

★ "Superb....A satisfying and bittersweet novel, perfect for those who enjoyed Markus Zusak's *The Book Thief.*" —*SLJ* (starred review)

★ "An extraordinary novel of injustice and xenophobia based on real history." —*Booklist* (starred review)

THE
WAR
OUTSIDE

THE
WAR
OUTSIDE

MONICA HESSE

LITTLE, BROWN AND COMPANY
New York Boston

Little, Brown and Company
Hachette Book Group
1290 Avenue of the Americas, New York, NY 10104
Visit us at LBYR.com

Originally published in hardcover and ebook by Little, Brown and Company in September 2018
First Paperback Edition: October 2019

Little, Brown and Company is a division of Hachette Book Group, Inc. The Little, Brown name and logo are trademarks of Hachette Book Group, Inc.

The Library of Congress has cataloged the hardcover edition as follows:
Names: Hesse, Monica, author.
Title: The war outside / Monica Hesse.
Description: First edition. | New York ; Boston : Little, Brown and Company, 2018. | Summary: Teens Haruko, a Japanese American, and Margot, a German American, form a life-changing friendship as everything around them starts falling apart in the Crystal City family internment camp during World War II.
Identifiers: LCCN 2018005733| ISBN 9780316316699 (hardcover) | ISBN 9780316316705 (ebook) | ISBN 9780316445238 (library edition ebook)
Subjects: LCSH: Crystal City Internment Camp (Crystal City, Tex.)—Juvenile fiction. | CYAC: Crystal City Internment Camp (Crystal City, Tex.)—Fiction. | Friendship—Fiction. | Japanese Americans—Evacuation and relocation, 1942–1945—Fiction. | German Americans—Evacuation and relocation, 1941–1948—Fiction. | Concentration camps—Fiction. | World War, 1939–1945—United States—Fiction.
Classification: LCC PZ7.1.H52 War 2018 | DDC [Fic]—dc23
LC record available at https://lccn.loc.gov/2018005733

ISBNs: 978-0-316-31671-2 (pbk.), 978-0-316-31670-5 (ebook)

Printed in the United States of America

LSC-C

10 9 8 7 6 5 4 3 2 1

For my strong Iowa grandmothers, Coral and Marjorie

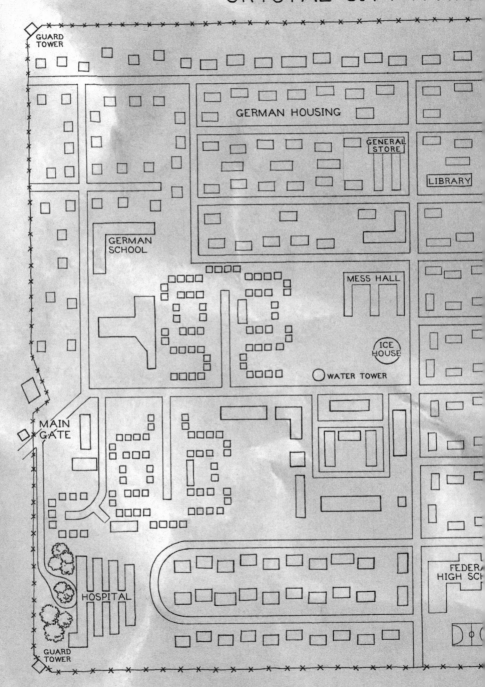

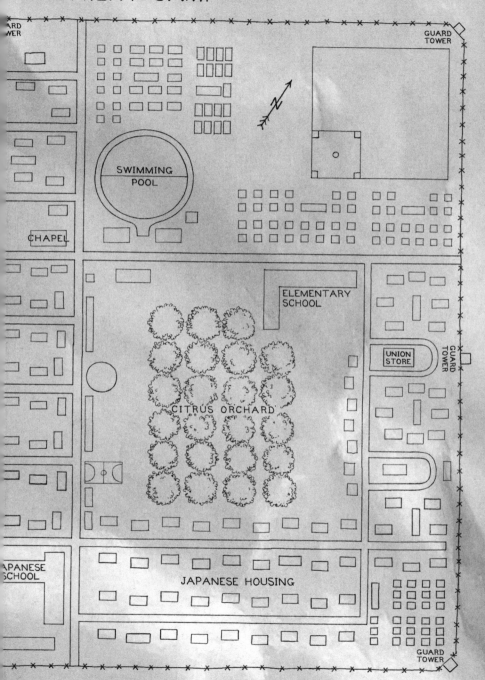

HARUKO

Of all the things that happened there, in that place full of enemies and dust and spies and sadness; of all the things Margot said to me—the calculations that sounded like friendship, the casual shattering of my life—out of all those things, I am grateful for only one: that I never loved her. If I had loved her I couldn't bear any of it, and so I am grateful for this lack of love, this one remaining thing I can bear. Because even if it's a terrible thing to have, if I didn't have that, I'd have nothing.

MARGOT

If Haruko said that, she was lying.
She did love me. I loved her too.

ONE

HARUKO

"I WISH WE WERE ALL HOME NOW," TOSHIKO WHISPERS, AS IF I'LL have a different response than I had the last time she said the same thing. She pokes my side to get my attention, which she knows I hate. But I stay serene because it's part of our unspoken pact, my sister and me, that we're polite because we're too afraid to be anything else. And because we promised our mother.

"Your little sister is not your enemy," Mama told me the last time Toshiko and I argued, which was the first time I learned about Texas. "I know that," I said meaningfully, and then I didn't say anything else because I didn't want to talk about who the real enemy was.

Now my mother sits across from us, wedged beside our stack of suitcases, keeping her back straight so her hat doesn't get crushed against the seat of the Pullman car. Her eyes are closed. I can't tell whether she's sleeping or train-sick, a kind of sick I didn't know existed until we got on the train and people started making retching sounds into the paper bags provided by the guards patrolling the aisles. For more than a thousand miles now, that hat has been pinned to my mother's head. Everything else in the car is wilted: her dress, my dress, my sister's entire body, pressing against mine as I decide not to respond to her last statement. Instead I lean my forehead against the window. Brown grass. Brown dirt. Dirty horses, ridden by men with bandannas over their noses across land that is unbearably flat.

The last time I saw Denver, the sky was clear enough to see all the way to the tops of the mountains.

"Haruko." Toshiko pokes my side again, below the rib cage.

"Helen," I correct her.

She rolls her eyes. "Everyone here is Japanese. They can pronounce your real name."

I will myself to keep looking out the window instead of glaring at Toshiko. "My friends call me Helen."

"About five people ever called you Helen."

We're becoming testy at the edges, not just my sister and me but the whole train, exhausted by three days of politeness and stale sandwiches. My head is pulsing with the screaming rhythm of the train's motion. It aches in my jaw, in my teeth; my nostrils are filled with oil and smoke. I cover my nose and try to take fewer breaths.

"Helen." Poke, poke. "Can I look at the letter again?"

I want to tell her no, not because I'm trying to provoke her but because I hate the letter. My mother has heard Toshiko's question, though, and opened one watchful eye to make sure I do what I'm asked. She loves the letter; they both love the letter.

The letter has an official stamp and a return address explaining the people who sent it are from the Department of Justice of the United States of America. I take it out of my handbag and hand it to Toshiko, who unfolds it reverentially. What does she think will happen if she tears it? They won't let us in? The whole point of the letter is that they won't let us out.

Dear Mrs. Tanaka,

You are informed that your application for reunion at a family internment facility with your husband, Ichiro Tanaka, has been approved. Please be informed that the only individuals accommodated through this agreement are Mrs. Setsu Tanaka (age 44), Miss Haruko Tanaka (age 17), and Miss Toshiko Tanaka (age 12). Arrangements will be made for such a reunion at Crystal City, Texas.

Crystal City. We are going to a place called Crystal City. I'd put faith in the name at first, because it leads you to believe you are going somewhere beautiful. A place where there might be a reason to pack nice things. My best dress. My new handbag. My bottle of Tabu perfume.

The train has other families on it, and we've gotten to know some of them.

Mrs. Ginoza and her little daughter, from Los Angeles. Old Mrs. Yamaguchi from Santa Cruz. Families with stories that sound exactly like each other's except for a few details. My mother still politely listens to everyone else's even though she must know by now how they will end: *And then we got on this train.*

We were sitting down to dinner; the FBI men didn't let him finish the meal.

They said it was because we were hiding Japanese correspondence. But it was letters from my mother-in-law that we saved in a hope chest. How could that be hiding?

We knew an attorney, but he said there was nothing he could do; it's all legal. President Roosevelt issued a proclamation.

Even now, I can hear my mother retelling our own story to the bride across the aisle, the one whose husband was taken two days after their wedding.

"They came on a Saturday morning when Ichiro was still at work and they sat in my kitchen until he came home," Mama is saying. "They wouldn't let me telephone him, in case I used a code to tell him to stay away. We had to wait for hours; my husband was staying late to help a guest arrange a hiking tour. He was always staying late to take care of things. The men said he was using his job to pass information between guests traveling overseas."

She leaves so much out of this story. She leaves out the fact that the Albany, where my father was a night clerk, was the nicest hotel in the city. That some of the guests were Japanese, but most of them were white, and they liked my father, and sometimes brought us gifts from places they'd traveled. Paper fans from Paris, a snow globe from New York City. She leaves out the fact that the governor came in once, and that my brother sold his secretary an orange soda in the hotel's pharmacy, and I gave her the straw to drink it with. Governor Carr's secretary told me I had lovely American dimples, and Kenichi and I spent the next week elaborately reenacting this scene as we mopped the floors at the end of the day. "Am-*er*-ican dimples are fine, I suppose, if they're all you can get," Ken would say. "Though I prefer my dimples to come from *France*."

Somewhere in the telling of this, when we imitated the secretary we started giving her a posh accent that she didn't actually have. "Did I say American dimples? *Heavens*, I meant American *pimples*." Nobody else thought it was as funny. Nobody else ever thought our things were as funny as we did.

On the day the agents came to our apartment, I wasn't helping out at the soda fountain. Ken had left to become an American war hero by then. Papa and Mama didn't want me to work there alone.

What I was doing was putting on my volleyball uniform

because I was going to meet some of the other Nisei girls from the California Street church. My mother called me out of the bedroom to translate for her; I still had rollers in half my hair. It took a while for me to figure out how to explain what the men wanted. Some of the terms I didn't have translations for. *What is subterfuge?* I asked one of the agents, who thought I was being cheeky.

When my mother tells the story, what she leaves out is my whole life.

A little while after the letter from the government arrived, a separate one came from my father, addressed to my mother but written to all of us—in English, I was sure whoever monitored his mail had insisted it be in English, so I had to be the one to read it out loud. *There is a beauty salon*, he wrote. *A grocer's. They are building an American school and a swimming pool: one hundred yards in diameter with a diving platform! People can have jobs, for extra money, but everyone receives housing, and tokens for food and clothing, whether they have jobs or not. You will like it.*

The least my father could have done would have been to refuse harder, to tell my mother he forbade us from coming to Texas. Instead when she insisted we were coming, we got cheerful snippets that sounded like a vacationer's postcards, with exclamation points that my father would have called vulgar if I'd used them myself: *So many Japanese people! Movies shown for free in the community center! Haruko, tell your*

mother that the hospital is looking for volunteers, and also that
some of the women have started a tofu factory, right in camp!

This is how my father tried to make us excited about the
barren desert of Texas. A tofu factory.

I did tell my mother about the hospital, and I watched her
light up. My mother, who graduated from the Tokyo Wom-
en's Medical Professional School, who never officially became
a doctor because instead she moved to America to marry the
stranger-son of a family friend, and who never became fluent
in English, and who instead made it her profession to worry
about the length of my volleyball uniform.

Personally I would worry about a place that allowed a
woman twenty years out of medical school to volunteer as
a doctor, but my mother lit up and so I said nothing. Serene.

Toshiko jabs me with her elbow. The train has slowed and
the brakes are creaking. "I think we're stopping," she whispers to me. "I think we're picking up more people."

"Maintenance break," I whisper back. "Window shades."

If it were an actual station, the guards would have told us
to pull down the window shades. They do that at every stop,
though they haven't said whether it's because they don't want
us to be able to see where we are, or because they don't want
people in the towns to see us.

But no, it turns out this time Toshiko and I are both
wrong. The train car has stopped, fully stopped, without anyone making us pull down the window shades and without any

new people standing outside waiting to board. The train is finally quiet, and the quiet is heaven. We all press our faces against the hot glass and nobody yells at us.

The short, pale guard walks the aisles, counting our heads, murmuring the numbers under his breath. When it's clear he has the number of people he's supposed to have, he tells us to line up. Keep orderly, no need to rush, leave the suitcases, someone will bring them.

I feel the shove of the heat as soon as the train door opens. It can be hot in Colorado sometimes, but this is hot like putting your face in front of an oven. It feels unnatural and stagnant and rolls thick into the train. I watch as every person ahead of me pauses at the door, swaying against the force of the heat, before they step down.

We're at a station. Or, really, more of a stop because there's no station building, just a sort of gazebo: rusty beams supporting a metal roof with a bench in the middle of the open space. A hanging sign: CRYSTAL CITY.

After we've all finally gotten off the train and been counted again, there's confusion. A bus was supposed to be here to take us to the camp, but apparently it's broken down in the heat and now we're stranded. The man who delivers this news, a Caucasian man in a suit with sweat at his temples, is apologetic about this "development." He keeps telling us that if we're willing to be a little patient and wait—

If we're willing to be a little patient and wait, I translate for my mother.

"Then another bus will come," the man says. He has thinning hair and a round face; he's tall and blocky looking. I can tell that he's a boss of some kind. He has a clipboard; other people who look like employees scurry over and whisper things while he makes notes.

Then another bus will come.

Here's what's around us: A post office with an American flag. A tiny weathered restaurant. A boardinghouse I wouldn't want to stay in. Low one-story houses, standing far apart from one another. In Denver we lived on the upper floor of a duplex. In Denver you were never more than a flight of stairs away from borrowing a needle or a tin of shoe polish.

While I've been orienting myself, other passengers have been talking. The more vocal ones, like Mrs. Ginoza, who persevered in asking for extra water for her daughter while my mother told Toshiko and me to swallow our own spit, have decided they don't want to wait for the bus. Somehow it's been decided we'll walk to camp: What's one more mile after the thousand we've already traveled?

The sweaty Caucasian man doesn't like the way it looks to have a bunch of tired women and children marching in their best traveling clothes, but we're already doing it. Mrs. Ginoza has spotted a sign so we follow her out of the tiny town, which has no glass buildings, nothing resembling crystal. Past some fields, which the man says are spinach. "Crystal City is the Spinach Capital of the World" is actually what he says, like he can regain control of the situation if he pretends it was his idea to be a walking tour guide. "We're very famous for our spinach here; we have a statue of Popeye the Sailor," he says, and I'm almost embarrassed for him. The sun is directly overhead and my dress is damp with sweat, first under my arms, and then as we walk farther, all of it, clinging to my legs and my waist.

And then, when my tongue is so swollen from thirst that there is no more spit to swallow, we're standing fifty yards from a gate. Behind it, a swarm of faces, the reason we're all here to begin with.

Our fathers and husbands crane their necks. They must have been told we were coming; a few hold up a welcome banner. Vaguely, through the sweat pouring down my face, I am aware of a brass band playing, and even more vaguely I see that it, too, must be part of our welcome ceremony.

At first I think my tired eyes are playing tricks on me, but it's true: A few of the men in the background have light hair and Caucasian features. German prisoners. Something else Papa told me about the camp. We'll share our space with Nazis.

"I don't see your father," Mama whispers anxiously.

I scan the crowd, landing on a fence post. A girl sits on it, frizzy blond hair, bony knees balancing a notebook in which she's recording something. She looks official like a camp employee but too young, close to my age. I should have realized that the German detainees would bring their own children. She scans the crowd, too, gawking at the new arrivals, and her eyes lock on mine for a brief moment before she bows her head and writes something else. I raise my eyebrows in annoyance. I have had too many people with notebooks check me off their lists. Too many noting when we've eaten, slept, used the bathroom.

"Haruko! Haru-chan!"

It's my father. *My father.* I haven't seen him in five months. My heart jumps before I remember that I'm not sure how I feel about seeing my father now, that the last time I saw him was strange.

He seems thinner, gray at his temples, standing near one of the other fence posts and waving a handkerchief over his head like a flag. I hear him before my mother and sister do. When he catches my eye, the handkerchief falters and I see something in his face that looks like uncertainty. "Helen," he tries again. It's not uncertainty, it's hopefulness, willing me to look in his direction. Toshiko was right. Only the other popular girls at school called me Helen. My family never did. He is trying so hard. I should be so happy. "Helen, I'm over here."

I nudge my mother. "There's Papa." My mother's eyes scramble until she finds him. Then she breaks into a smile and, with my wrist clamped in her hand, she rushes toward the entrance gates, toward the fence.

The chain-link fence surrounds the camp on all sides. Ten feet tall, topped with barbed wire, and the corners that I can see are occupied by guard towers and soldiers with guns.

My father didn't mention this in any of his letters. It must have slipped his mind. *Here in Crystal City, Haruko, we have outdoor movies, a tofu factory, and jagged, sharp fences guarded by men who will shoot you if you try to leave.*

It's funny the things you can leave out. It's funny the way you can paint a picture that is both completely true and the falsest thing in the world.

My father doesn't come out to greet us because he lives inside this fence. He brought us to this fence. And even though I know that I'm supposed to be excited to see him, I can't help but think that when my mother said, *Your sister is not the enemy*, what I wanted to ask was, *Is my father?*

Suddenly, my left arm wrenches. While my mother is trying to move us forward, Toshiko is pulling my other wrist back, her mouth a wide O of panic.

"Stop it, Toshi, you're hurting my arm."

"I don't want to go in."

"Don't be silly, you've been talking about it for days."

"Now I don't want to," she shrieks. I can feel her about to cry.

"Toshiko, stop it. If you want to see Papa, you have to come this way."

My mother is still trying to press us forward. Through the crush of bodies, her hat tips forward; a sprig of blue petals bobbles like it might come loose. I turn back to my sister, who is still a mule in the mud. "I wish we were all home now," Toshiko says. "I wish we were picking up Papa, and then we were all going home."

She's crying, wet and sniffly, and as she tries to enlace her fingers with mine, I jerk my hand away. Without meaning to, I pull that same hand back and slap her across the face.

My fingers sting at the contact with Toshi's soft baby skin. Her mouth falls open and she reaches to where there are four white finger-shaped lines appearing on the side of her face. "Haruko—" she starts, because I've never hit her before, and because I did it hard.

I'm breathing heavily, we both are, and the regret I feel is mixed with a nauseating kind of relief, because slapping my sister feels like the first true thing I have done in months.

"This is home now," I tell her, as she gulps back new sobs. I pull out a handkerchief, waiting while she wipes her face. "No more wishing. This is home."

TWO

MARGOT

August 24, 1944
Arrivals:
Women: 44
Children: 63 (girls—37; boys—26)
Total arrivals: 107
New total in Crystal City: 3,368

ALL THE NEW DETAINEES ARE JAPANESE THIS TIME. I PUT THAT IN MY
notebook, too. *Total Japanese detainees: 2,371. Total German
detainees: 997.*

Within my totals, there are subtotals: German-born
prisoners who have come from Costa Rica. Japanese-born

prisoners from Peru. America has agreements with those countries, saying that Crystal City will house their enemies of the state in addition to our own. One of these girls has a Betty Boop decal on her handbag, so they must be American.

I check my notes from the last arrivals. This is the smallest group since I've been here. *Smaller train?* I write. Not enough housing for more people?

All the new detainees are inside the gate now. The fathers who have already hugged their families proudly introduce them around. One of the camp nurses, in a white uniform, funnels people through the medical tent for vaccinations and exams. Whooping cough. When my group came, fifty-four of us had whooping cough.

Mr. Mercer, a head taller than anyone else and looking upset, has taken off his suit jacket. There are circles of sweat under the tan of his shirtsleeves. His shoes are dirty. The bus must have broken down.

Is this shipment smaller because the country is running out of Japanese people to put into camps?

"Good morning, Margot."

I swivel to a man's voice, shielding my eyes against the sun. Thin lips, dark hair, a little older than my father. He starts to raise his right arm. "He—"

"Hello, Mr. Kruse," I interrupt, because I can tell how his greeting was going to end, and I'm still not used to it.

"Keeping an eye on everything for us?"

"Staying occupied. School will start soon," I say, though he probably knows that already. He has a daughter. "There was a delay, I guess, but they finished the buildings."

"The German school for you, correct?" When I shrug instead of respond, he raises an eyebrow. "*Not* the German school?"

I wonder if I should have nodded. The camp's chapter of the Bund advised German parents to send their children to the German school instead of the federal school. It's been published in *Das Lager*, spread among housewives. But Federal High School will be certified, with American teachers, like every other school in the United States. The German school will use a curriculum the Bund decides is appropriate. Mutti and Vati would never make me go to the German school.

"Heidi will be disappointed," he says. "She still talks about you. I'll send her to visit sometime, if she won't be a bother."

"Of course not, I like Heidi." She and I came on the same train; she'd been staying with an aunt until her parents sent for her. I helped unwrap her sandwiches; I told her stories about a girl from the Swiss Alps who shared her name.

Over by the fence, the newly arrived women straighten their children's collars and smooth down hair. After vaccinations, the next part of orientation is a family portrait. Every family is given one to hang in their Crystal City hut. Nobody ever expects it.

"What has your father been up to?" Mr. Kruse takes a cigarette out of his breast pocket and lights it, turning his head to blow the smoke away from my face. It's so hot it's hard to tell the difference between his cigarette vapors and the wavy lines of heat on the horizon.

"He keeps busy," I say neutrally, but his question has put me on alert. "Mutti got permission for a garden but she can't be on her feet much. Vati's building planter boxes."

Mr. Kruse looks amused. "Spending money on seeds when the US provides food for free? I wouldn't. Might as well take advantage of this prison. Drain their resources."

"*Wer rastet, der rostet*," I say automatically.

Mr. Kruse bursts into laughter. "He who rests *does* grow rusty. I'm glad to hear young people speaking German. Listen, have your father come find me. We could use another man at the swimming pool, especially with his training. We never see him at meetings. Tell him that, too. And your mother if she's up for it."

My insides tighten. Now the conversation has officially changed. Mr. Kruse will never see Vati at meetings. One meeting brought us here. He would never go to another. *Why did I not just say I was going to the German school?* I pretend to look for something in the crowd.

Straight ahead of me, a shock of bright blue. It's the flowered hat of a tired mother. She is tucked into a tall man's arm, and her younger daughter is wrapped around his waist.

But she has an older daughter, too, lean and pretty and

athletic-looking in a lavender dress. The older girl's shoulder-length hair is pinned back in a style I could never get mine to behave for. She hangs her arms stiffly by her sides, while her father tries to pull her close.

Don't be rude. Look away, I tell myself, but I can't.

While I watch, a piece of blue falls to the ground: a few of the fabric lilies. They land by the lavender girl's foot, silky and cool against her dusty shoe. She looks down but doesn't pick the flowers up. I would. We don't see beautiful things here. I would pick them up and bury my face in them, the way I used to with flowers on our farm. The girl's dress isn't quite the same color as the lilies, but almost. Another cool, beautiful thing dropped in the dust. I swallow.

The girl's cheek is now pressed against her father's sleeve, and a look flashes across her eyes. Something lonely and defiant that her family isn't meant to see, that nobody is meant to. Only, I *am* seeing it. The way her muscles tense. How she keeps her weight on her own feet instead of leaning in to her parents. In the middle of this dust, in the middle of these chaotic arrivals, I feel like I am watching a secret.

I shouldn't let myself think like this. Not about the girl, not about how much I miss home, not about any of this, so instead I make myself count the lilies on the ground.

Eight lilies. My lips are so dry. It's so hot.

She pulls away from her father, scanning the camp, and stops when she sees me. She's noticed me staring. My face flushes red and I quickly look down.

I don't understand what it would feel like, to finally be reunited with your father and refuse to acknowledge him. On my arrival day, I was sobbing. Vati, too. Only my mother was not, because she was still too hollow to cry. It had been six months since the two of us had seen my father.

I can't understand not wanting to hold on to your family and never let go.

Mr. Mercer has peeled himself away from the crowd, clutching his clipboard, searching for someone until he spots me and decides I will do. "Miss Krukow, isn't it? Could you do me a favor?" He wipes sweat from his forehead as he approaches, hesitating when Mr. Kruse coughs next to me. "Am I interrupting?"

"No, you're not." I stand and brush off my skirt, relieved that he's blocking the awkward stare of the lavender girl, relieved to have an excuse to leave my conversation with Mr. Kruse. "I mean, pardon me, Mr. Kruse. I don't mean to be rude."

"It appears we've had a bit of trouble with the arrivals," Mr. Mercer says. "The luggage is stranded, and meanwhile there was an outbreak of nausea. We need a spare set of clothing."

"Do you want me to get some from the commissary?"

He's already producing paper from his breast pocket and writing something down. "Here's permission for one skirt and a set of underthings. I think a women's size medium."

When he leaves, I realize I forgot to ask him which commissary. The Japanese have one, the Union Store, and we have another. Ours, the General Store, has cigarettes, dry goods, American soft drinks, and German beers. The Japanese store must have mostly the same things, but I've never been inside. I've also never been inside one of the Japanese houses, or even on one of the Japanese streets, not after four months here.

In the German store, I show the clerk Mr. Mercer's note instead of the cardboard token I would normally use to buy things. They used to hand us clothes, based on sizes we wrote out on slips. Then they decided that shopping would be good for our morale. Now we get choice, but not too much. Curtains, dresses, tablecloths, all sewn from the same few fabrics. When a new pattern comes in, a line forms halfway across camp: women pushing homemade wooden carts, desperate to look at something new, anything new.

By the time I get back, the lavender girl's family is gone. The clothing I've just purchased is meant for an exhausted young mother. Her skirt has a blotchy stain and a sour odor rising from it. She dabs at it, embarrassed, with a wet towel.

"Good. Lovely," Mr. Mercer says, as I hand the woman the brown paper parcel. "Thank you, Margot, I'm sure that Mrs."—he checks his clipboard—"I'm sure Mrs. Menda will be relieved to be out of her soiled clothes."

After he leaves, the woman holds up the skirt I've brought her and looks at me.

"The nurse can probably show you a place to change," I tell her, realizing too late from her confused expression that she doesn't speak much English. "The nurse, that way." I point toward the vaccination tent and keep pointing until the woman heads in that direction.

"Margot!" a voice says, and my insides curdle a little. I didn't realize Mr. Kruse was still around. "Did we make sure to be very helpful for the camp director?"

"It was just a small errand."

"Of course. We're all looking for ways to be useful. You know, I was thinking that if I brought Heidi around for a visit, I might also talk to your father myself about coming to some of our meetings. Do you think that would be a good idea?" He winks. "I'm asking you, because I know if you have a daughter's ear you have her father's."

A drop of sweat trickles down my inner arm, past the dusty crease of my elbow and the fold of my wrist before falling to the ground. *Do I think that would be a good idea?*

I'm not good at this. I'm not good at saying one thing and meaning another, at knowing how much I can disagree with Mr. Kruse, my elder, a man in an elected position.

"That's a lot of trouble for you," I say.

"It's no trouble at all. So could you tell him that? That I'll stop by? Wonderful."

And then he clicks his heels together, raising his arm parallel to the ground and poker straight. The gesture makes me sick. Even when it's not accompanied by words, which, thank God, it's not. He waits expectantly, but I can't return the salute. I can't look at it. I bury my face in my notebook again, hoping I can pretend I didn't see it.

"Good day, Margot," he says.

"Good day, Mr. Kruse."

I stare down until I think he will be gone. Mr. Kruse has that kind of voice, where even when he's not speaking very loudly, you can hear it from a distance. When I hear it, it always reminds me of the time when Vati took me into the empty grain silo and had me close my eyes and guess where he was, by the sound of his voice. It was a lesson about acoustics, he explained. Curves can amplify sound, making them seem closer than they are.

Here in Crystal City, I can always hear Mr. Kruse. It doesn't matter if he's shouting or whispering. His voice arrives to me like it's carried on the curved walls of a silo. By now he must be yards and yards away. Still, I can hear his words.

"Heil Hitler," he says to every man he passes, the greeting invented to honor a dictator who lives halfway around the world, but who is why we are here.

"Heil Hitler," Mr. Kruse says again, but this time it might be amplified in my imagination. *Heil Hitler. Heil Hitler. Heil Hitler.*

THREE

MARGOT

"BOOKS?" MUTTI ASKS AS I WALK IN THE DOOR. THAT WAS THE original goal when I left two hours ago: checking whether the books we requested came into the camp library.

"How are you feeling?" I say, pretending it doesn't drive her crazy to be asked all the time.

She waves her hand dismissively. "Books?" I give her the volume from the top of the stack I'm carrying, *Texas Gardening*, and she flips through it. "Good news and bad. Good news: Your mother is not batty. No wonder I couldn't get flowers to grow from the seed packets I bought here. This climate is all wrong."

"That's the bad news?"

"No, dead flowers are not bad news, just bad luck. The

bad news is this confirms that the clerks ordering for the General Store are incompetent boobs. Maybe we should have yards full of spinach instead of trying to grow anything useful, or God forbid, pretty."

"I guess that could work—" I start, but Mutti sticks out her tongue.

"Joking. Don't be so literal, Margot." She presses her lips together as she goes through the pile. "Latin, good. Advanced geometry, good. You and Vati mostly taught yourself back at home anyway, right? That's how you managed to place a year ahead." At the end of the stack she looks up. "I thought Vati requested a chemistry book."

"It didn't come."

"Maybe next shipment."

"No, I mean—it's not coming."

It takes her a minute to understand. There's usually only one reason for books not to come at all. "Well. You didn't want to be a chemist anyway, did you?"

I shake my head.

She tilts her head and looks at me. "Are you excited about school?"

This time I nod, but too slowly and my mother notices.

"It will be *fine*." She sets the pile firmly on the table. "At home, they were intimidated. Because you were more advanced. And too *serious*. That's why you didn't have many friends—here it won't matter. Everyone's new, everyone will have better things to worry abo—"

Suddenly, my mother pulls a handkerchief from her dress pocket, pressing it against her mouth.

"How are you feeling?"

The moment passes and she swallows. "More morning sickness. Which is actually evening sickness and afternoon sickness, too, as it happens. With you, I was vomiting all over the place. Remember Mrs. Loeb at church? Every week I would smell her perfume and, *blech*."

With me she was sick. This time she is sick. This is a good sign. There is at least one way in which this time is not like March. Many ways, I correct myself. Nothing at all alike.

"Did you see anything else while you were out?" my mother asks. "Here, come help me." She nods me over to the army cots she and my father sleep on, picking up the blanket. My cot is on the other side of the room, and so is my trunk, which serves as a bureau, bench, and nightstand. Between us is the table; on the table is a porcelain bowl that we use as a washbasin. Our room is sixteen by sixteen feet, in a building with three other units of the same size. We share the common kitchen facility with the other families. The smell of most cooking makes my mother vomit. At least our house has a kitchen.

"Why don't you sit down?" I offer.

"Because I'm making the bed."

"Why don't you let me make the bed?"

She doesn't relent, just looks at me expectantly until I pick up the other end of the blanket. "A new busload of people came," I start. "I helped Mr. Mercer run an errand. And also..."

"And also?"

And also there was a girl in a lavender dress, I almost want to say, but it makes no sense to mention that; I will probably never see that girl again. "And also I talked to Mr. Kruse. Or, I guess he talked to me," I add hurriedly.

Mutti's jaw stiffens and she gives the blanket a violent shake. "What did he say?"

Before I can answer, the door behind me creaks open. "What did who say?" Vati removes his hat and works the door shut again. It doesn't close right. The walls bow in a curve, something to do with the heat. At home Mutti would have had him wash off in the spigot out front before he came inside, but now he would be stripping naked in a dirt road so narrow that at night I can hear the snoring of four families.

"Margot was telling me about some new arrivals," Mutti says breezily. "Japanese?"

Vati nods, going to the basin and scrubbing his face. "Did they have news?" The war outside moves in leaps of time since our news is so censored. When my mother and I arrived, our train got to share news of Monte Cassino, an abbey near Rome the Allies kept attacking. A few months ago, a train arrived and the people on it said thousands of American soldiers had landed on a beach in France. *So it might be over soon?* we wondered, but nobody let us out, so the war must not have ended.

"I don't know if there was news," I tell Vati. "I didn't really talk to them."

"Then what did *who* say?"

Behind him, Mama's eyes dart in a warning.

"Mr. Kruse," I say after a beat, because I haven't been able to think of a lie in time. "After I got the books."

Vati nods. "Did he happen to mention how the swimming pool was going?" He asks it in a way that could be casual, but Mutti is shaking her head, telling me not to answer.

"He—he said they're working on it, but we really didn't talk for very long."

Vati sighs, sitting down at the table. "They're not using the right material for the lining. It's black, which makes it impossible to see the bottom. I honestly don't think they have any engineers consulting on the whole project."

Last year when Vati sent his first letter from Crystal City, he told us there were plenty of good, decent men, and "a few delusional Nazi sympathizers." In his next letter, he told us, bemused, that one of the delusional men had been elected German representative. In his third, he said that, as representative, Mr. Kruse got to give out work assignments, and he chose the men who came to his meetings.

It doesn't matter, Vati had written. *As long as I have my family here, none of it will matter.* But then we came here, and it did matter, because there was only so much furniture he could build for our small room before he ran out of things to do.

"So it sounds like you've gone there, then?" I ask tentatively. "The pool. It sounds like you've been spending time at the construction site?"

"I'm not going to join up with him, Margot." His shoulders stiffen.

"I didn't mean that. It's—I know it bothers you to think they're not doing it right."

"I *know* they're not. You see the furniture I built here. Did I cut any corners?"

"Right, that's what I mean."

"Why would you think the worst of me? Why do you act like I need to be babysat?"

Mutti closes her eyes. *Not now*, her face says. *Please not this now.*

His hand slaps the table. "The pool is inside the camp. When I go for a walk, I am also inside the camp, if you haven't noticed. The camp is less than half a square mile. I have walked every foot of that, including the pool, on multiple occasions. I am not specifically seeking out the pool, but there are a limited number of locations where one can walk and still be inside the camp. And, again, staying inside the camp is the only way to not be shot dead."

On the other side of the wall, I hear what sounds like someone tiptoeing, and a chair scraping. The neighbors can hear that we're fighting. Laugh, I tell myself. Laugh so the neighbors know we're fine, it's an absurd joke. Laugh so my father knows everything is okay.

"Somebody should talk to Mr. Mercer about holding another vote for the representative position," my mother says. "The Japanese don't seem to have trouble: They're organizing a kite-flying event for their national holiday. What is our leadership doing? Negotiating how many times they can parade a swastika around on Hitler's birthday. Building secret distilleries to get drunk on grain alcohol."

"I thought you didn't like the Japanese leadership, either." Vati sighs, the anger in his voice deflating. "The voting. Because they won't let women vote as they're not technically prisoners."

"It's a stupid rule. Not prisoners? So they're guards, then?" Mutti says archly. "They're camp employees? They're Texans who accidentally wandered in through a barbed-wire fence and said, *Well, this seems lovely, I think I'll stay awhile.*"

I think for a minute that he is going to yell again. Instead, he snorts. The knot in my stomach loosens as the snort turns into a laugh. At the fact that we're all behind this fence together, but some are considered prisoners and some aren't. "Can you imagine?" Vati plucks the air in front of him, picking up a pretend telephone receiver. *"Hello, Crystal City? This is the Jones family in Houston. We'd like to make a reservation. How long? Is* indefinitely *available? We'd like to make sure we stay indefinitely."*

He's still laughing when he looks down at the pile of books on the table. "I forgot that you went to the library! Did they get the newest edition for the chemistry book? I wondered if it would have curium."

"Not chemistry," I say finally. "There's no chemistry book."

"Margot hates chemistry now," Mutti adds. "Me too. I forbid her from bringing chemistry books into the house."

It takes my father a second longer than it took my mother. "Did the rejection slip say anything in particular?"

"Just what it usually says," I tell him.

What usually happens is that my father requests books from the camp library. For books that aren't in stock, the requests travel to the University of Texas a hundred miles away. Sometimes we get the books.

Sometimes the requests come back: *Denied by the US Government*. Those replies mean that my father isn't allowed to read the books. Books about building things or about revolutions are considered too dangerous for enemy aliens. Books about chemistry also, apparently. "All the other books came," I offer hurriedly. "I wouldn't have had time to study more."

"Anyway, it's done. No use crying," Mutti says, untying her apron. "I'm going to walk to the entrance and watch the new arrivals. I won't be on my feet long," she adds, before Vati or I can protest. "I just want to stretch my legs."

She leaves, and my father sighs. He took the news about the book well. He seems mostly his old self again, with a fraction less happiness. An infinitesimal fraction, the weight of a feather. But I wish I knew how to quantify it. If I knew how much the happiness weighed, I'd know how much my father could afford to lose before he disappeared.

"Latin or geometry?" He straightens in his chair, shaking tension out of his shoulders.

"Are you sure?" I say uncertainly. "We don't have to."

"Should we do Latin or geometry?" He wiggles his fingers at me so I'll hand him a book, the same as he has done a hundred times, until I hand him the right one. "Of course I want to, *kleine Schnecke*. We can't have you fall behind, because the war can't last forever."

FOUR

HARUKO

THIS IS JUST A SCHOOL. THIS IS JUST AN AMERICAN FLAG, POKING out of the ground in front of what is just a brick building, and this could be anywhere, really. Except it's not.

"You look darling," Chieko says, clucking approvingly at my rose seersucker dress.

Chieko lives two Victory Huts down from us, and I met her last week, a few days after my family arrived, at the mess hall. "It's Chinese rice," she said, watching me try to make sense of the strange texture. "They don't know that there's a difference."

Chieko plays tennis back home in San Francisco, she told me. And she has all the Glenn Miller records, and her father owns a film projector which, she explained when we met, is used once a week to screen movies outside. The camp employees choose—Westerns, musicals—and keep track of which we like. I learned this at my first movie night, when a guard with blond hair and freckles told his superior that my row yawned six times during *Dancing Pirate*. Nobody yawned during the newsreel that came before it. Edited propaganda, maybe, but it was still a sudden sharp taste of the outside world.

"Tell your sister to walk closer with us," Chieko says. "It looks bad, her being back there all by herself like she couldn't find anyone to be friends with."

Chieko is exactly the right kind of friend for me to have here. She lent me a pair of anklets with pink trim because they complemented my dress. She's been here since the beginning of summer; she knows everything about the camp. I should be so grateful to be friends with Chieko.

"Toshi, come walk with us."

My sister can hold a grudge, and she hasn't forgiven me for slapping her. Every night we've been here she's dragged her cot away from mine to sleep next to our parents in the next room. So instead of walking to the washrooms with Toshiko in the morning, I walk with Chieko, who knocks on my window before it's even light. Someone is always there before us, holding their piece of cardboard to use as a privacy screen. *It will feel normal*, Papa told me the first day, when I didn't know about the cardboard and my mother and I took turns holding our skirts wide to block each other's stalls. *It will never*, I thought. A week later, I check the latrine for crickets, and I urinate behind cardboard, but I tell myself every time that it's not normal.

The school is one-story, redbrick, shaped like a U. In the middle of the U is a courtyard with a small playing field, and on the other side of the courtyard, facing the U, is one of the guard towers. As we walk past it I hear the sound of a whistle. Not angry like a police whistle, but friendly. The three of us look around.

"Good luck!" a voice calls.

I've now turned in a full circle looking for the source of the whistle and the voice.

"Up here." The guard leans out of the tower so we can see him. "Here, catch." A handful of small square things flutter down. Chewing gum, wrapped in waxy paper. Chieko shrieks and covers her head. "Sorry it's not Wrigley," the guard says. "Wrigley is shipped away for soldiers."

He's young. Wavy blond hair bleached from the sun, tanned skin with freckles across his nose, the same guard who was observing me at movie night. Ken's age. I wonder how he managed to get this job, guarding us, when so many of the men his age are off fighting. Most of the guards here are older than my father. Sagging, slow, unfit for combat duty.

"Thanks," I call back cautiously, wondering if he should be talking to me.

"What?" He shifts his body so his right side instead of his left is facing us, and leans out of the tower. "Sorry, I'm a little—in this ear I can't—what?" He cups his hand over his right ear.

So that's why he's here instead of somewhere in Europe or the Pacific. He couldn't pass the hearing test. Ken has perfect hearing. Ken and his stupid perfect hearing.

"I said, thanks," I yell, making sure to enunciate my words. "But are you sure that's—" And then I don't know how to finish my sentence. *Is that legal?* I want to ask. *Is that appropriate, for you to be throwing us chewing gum?* Instead, I notice a black-and-white logo affixed to the side of his helmet. "Is that an M&O Cigars sticker?"

"It sure isn't Elitch Gardens." He grins. "Who do you go for in the Denver tournament?"

"Baseball isn't really my fav—wait, how did you know I was from Denver?"

"I heard you, last night at the movies. I am, too. Well, when I was a kid. Do you think we'll get a pro team soon?"

"My brother says no," I call up.

"I'd take that wager."

Who are you rooting for? Let's meet at Merchant's Park. I heard the Nisei All-Star team might visit next year.

I wasn't lying to the guard, I never followed baseball; I could not care less whether Denver ever got a professional team. But I overheard a hundred versions of this conversation between the boys at home: Japanese boys who took me to Nisei socials, white boys who sat next to me in school. I ignored a hundred versions of this conversation, because I didn't realize I might never get to hear them again. Now, I rack my brain for anything to say about baseball, anything to keep me in a normal conversation about normal things from home.

Chieko nudges my shoulder. "We're *late*."

"The Cigars," I say hurriedly. "Obviously, I'd root for the Cigars over Elitch Gardens. But the Grizzlies over everyone. And thanks for the chewing gum."

"Thanks, *Mike*."

"Thanks, Mike," I say, as the bell rings and Chieko pulls me toward the school, where dozens of others swarm into the building.

"Where are all the German kids?" I whisper as we walk through the double front doors, elbowing past a cluster of younger boys, finding the right hallway for Toshiko to turn down.

"Hmm?" Chieko looks for our own room number in a corridor of black-haired students.

"The German kids. Do they have a different entrance?"

"Come on, let's get inside and get good seats." She pulls my arm, maneuvering me into the classroom she's decided is ours. Inside, she waves to some of the people she knows, promising to introduce me later but unwilling to commit to a desk until she's made a predatory lap around the room. I know how this is played, how to choose the right seat and say the right things. I'm trying, here in Crystal City. I'm trying hard.

"What about those seats?" I point to a row with only one other girl in it. Close enough to the back to avoid seeming too eager, but not the very back row, which should be reserved for the boys to pass us notes. This was the row the popular girls would have sat in at my school, the row it took me years to sit in.

Chieko sees who the other girl is and makes a strangled, disapproving noise, shaking her head no. "Why not?" I ask.

She's a repat, she mouths. *She might leave soon.*

"What are you talking about?"

She grabs my elbow again, steering me to a corner where the girl won't overhear us. "Her family volunteered to go back on one of the ships to Japan."

"There are no ships going to Japan," I say, confused.

"The government wants to bring the American soldiers home. So families here, they can volunteer to be repatriated back to Japan. An exchange." Chieko looks impatiently over my shoulder, watching the seats fill up.

"We aren't soldiers—why would the Japanese government accept us? Why would we volunteer?" The thought bothers me. "Are the Americans making her leave? Isn't *she* American?"

"Can you ask me this later?" Chieko says. But the conversation has already taken too long. No empty rows are left, and now we're going to have to sit next to the repatriating girl. Chieko sighs.

Sorry, I mouth, but I can't stop thinking about how she

said *go back*, when you can't go back to a place you've never been.

Our teacher, Miss Goodwin, is younger than I expected, with clothing and makeup nicer than Crystal City requires. She gestures to a box of textbooks and it's not until the last of us has collected our books that the classroom door bangs open, and all of us turn to stare.

A sunburned white girl with frizzy hair. The girl who documented our arrival in her book.

"Yes?" Miss Goodwin asks, because the girl is still standing there clutching her books to her chest and hasn't said a thing. The boy behind me starts to laugh; a second later more join in.

The girl blushes, reaching into the pocket of her skirt for a folded piece of paper. "I'm sorry I'm not on time. They didn't believe I was supposed to be in this school," she says, handing the note to Miss Goodwin. "But I am. Supposed to be here."

"Margot Krukow," Miss Goodwin says, handing the note back. "Take any empty seat."

I don't know if she doesn't hear the other students whispering as she walks down the aisle, or if she's very good at pretending. Her eyes are dark gray and they're hard to read.

Chieko told me yesterday that the Nikkei community in California was so big that her school was almost all Japanese students. Mine wasn't. I have been the student that Margot is now, walking down the aisle while other students laugh under their breath. I have worked on ignoring the whispers.

Even though I hated that she wrote in her notebook about my incoming train, even if her father is a Nazi, I have been that student enough to feel like I should smile at Margot now, as she holds her books tighter and searches for a seat.

I have also been that student enough to decide not to smile now, to instead feel myself tense as she walks closer. Next to me, Chieko does the same, willing Margot to choose a different row. We don't need to be the row with the Nazi girl on our first day.

But there are no other seats. Thanks to my mistake earlier, the empty one is next to me.

"You dropped these."

She's talking to me, touching my hand to get my attention. Her fingers are rough and calloused. I turn to tell her she can keep it, whatever it is, my pencil or book cover, because as long as her hand is on mine, people are whispering about me, too.

"You dropped these last week so I brought them for you," she says.

"That's a little strange." Chieko laughs, to break the tension in the room. I make myself laugh, too, until Margot turns back to her own desk.

Except it's not a pencil, what she leaves on my desk. It's a bunch of lilies. Made of silk, but for a minute when I see them on my desk, blue and soft, and I see the way Margot handles them, like they are the most precious thing she'll ever touch, I forget that they're not real.

MARGOT

Haruko remembers things wrong. She told you what she wished was true. I didn't put the flowers on her desk. That would have meant that I brought them to school, expecting to see her. That doesn't make any sense. I didn't expect to see her. I didn't put my hand on her hand and say, You dropped these. *I never would have. I was careful to barely look in her direction.*

I think Haruko prefers her version because it makes it seem like she had no choice in the matter. Like I forced myself into her life.

I did have the flowers. That part was true. I had them pressed between the pages of my book, but she didn't see them until later, much later. She said, They were my mother's. *She said,* You can keep them to remember me.

I kept them.

I know this correction seems like it's a small difference. It's a big difference. I know the way I am telling these stories seems mundane and boring. Horror grows out of mundanity. If you're paying attention, it always starts small. We all tell the versions we wish were true.

None of this matters anyway. Whether I tried to give her the flowers then or later. She doesn't know my version of the story; she'll never know it. She can remember things however she wants.

But it's a big difference. You can't change endings by going back and changing beginnings.

FIVE

HARUKO

I WAIT FOR TOSHIKO AFTER SCHOOL AND WE WALK HOME together, down the narrow dust paths that pass for streets. "How was your first day?" I ask, but I don't press when she shrugs. Before I turn away, she makes sure I see her wrinkle her nose at me, though, so I know she's almost done being angry.

Our parents are in our Victory Hut. Both of them, since my mother has evening shifts at the hospital, and my father is already home for the day. There are no natural roles for a hotel clerk at a camp for enemy aliens. The Japanese council here has promised to look for something suitable, but in the meantime they have assigned him to work in the spinach fields. It's a hard job to get, Chieko told me, since it's outside the fence.

"How was school?" my mother asks, but she's barely paying attention to Toshiko's answer, murmuring, "Good, good,"
before Toshiko is through the first sentence. Mama got her
uniform last night, a white coat to wear over her clothes. My
father called her Dr. Tanaka when she tried it on, but she
couldn't stop worrying over the sleeve length, and she spent
the whole evening with her head bowed over a Japanese text-
book lent by one of the other internee doctors, murmuring to
herself: *Lacrimal. Ethmoid. Zygomatic.*

"My day was also fine," I say, since she hasn't bothered
to ask.

Instead of responding, she hands me a manila envelope
with *War and Navy Departments, V-Mail Service* written on
the sender label.

My heart thuds.

"It's from Ken," she says, as though anyone else in the US
Army would be sending us mail. "We waited for you to read it."

Ken. It's been months since we heard from him. Months
since he wrote from some training camp in America that we
weren't allowed to know the location of. He made jokes about
his commanding officers in that letter, how one of them
walked pigeon-toed with a waggling rear end, and we read it
around the table and laughed.

The last time we heard from Ken, the FBI hadn't come
yet. I'd written Ken back, telling him I'd stopped going to
the soda fountain because the new people who worked there
were morons who couldn't make a simple phosphate, and that

my friends who thought he was a loser before now found him attractive in uniform. My parents wrote him when we learned where we were going but we never heard back. "He has more important things to worry about," my mother said then.

The letter now has already been opened—all of our mail is inspected—but Papa nods that I should take it out of the envelope. The sheet of paper in my hand is small, half the size of a regular letter, with Ken's handwriting shrunken, too. V-mail: Ken wrote this, wherever he is, and the government copied it onto a roll of microfilm with thousands of other soldiers' letters to save on shipping costs, and then it was printed again, but smaller.

Cursive. The letter is in cursive; that's why my parents haven't read it yet. Mama can't read English. Papa's speaking English is almost perfect, his printed English is very good, but aside from the signature he mastered for forms at the hotel, he barely knows cursive. The letter is addressed to all of us, but Ken must've known I would be the one to read it.

I run my hands over the page because it's the same page my brother once touched, before remembering that's not how V-Mail works. He never touched this. It's a copy of the real thing. "Read it!" Toshiko bounces on her toes, and I clear my throat.

"*Dear Papa and Mama, Haruko and Toshi,*" Ken writes.

> *Boy, is it good to have a minute to sit down and write. I just sat down after the longest bivouac. That's when*

44

we hike and make a temporary encampment and sleep in the dirt. It's not so bad and at least it comes with plenty of fresh air. Nothing like filling your lungs with some fresh air from the countryside! Plus, the towns we pass are pretty, almost like postcards.

What kind of town, you ask? Tsk, tsk, I'm not allowed to tell you! What I can tell you is that all the kids who live here have learned to recognize American soldiers, but they are confused as the devil when they see a bunch of Japanese-looking guys in American uniforms. We try to tell them, mostly through hand gestures, that we're American, but they usually don't believe it until we pull out a real Hershey's bar. Then they're clambering all over us. It's a hoot.

The other fellas here are swell. I've made so many friends. Most of them are from California and I can't wait to visit them there one day. Boy oh boy, we'll paint the town.

Anyway, I am fine, and I hope you all are, too. I sent this letter to Crystal City because Papa told me in his last letter that he thought you'd all be there by now. Write soon.

Kenichi/Ken

I finish and my family is still while I refold the paper and hand it to my mother.

"That was a good letter, don't you think?" She smooths it between her fingers. "He seems healthy."

"A very good letter." My father sounds even more relieved than my mother. "He's doing us proud."

"Where do you think he is?" Toshiko asks. "Germany?"

"Nobody is in Germany yet, Toshi-chan," my father explains. "Except the Germans. We haven't invaded there yet."

"Unless it happened since we got here. No other trains have come with news. All we know is we hadn't invaded Germany before we left home," Toshiko says.

My tongue is numb. I can't join in because I don't know what they're talking about.

Ken sounds healthy, for someone who is not Ken. It is a good letter, for someone who is not Ken. *It's a hoot?* Ken never would have talked like that. Ken didn't use slang. He wouldn't be making lifelong friendships with a bunch of *fellas*. I once watched my brother spend an entire school dance sitting alone under the bleachers because he said the comic book he was reading was more interesting than getting all sweaty on the gym floor.

I was the one who cared about making friends. I was only under the bleachers because one of the white girls at the dance had asked me if my father was bucktoothed like the advertisements showing pictures of General Tōjō. The cartoon ones that read: *What have you done to help save the country from THEM?* The ones that had a drawing of the Japanese general as a captured mouse, with the words "Jap Trap." I'd forced myself to laugh at her question because Jennie was laughing, too, because in order to be popular at a school with barely any Japanese students, you had to make yourself laugh at things like this.

Stay here with me, who cares? Ken had said as I crouched in the new cap-sleeved dress I'd promised my mother I would wear to every social event for two years if she would let me buy it, if she would let me go to a regular school dance instead of the socials at the Japanese church. It was my father who convinced her in the end, my father who liked that I was pop-ular at school, who listened to American big band music, and learned American dance steps, who conspiratorially told me to let him handle convincing my mother.

We don't need to tell our parents everything, Ken said. *I'll say you danced all night long.* He handed me a handkerchief and went back to reading, pretending he wasn't watching me.

My brother could not have cared less about walking through the beautiful countryside. Ken loved the indoors: word puzzles, backgammon, long games of criss-crosswords where he arranged letter tiles into fiendish combinations. Ken would only use the word *bivouac* to talk about how *bivouac* is a useful word if you're playing criss-crosswords and have drawn a lot of vowels. But now here that word is, in a letter that is apparently from him.

Ken, the American army's pride, one of the Nisei boys who convinced the government that they could be trusted to join the service. He joined when he turned eighteen. Nobody expected him to, but my skinny, sarcastic brother did anyway.

"We can be very proud of Ken," my father says again, but hearing it makes me bristle.

Ken didn't join just because he wanted to. Ken joined so our family could hang a yellow ribbon in our window. So I could tell the girl from the dance that my brother was off fighting. So it would be clear, in a city that had only six hundred Japanese people, that we were as American as everyone else.

But when the FBI men came to our kitchen, did my father say that? Did he talk about how his son was in the 442nd division, and how Ken had left for boot camp on a bus waving a handkerchief out the window?

He didn't tell them anything about Ken at all. He didn't explain anything or defend himself. He offered them a drink, the good hotel clerk my father had always been. He told my mother and sister and me to sit at the table and not move. He apologized for the desk drawer sticking. He was so deferential, while the FBI went through that drawer and opened our closets. As if he'd done something wrong, as if we all had.

And then something happened. Something suspicious, something strange. While the federal agents were rolling up our living room rug to check underneath, my father caught my eye. He shook his head slightly. To me, to no one else. To a question I hadn't even asked, he shook his head. I had never seen him make that gesture before. I didn't know what it meant.

I've spent every day since then replaying that head shake. Every single day since the FBI took Papa and left behind our ransacked apartment, wondering what my father wasn't saying, and thinking of the fearful look in his eyes while he wasn't saying it.

Ken is going on bivouacs for nothing. Ken left for nothing. We are getting letters that pretend to be cheerful but only sound wrong, and my family is too desperate to acknowledge it. How can they not see that cheerfulness is something to worry about, too?

"He sounds great!" is all I say, though. Because even now, I know I don't need to tell our parents everything. "Boy oh boy! What a time he must be having. I can't wait until he comes home so he can tell us all about it, can you?" My family nods along as I coo over the letter. I make sure my voice is very cheerful.

"I'm going for a walk," I say. "I'm going to listen to some of Chieko's records."

"Help me set the table first," my mother says. "And make sure you're back in time for roll call."

This is not a normal place. This is not a normal time.

I manage to stay cheerful for as long as it takes to set the table, and for as long as it takes me to tell Mama the gingham she bought for the tablecloth is very nice, and then I go outside where I make it to the end of our dirt road before I burst into tears.

SIX

MARGOT

September 4, 1944

Number of people who thought to bring chairs from
   their houses for our first roll call: 0

Number of people who have brought chairs today: 7

Number of people who have also brought bottles of
   soda: 15

Temperature: ? (We're not allowed a thermometer.
   A thermometer might be considered a dangerous
   tool.)

WE ARE COUNTED. TWO TIMES A DAY. THE GUARDS DO IT EFFI-
ciently. It happens in rows and columns while we stand in

a clearing near our houses. Once in the morning, before the temperature gets too high, and then once in the evening, when it drops.

The camp's main entrance is on the west side of the compound, which is also where the hospital and the laundry are. On the south side is Federal High School, the tennis court, and most of the Japanese housing and Japanese facilities and businesses. The east is a small orchard and the site of the swimming pool; the north has the mess hall off a street called 11th Avenue, a recreation hall off Lincoln Avenue, and the library off Arizona Street. The north and central part of the camp also have German housing as well as the German establishments and school, and the space between the houses and school is where we are counted.

Women bring knitting, children bring schoolwork to stay occupied while we wait. I should mind it: the hot sun, standing on one leg and then the other so my feet don't fall asleep. But I find comfort in order, knowing where my family is and that we're here together.

Tonight we are counted hurriedly. Not quickly, exactly, because the guards try not to be sloppy. But in a way that feels rushed. It's because of the sky. Overhead are mackerel clouds that mark a coming storm, the kind of weather that would make Vati and me rush to put the cow in the barn. The wind bangs a loose shutter against Mrs. Schmidt's tarpaper shack. *Mrs. Schmidt has shutters*. I turn to share that new information with my mother, before remembering I came straight from the library and I'm not standing where I normally do.

"Four ninety-five?" the guard with the shiny forehead calls to the other.

"Four ninety-four," the guard with the big mole calls back. Around me people groan, because it means we'll start over. It should be 495. That's how many German prisoners are counted every day here. It's 495 today, too. The second guard didn't notice that when he passed the row in front of me, Mr. Fuhr was squatting down, resting his knees. I would explain this to one of the guards, but they wouldn't be allowed to take my word for it.

The guards start again from opposite ends, irritable now. Mrs. Schmidt's shutter bangs. I'd taken out my Latin book planning to memorize a few verbs, but now I'm doing what everyone is: measuring the sky and wondering if the weather will hold before the count is done.

Out of the corner of my vision, a flash of movement. It's a girl, running toward us.

For a minute I think that means I was wrong: Maybe it was actually 494 people before. But I'm never off in my counting, and the running figure isn't German, either.

It's Haruko, the lavender girl. Her dress today was pink and she didn't say a word to me the whole day though my desk was eleven inches from hers. I don't know if she knows my name.

"Hey," one of the guards calls out to her, breaking off in the middle of his counting. "Whoa, there. Hold on a minute."

Her eyes are puffy; she looks like she's been crying as she stops to talk to the guards. Haruko shouldn't be here. She should be counted later, on the Japanese side of camp, that's how it works. *Where are her friends, the people she ate lunch with, who I can already tell will be popular? Why is she here, and alone, and crying?*

I'm studying her again, like I was at the entrance gates, only now others are watching, too. *Stop it,* I want to tell them, because I feel like whatever is making her cry now must be whatever was making her angry when I first saw her, just boiled over, finally. We're all invading her privacy.

I know what it's like to want your thoughts and feelings to be contained, and to be afraid the whole world will see them.

The guards are looking at their watches and then toward the darkening sky as they try to figure out what to do with Haruko, and how to finish the count before the storm comes. Finally, one points over to the rest of us, telling her to join the row in front of me.

She has to walk directly past me to take her place, and as she passes, I surprise myself by calling out her name: "Hi, Haruko."

She glances over to me for a second before dabbing her face against her shoulder and then dismissively staring ahead again. I'm embarrassed I said anything at all.

My parents told me their one fear about me going to the

federal school was that because there were so few German students, it would be hard for me to make friends. I didn't say it would be a relief for me to have that excuse. At home I'd always wished it really *was* because I was a year younger than the other students, which is what Vati said. Or because I was too reserved like my mother thought. But part of the reason I was serious and literal is because, when you can tell you are different, it's safer to be careful. To keep things in a box. To respond to what other people are actually saying, not to what you think they might mean.

And I *was* different. I was odd in a way they didn't know how to describe and I didn't know how to fix. The people in my class said I stared too long and too much at the visiting student teacher. I didn't, though, not how they meant, not that time. She was just nice to me.

The wind plasters my skirt to my knees. Two women ahead of me produce scarves from their apron pockets and tie back their hair. "Four ninety-six," the second guard calls out over the howl. All of us who are supposed to be here plus Haruko.

"Y'all might want to hurry home," the first guard calls out. "Sorry this one took so long."

People barely acknowledge him before starting to run back to their houses before the storm. I stall for a minute wondering if I should try to find my parents, but there's something wrong with the sky. For a thunderstorm, it should be dark gray; the air should feel heavy. This sky looks greenish orange, the color of a faded bruise, and the air is sharp. Almost like the sky before a tornado, but it's September and tornado season is early spring.

"Wait," a voice behind me calls, just as I've decided to go home. "Margot, wait." I turn. Haruko looks around, panicked.

"Behind us and then turn left," I yell over the growing howl, barely registering that she does know who I am as I direct her to the Japanese side. *Why is the wind so loud?*

"What?"

"To get to your house. You need to turn—"

"What?"

I run over and grab the sleeve of her cardigan, pivoting her in the right direction. I mean to let go, but as soon as we're facing east, my throat drops.

It's not rain. Across the flat land, half a mile away but moving fast, a black wall as long as the horizon is rolling in our direction.

"It's a dust storm," I shout. *That's why the sky felt wrong. Not water. Dust.* Haruko stares at me, rooted to the ground. She hasn't seen it. *"A dust storm,"* I say, pointing to the black wall, and I no longer feel shy talking to her, because the storm is something I understand, and it's bigger than my own fear.

Finally, Haruko turns in the direction I'm pointing and her eyes get wide. The sky flashes. The wall of earth is more than a mile high; these storms can choke people, blind them.

We're on the edge of the German side, in front of the German school. My house is blocks away, too far to run to.

"This way," I yell, trying to pull Haruko toward the school, but she doesn't follow until I start to let go and run without her. I use the hem of my skirt to cover my nose and mouth, but I can barely see a yard in front of my face. At the school's entrance I throw my shoulder against the door. Locked.

Around us, buildings have become big, shapeless shadows. I hear Haruko yelling something, but I'm busy trying to hold the map of the camp in my mind, figuring out where we should run next while my hair whips around my face and the wind is screaming.

Keeping my right hand on the side of the building and my left holding a bunch of Haruko's sweater, I snake along the wall until I get to the corner. "Seventy-five yards—" I start to call out, but as soon as I open my mouth, dust pours in and I'm burying my face in my skirt again, gasping for air and tasting only cotton.

We run, slipping over loose stones and branches, and all I can see of Haruko is her feet stumbling next to mine, her own outstretched arm disappearing into the dirty air.

Did I miscalculate? We keep running south, and after a second that feels like an hour, my hand meets a wall of brick.

The icehouse.

It's supposed to stay locked but it usually isn't; detainees from both sides of camp use it. Still, I hold my breath until the handle turns, and then I shove Haruko ahead of me and wrench the door closed with a cold, metallic *click*.

We're both panting. My throat and nose burn and I rest

my hands on my knees until I can catch my breath. *Water*, I think, but there isn't any. It's all ice and no water. I spit on the concrete floor of the round shed, trying to empty the taste of dirt. When I look up again, Haruko is still standing where I pushed her. Her eyes are glassy and her hair has come loose from its pins; there's a hole in her sleeve I must have accidentally put there.

"You should, too," I tell her finally. "Spit. You don't want to swallow the dirt."

After a minute she clears her throat and spits.

"Better?"

Instead of answering, she wipes her mouth and goes to the small window in the door, still unsteady on her feet. I start to pick my way around the perimeter of the shed, seeing if there's a thermos or something else with water. There's not, but toward the back I do find an oil lamp and a work blanket, which I spread over one of the hay bales buffering the ice blocks.

"I've never seen anything like it," Haruko says finally, her voice cracked and dry.

"This is a bad one. Usually it's light dust, like beating a rug with a broom. Do you think you should sit down?"

"It looks like the mountains. When it's a clear day in Denver. That's what that dust storm looked like. A mountain. And then when it was on us, heavy snow."

"In Iowa we have tornadoes," I offer. "They're worse than this. The science is the same with dust storms and tornadoes.

Instability in the atmosphere, when dry air meets moist air. I don't think it's the same with snowstorms."

She looks at me oddly. "I wasn't talking about the science. I just meant that for a second the storm reminded me of home."

My face turns red, because of course that's what she meant. *Don't be so literal, Margot.*

"In a way, this reminds me of home, too," I tell Haruko finally, trying to make a joke. I gesture to the other blocks of ice. "I haven't been cold since I left Iowa." I don't wait to see if she smiles before I take my Latin book from my pocket and shake the dust from between the pages. "Anyway, even bad ones usually don't last more than twenty minutes."

After two or three, Haruko leaves the window and mimics what I've done, finding her own blanket and spreading it over her own bale, across from me with the oil lamp between us.

"That was nice of you," she says. "To help me."

"It's fine." I stay focused on the page.

"Especially since I was...especially because of school today."

"It's fine," I repeat, not sure what else to say. "You were lost and the storm came fast. I didn't know if you'd be able to get home."

"I didn't mean to end up on the Naz—on the German side of camp." She looks away, embarrassed, and I pretend that I didn't hear what she said. "I was turned around."

"Why were you crying?"

"When?"

"A half hour ago. You were running and you looked upset. I thought I could see when you walked past me that...Never mind."

"I *wasn't* crying." She takes the disheveled bobby pins out of her hair and lines them up on her lap, blowing dust off each one, slowly putting herself back together. I don't know why she's lying, but it's none of my business. I turn another page and try to memorize verbs.

Her hair rustles as she combs it with her fingers, working through the waves section by section. After a minute, she clears her throat. "Margot—it's Margot, right? You pronounce the *t* at the end? How did you come to Crystal City?"

"Through San Antonio," I say. "Like you did, probably. And then into Crystal City. The bus wasn't broken when we got here. We took it all the way in."

She shakes her head. "No. I mean before that."

I blush again, the second time I've misunderstood what she was saying. "Why?"

"We're stuck. I was just making conversation."

"Why? Is it because your other friends aren't here?"

She winces, but I didn't mean to accuse her. It's that I need to be careful to make sure I understand the terms of this conversation. Is she bored? Is she looking for something to repeat to everyone else back at school tomorrow?

"I suppose I'm asking because it's easy to end up in a camp if you're Japanese. That's all the government needs to know about you. But there are tons of German immigrants in the United States. They didn't lock up all of you. Only the ones..."

She doesn't finish her sentence. What she means is, to be German and end up in an enemy camp, you must have done something really wrong.

I wish I did not want to answer her. I wish she wasn't being curious about me. I wish she wasn't pretty. I wish I wasn't so aware that this is the longest conversation I've had with any other person my age in Crystal City and that she doesn't know anything about me, and so maybe because of that, we could be friends.

"My father is a farmer," I start carefully. "An engineer in Germany, but—there were a lot of German farmers in Iowa."

A whole community. Barn-raisings. Parties on St. Thomas's Day. She is right, they didn't lock up everyone. They barely locked up anyone.

"There was a hall the next town over where we went to hear a band play every Friday. The owner invited my father to hear a speaker from Chicago talk about the American Nazi party. He said he was inviting just a few friends."

Mr. Schweitzer had been good to my family. Was he good enough to warrant my father agreeing to see the speaker? I don't know. It doesn't matter. Chapters of the German-American Bund were all over the United States by then, giving lectures about the American Nazi party. Twenty thousand had gone to Madison Square Garden to listen to a man named Fritz Kuhn talk about preserving the Aryan race in the United States.

"So you *are* here because your father's a Nazi," Haruko says.

"He's not a Nazi."

She doesn't respond, but I can hear her doubt.

"Vati just went to the *one meeting*, as a favor to a friend. He didn't believe in what they were saying." I try to keep my frustration in check; this isn't how I wanted the conversation to go. "He came home and said the meeting was a dozen old, wrinkled men talking nonsense. But later, when the FBI came, they said he had signed in at the meeting. They had a sign-in sheet, so he signed in. So the FBI took him. And we followed."

I try to remember the story calmly. The facts. First, there were two months of us not knowing where he was, if he was even still in this country, if he was even still alive. Then, there were four months where we were trying to join him, but those four months are another thing in my life I don't like to talk about.

Haruko whispers something. I can't tell if I'm meant to hear. "And then you got on the train" is what she says. "And then all of us got on the train."

There is no point in looking out the small window anymore. It's nothing but a swirl of dirt. It must be barely after seven, but outdoors it looks like midnight. Indoors the oil lamp casts a weird glow on everything in the room. I can make out the contours of Haruko's face enough to know that she's not sneering, the way I worried she would be. She takes in a breath, hesitating before she speaks again.

"I was crying because we got a letter from my brother," she says. "He's in the 442nd. Do you know what that is?"

"The army?"

"Japanese division. Boys like him wanted to fight for their country." She juts her chin out, like she thinks I'll contradict her.

I've never heard of the 442nd, but I don't think this is the right time to say that. "If you got a letter, then that means he's okay, right?"

She bites her lip. "He says he is. My parents think he is."

"You don't?"

"I wish I did, but I don't. I can tell."

"How can you tell?"

"Because I just can."

She uses the corner of her work blanket to quickly wipe her eyes. I think she is hoping I won't notice, but this girl, who was stone-faced when she was reunited with her own father, who was confident and laughing in school, can't stop crying when she talks about her brother.

"What's he like?"

"Ken?"

"Yes. I've never had a brother. I've almost, but—I don't have any brothers or sisters."

Haruko sucks in a quick breath, and the noise that comes

out next is halfway between a laugh and a sob. "He is like—
he is like, if he were not my brother, I would probably not be
friends with him. We're not interested in the same things.
He never cared about what other people thought. He would
make up the stupidest—and it was okay. When I was with
him, I did, too. Because I didn't have anything to prove. He
understood me. He understood what it was like to be—and
our parents did, too, of course, but they were from Japan so
it was different, they didn't need to fit in the same way. Ken
understood what it was like to be both things, to be—"

She cuts herself off and looks embarrassed. Tears roll down
her face, making little wet streaks in the dust. "Nobody here
has asked me about who Ken really is, besides that he's a soldier." She shakes her head. "I know I'm not making any sense. I
know I'm not—why am I telling you all this?"

"Because I asked," I say.

She laughs, like my answer is funny, and I realize this
was another question that I wasn't supposed to answer liter-
ally. "That's not what I—" She stops, and her breath comes
out chopped and ragged as she tries to stop crying. "I guess. I
guess because you asked."

She looks down at her lap, twisting the blanket between
her hands. "Margot, earlier at school. I'm not a mean person.
I just..."

"It was easier for you not to talk to me."

She twists the blanket harder. "Yes. It was easier for me
not to talk to you."

I want her to add something to that. To say that she's sorry and things will be different in school tomorrow. But she doesn't, and I try to fight my disappointment because honestly I shouldn't expect her to. Why would she?

It will just be this, then. Those are the terms. We'll have this one time in the icehouse and we'll never talk again.

I keep my eyes on the ground, where I see something metallic. One of Haruko's bobby pins. I pick it up and clean it against my dress. It's a new thing, a shiny new thing to look at. There are no bobby pins in the general stores. *You should keep this*, I want to tell her. *You should make sure you hold on to this. You won't be able to get another.*

Haruko is watching me. "Why aren't you angrier?" she asks me. "When you talk about how you got here, you sound so matter-of-fact about it. Aren't you mad, if you think your father doesn't deserve to be here?"

"I can't be angry," I say without having to think about it. "After they took my father away, I thought I would never see him again. But then I saw him again. So it could have been much worse."

I wish I knew how to explain more, why anger isn't an emotion that makes sense for me to have. How, in order to survive here, you have to decide that you chose to be here. You have to find a way to put Crystal City into a box, instead of letting it box in you. Count the new inmates. Notice the new things. My family will get out of here intact, and we will go home to Iowa, and that is what matters. The rest of this is something to be observed. The bad parts don't have to be remembered and they can't be explained.

It could be so much worse.

"Haruko. I saw your family on the first day you came." It's a risk, to tell her this, but she seems so upset, and if we're never going to talk again, it might not matter what I say now. "I saw you and I thought...." I hesitate, because I don't want her to think it's strange, how much I remember about that day. "You didn't look happy."

"Why would I look happy? I was reporting to a prison."

I blush. "I mean, you didn't look happy to be seeing your father. You looked alone."

"You thought you saw that?"

"Maybe I was wrong."

A pause that feels like it lasts forever. Then Haruko's shoulders suddenly fall and she slowly shakes her head back and forth.

"You weren't wrong," she whispers. "I'm so angry. I'm so angry all the time."

"I know it's hard, what they did to your fath—"

"I'm angry *at* my father," she interrupts. The words come out harshly, in a rush. Her voice echoes off the wall of the ice-house and it's a different tone than she's had until now.

"Why?" I ask, trying to keep up. "Did he make your family follow him?"

"No. I mean yes, but no. It was my mother's idea. She was the one who put in the request."

65

"Then I don't understand. Do you think *your* father *does* deserve to be here?"

I say it because I couldn't immediately think of another explanation, but I don't expect it to be true. I expect her to explain how I'm wrong, the way I did when she asked about Vati.

But instead, Haruko's face breaks open. Her mouth twists in anger at my question, but she can't manage to yell at me for asking it.

"You can tell me, if you want," I say softly. "I don't have anyone else to tell."

I mean, I don't have anyone else to tell in this camp, but I also mean, ever. I've never had secrets with anyone.

Haruko looks pained. "I think," she whispers.

"*What* do you think?" I lean forward. The straw under my blanket digs into my thighs.

"I think something happened on the day they took my father that I don't understand."

As soon as the words have left her mouth, she buries her face in her hands, like she is ashamed. She's crying again; it hurts her to say what she just did. It seems that it hurt her the way it hurts me to ask my father if he is going to ask for a job at the swimming pool. But I can't bring myself to talk about my father. And I don't know what else I should say, or how else I should offer comfort, or whether she would want me to.

I still have her bobby pin, making wavy indentations in my hand. When she lifts her face again, I hold the pin up.

May I, I gesture, since it's the only thing I can think of to offer.

She doesn't say no, so as carefully and non-clumsily as I can, I slide off my ice block and kneel in front of hers. I take a piece of her hair, and I smooth it back against her head, sliding the pin into place. I feel the dust coating her scalp on my fingers, but beneath that, I feel how her hair is soft and thicker than mine.

We are still. Both of us are completely still.

"Please don't tell anyone I said that," she whispers. "I don't know why I did. It's not true. I just want to go home. I want to go home so badly."

I want to tell her that I know what it is to be terrified for your family. How I make my father drill a hundred Latin verbs every night because I am trying to make sure his head is filled with that instead of with sadness.

"Whatever you say to me," I start, "whatever—"

A rattle pierces the air. Someone outside is jiggering the handle of the door. It hasn't opened yet; it must be jammed with dust. Haruko looks at me, scared.

Before I can think about why I'm doing it, I blow out the lamp and grab Haruko's wrist. We both scramble over her ice block, crouching in the blackness.

The door jerks open and a flashlight sweeps over the shed. It's a camp employee, probably checking to make sure nothing was damaged in the storm. We hold our breath as the light sweeps the floor.

Haruko's arm is cold against mine, and I can feel her soft hair brushing against my neck as we crouch behind the ice block. The guard whistles, taking his time, moving his flashlight in a methodical pattern. He reaches our side of the room and Haruko clutches my knee, trying to make herself smaller, and my leg burns where she's touching it.

I want the guard to hurry, but in that moment I also want him to take his time, in that moment it would be all right if he took forever. I know my face must be red. I don't know what is wrong with me. I don't know why I wanted to put that bobby pin back in her hair instead of handing it to her.

The guard finishes his inspection and turns away, still whistling the same song. As he leaves, Haruko's fingers slowly loosen from my knee, but I can't move anything until her hand is gone. I can't even breathe. I don't even need to.

Then the door swings closed. A rush of stale air pours in from the outside. The latch clicks, a final-sounding noise, and something has changed. Or something has disappeared.

I'm suddenly aware again of how cold it is in here. The dust under my collar and in the creases of my knees itches in a way it didn't a few minutes ago. My mouth feels unbearably dry.

Haruko stands up again, brushing off her skirt, feeling her hair to make sure the pins are in place. With the light from the lamp gone, she is just a silhouette.

"I guess it was silly to hide," she says, rolling up the sleeve of her cardigan so the hole doesn't show. "We had to find someplace to go in the storm; it's not illegal for us to be in here."

"That must mean the storm is over, though," I say, trying to busy myself by searching in the dark for my book.

"I lost track of the time. How long were we here?" She makes a show of slapping her forehead. "Why would you know—you don't have a clock, either." She laughs nervously; she's not acting like the same person she was before the guard came in, but neither am I.

"I don't think it's been more than half an hour."

In the dark, I can't figure out if she wants to say anything else, or if she wants me to say anything else. In the dark, I don't want to risk saying, *I'll see you tomorrow*, when I shouldn't make assumptions. "I'll fold up the blankets" is what I say finally. "You can leave first."

The sun is setting outside. I make myself jog, first because my body feels filled with loose, confusing energy, and then because I'm thinking of my parents, who must be at home and wondering where I am. But Mutti and Vati aren't there when I get back to our house. I worry that they're looking for me, that when I didn't come home they went to find me in the storm. Then I see the table, where my father has left a note with one word on it:

Hospital.

SEVEN

MARGOT

I REACH THE HOSPITAL PANTING, MY CHEST STABBING AS I RUN UP the dust-covered pathway marked with two sets of footprints. *At least that means my mother walked here by herself. At least they didn't have to wheel her in on a stretcher.*

Inside, my eyes search the big room: Rows of white beds. Two patients with thermometers in their mouths. Young nurses' aides in caps.

"Margot!"

Thank God. Thank God. Gott sei dank.

Vati and my mother are at the bed near the end of the room, the most private setup this building allows. She looks pale, but smiles when she sees me.

"It's nothing." She makes a calming gesture with her

hands before I can say anything out loud. "It's nothing worth this fuss. I fainted, but it was because I'd been standing and hadn't eaten much."

"Because you've been sick all day," Vati reproaches her. "It's worth more than a fuss."

I'm still trying to calm my racing heart when a new voice interrupts us.

"I agree with your husband," the voice says, and the three of us turn toward a sandy-haired man in a white coat, carrying a clipboard.

"It's always good to be on the safe side, and I'm glad you came in, Mrs. Krukow," the doctor says. "That being said, it does seem like based on what you told the nurse, you're right: It was the heat, combined with an empty stomach, combined with the roll call. I'm going to recommend that you receive an exemption from participating. You shouldn't have to, in your condition." He makes a few notes. "After having your feet up for a bit, are you feeling any better? Anything we can do to make you more comfortable?"

"I don't suppose you're hiding any *Schwangerschaftstee* in your pharmacy, are you?"

The doctor looks at my father, like maybe my mother is one of the brides who came to the United States but hasn't quite learned English. My mother's vocabulary is bigger than my father's, but there's no English translation for this word.

"Pregnancy tea," I explain for the doctor. "It's a mix of herbs. I think it has stinging nettle and peppermint."

"And Saint-John's-wort, and a few other things," my mother adds. "All German women drink it. It helps with nausea. With Margot, my own mother sent me some special."

My father turns impatiently to the doctor. "Can you get her some of that?" he asks. "Some of that tea, can you send her home with that?"

I already know the answer will be no. Of course the doctor can't send her home with that. The doctor had never heard of that.

"I'm sorry, but we don't prescribe such, ah, regional remedies. For common nausea like your wife's, we would instruct her to have bed rest, fluids, and perhaps some soda crackers."

"My wife's situation is not common." He is furious. "My wife has already been through—my wife's situation is not common."

"Jakob." Mutti lays a hand on his arm, which he shakes off.

"I'm sorry, Ina, but it's not. Your situation is not common. This time it's got to—you've got to be more careful this time."

"Do you think I was not careful the other times?" Her voice is stony.

The doctor looks back and forth uncomfortably between them as he tries to figure out how to make peace. "Of course, if you feel it helped last time, there's no harm in trying it again. You said you arranged for your mother to send you some last time?" he asks. "Perhaps that could happen again. Where does she live? You are from Iowa?"

"In Heidelberg," my mother whispers. "My parents are still in Germany."

"Of course." The doctor looks embarrassed. No tea will be traveling to the United States from Germany, even if we weren't in Crystal City.

He murmurs something about soda crackers, about seeing if he can get her some to take home, and then excuses himself. As soon as the doctor is out of earshot, my father leans in.

"This is ridiculous," he says through clenched teeth. "A pregnant woman, held prisoner, and denied the treatment that she needs."

"They're not denying her treatment if they don't have the treatment to give to anyone," I reassure him. "They're not trying to help other people more than they're trying to help her."

"Yes, Jakob," my mother says. "He told me to do the same thing he would have told one of his American patients to do. Which is rest. Which is what I will do, like thousands of women have before me. If we weren't in here, we *still* wouldn't be able to get mail from Heidelberg, at least not without Red Cross assists."

What my mother is saying is true, I suppose. But what my father is saying is also true. We had German friends in Iowa. A whole network of busybody women, *Tantchens*, who would have canisters of tea in their kitchens or know how to make it themselves.

My mother's shoes are off and I can see how bloated her

feet are. She's barely far enough along to show around her belly; there's a bump only when she presses her dress flat against her stomach. She's not as far along as she got last time. But her feet and legs are bloated. That's how she knew, she said, that she was expecting again. I take one of her feet in my hands and rub it.

She nestles into the pillow. "This bed," she says. "I don't want to malinger, but I am perfectly willing to pretend to be as sick as I need to in order to stay in this bed."

My father stiffens. "I did the best I could with the beds in our hut," he says shortly.

"I know, Jakob." My mother sighs.

"You think I didn't do enough, but I did the best I could."

"I am not criticizing you, I'm merely saying that I am comfortable, finally."

But my father isn't listening anymore. He's barely paying attention to us at all, chewing his lip as he sorts through something.

"I bet I know who could get the *Schwangerschaftstee*," he says, taking my mother's hand.

My mother and I look at each other. "No, you don't," I say quickly.

"He knows everybody in the camp," Vati says stubbornly. "He's in contact with lots of people on the outside."

My mother flinches. "I don't know why you would talk about this. Nothing would make me feel sicker than accepting something that way."

74

"For God's sake, he believes crazy things but he's not a bad man. He has a wife who has been pregnant."

"Promise me you won't," my mother demands. "His gifts come with strings." We haven't mentioned Frederick Kruse's name, but we all know who we're talking about.

"Excuse us, we don't mean to bother you," a new voice says. The three of us whip around, acting like we've been caught in some conspiracy instead of trying to figure out how to get tea for a pregnant woman.

Standing by the side of the bed are two of the Japanese nurse's aides I saw when I first came into the hospital. Close up, I realize one of the women I thought was an aide is actually in a doctor's coat. She's not a teenager, either, but a middle-aged woman, petite and shorter than I am. I have never seen a woman doctor before, much less a Japanese woman who is obviously a detainee herself. But I recognize this woman. Her face is more angular, but they have the same forehead and chin.

"Mrs. Tanaka," I blurt out.

My own mother looks at me, confused. "Have you met?" she asks.

Haruko had been so focused on talking about her brother that I almost forgot about the rest of the family with her.

I spent the storm with your daughter. She told me about Ken. I watched her cry.

I don't say this. "Her name is on her coat" is what I say. I don't entirely know why I told that lie. I just know the ice-house is a secret.

Mrs. Tanaka—Dr. Tanaka—says something to us in Japanese, and the nurse's aide, the one who had spoken to us before, quickly translates.

"She says she heard what you were looking for," the aide says. "She says that some tea is sold in the Japanese commissary. It's bad American stuff, not like what you are looking for, but you might find it soothing anyway."

My mother smiles. "What a kind offer," she begins, at the same time my father shakes his head.

"We don't need charity," he says shortly. "From other people. I can take care of my family, thank you."

"It's not charity, she's a doctor and she's trying to be nice." I put my hand on his arm. It diffuses things sometimes to put a hand on his arm.

"She should be doing her *job*."

"This is her job."

"Her job is interrupting family conversations?"

"Please, grosse Schnecke."

Grosse Schnecke. Big snail. I am calling him by the nickname I haven't used in years, because of how much it made him laugh a few weeks ago to call me *kleine Schnecke*, little snail.

"It's not what your mother was looking for, and we don't need it," Vati says again.

"Jakob."

"I know how to take care of you and Margot!" he explodes.

"Why do you both always act this way? These worried looks that you always exchange behind my back? I am a part of this family!"

"We don't *always* do any—"

"You think I am weak."

My father's voice raises in a growl, a sound I have never heard come out of his mouth before. He flings my mother's hand away roughly, and she immediately cradles it with her other hand.

Dr. Tanaka looks concerned before the aide finishes translating; she hasn't needed to understand English to know what is happening. I wonder if Dr. Tanaka talks about her patients at home. I wonder if tonight at dinner, she'll tell Haruko about the fight between the German parents with a daughter her age. The thought fills me with dread.

"Come for a walk with me, Vati," I say abruptly. "Mutti can rest for a minute and we can stretch our legs."

My mother is still trying to smile at Dr. Tanaka, but it's so forced.

"A walk. Please, for me."

"This bed will not fly away while you're gone," Mutti says. There's a tremble in her voice, desperation for us to leave. "I will be right here. They probably need to talk to me about private woman-things."

I lead him out of the building to the hospital courtyard, which is filled with mesquite trees. Branches litter the grass, blown off in the storm; the two benches are too dusty to sit on. "What is wrong?" I ask my father as we walk laps around the yard.

"What do you mean, what is wrong? I'm worried about your mother. I have to care for my family."

"The doctors are caring for her now."

"The American ones aren't. They won't do it."

"The...the Americans?" I say, confused.

"It's other Germans who are always offering to help. What have the Americans done besides hurt us? Would we be getting this treatment if I were home in Berlin?"

Other Germans? Home in Berlin? "Vati." I am calm. I am steady. Inside I am trying to pretend what he's said is normal, but I know it's not, because if he'd talked like this earlier today, I would have been too embarrassed to admit it to Haruko in the icehouse. "Vati, what happened? This doesn't sound like it's about Mutti."

He kicks at the landscaping underneath the mesquite trees. "I got a letter." He cuts off, glancing to the hospital door, where a nurse has brought out a patient in a wheelchair. He nods for me to follow him farther away, and starts to talk again when we're out of earshot. "I got a letter from Mr. Lammey. He wants to lease our land to someone else. He can't have it sit."

"Oh," I say, as lead fills my stomach. "Oh. I see."

Our land. That's how I've always thought about it. How my parents have always talked about it. We were the ones who decided where to plant corn and where to plant barley. We plowed it in neat rows. We worked after dark, because Mutti and Vati wouldn't let me stay home from school in harvesting season the way other students did.

But of course it wasn't ever our land. It was Hank Lammey's land. We rented it; we paid him in crops. That's what this is about—the profits, I tell myself. Mr. Lammey can't make a living if nobody is farming that land.

"He said it's too difficult, to have a German enemy alien as a tenant. He said that he doesn't feel that way about us personally, but the way other people feel..."

"But you're going to write him back, right?" I say. "And remind him that we have friends in town, and that it wouldn't be like that?"

"I've already written the letter. I sent it this morning."

Mr. Lammey owns the land, but we built the house. Year after year, starting when I was small and they first settled in Fort Dodge and began working that plot. They saved money, and they bought lumber and built our house, room by room.

"I learned how to swim in the Lammeys' pond," I say. I don't know why I'm remembering this now. "Remember? Mutti and I were both in our underthings when she taught me. I kept being afraid the Lammey boys would see, but Mr. Lammey said if he caught them looking, he would whip them."

"I think your mother would have whipped them herself."

"Scolded them, at least."

"Did she ever tell you about the landlord of the first room

we rented in Iowa? You might have been too small to remember it."

I shake my head. I don't think I've heard this story.

"We had barely started building the house," Vati says. "The three of us were crammed into a shabby room in a boardinghouse, and there was a hole in the door. Your mother became convinced the landlord was spying on her when she got dressed. I wanted to have a word with him, of course, but she told me she would handle it. When I came home the next day she'd hung a sign covering the hole that said, *Ten cents a peep*. Or maybe it was an envelope with, *If you must peep, have the decency to pay*."

"Was there a cat who lived in that house? A big orange one that used to scratch me?"

"Jingles. I'm surprised you can remember that."

Barely. I remember the cat, and a bedraggled yard that my father would chase me in, and how he would come home from working on the farmhouse caked in dirt and my mother would pour bucket after bucket of boiled water into a metal tub for his bath. She never complained. Even when it was so cold that she had to throw rocks into the well to break the ice before drawing up the bucket, she never complained. "What did you do when you saw the sign, the one that Mutti made?"

The corner of his mouth tugs. "I slid a dime through the hole."

"Vati!"

"And the landlord never looked again. At any of us,

actually; he spent the next three months avoiding us in the breakfast room."

"And you didn't have to fight him," I say.

My father shrugs. "I wonder if I should have protected her instead of letting her deal with that on her own."

"She protected herself."

"She was so tired, and you were sick that winter, and none of us were getting any sleep." He swallows hard. "But we would pile under the blankets and stare at you for hours and talk about what a life we were going to build."

I search for the right things to say to my sad, breaking father, but there's nothing. I can't think of anything. The sun has gone down while we've been talking; it's almost all dark now.

"Should we go back?" my father asks, and I nod because the anger has left his voice.

Inside, my mother is still talking to Haruko's mother. She looks up when she sees us. "I was telling Dr. Tanaka again that her offer to find me some tea was very kind. *Very kind,*" she repeats, this time looking at Haruko's mother. "Which I may be happy to take you up on, if I find myself again feeling as badly as I did this afternoon. Right now I'm feeling much better."

She waits for the aide to translate before she continues. "And I know my husband is also very grateful. We were both so affected by the heat."

Dr. Tanaka doesn't protest about the tea anymore. She

gives a polite nod, and then gestures to the aide that they should give my family privacy again. Before she leaves herself, though, she steps closer to my mother's bedside and begins to rearrange her pillows, moving one so it's lower behind my mother's back, creating more support for her to lean on. When she speaks again, it's in English, and low enough that I'm wondering if she's trying to talk privately to my mother, or if she wishes my father and I weren't around. "Need tea, need anything," she says. She enunciates each word carefully. "Need anything, come to me."

It's so kind. It's so humiliating, because in her concern, I see how she sees my family.

EIGHT

HARUKO

THE OPPOSITE OF SERENE, I THINK TO MYSELF AS I WALK HOME
through the dust. Whatever I was in front of Margot in the
icehouse was the opposite of everything I have tried to be
since coming here. I said more than I should have said and
asked more than I should have asked, and let myself be so
much more raw than I should have let myself be. She listened
to me talk about Ken, she listened to me talk about my father.
I shared my secrets and she barely told me anything in return.
Why did I pour everything out?

I arrive at school the next day debating what to say to her,
but it turns out I've worried for nothing—Margot isn't there.
The desk I'd so desperately wished empty the day before
stays empty all day long.

And she's not there the day after that, and a crazy part of me wonders whether I made everything up, whether I really hid behind a block of ice praying a guard wouldn't find me. When I finally ask Miss Goodwin, on the third day, if she knows what happened, she seems surprised I care Margot is gone. "Her mother has been sick," she explains. "Margot is looking after her."

I could try to find her house; it wouldn't be against the official rules. But some rules are official, and some rules are quietly understood and everyone knows to follow them. The Japanese people that I know here—they are businessmen and doctors and teachers. The first round of German prisoners, my father said, came here because they were the ones who built the camp. They're laborers, farmers, construction men, who asked to stay in Crystal City when it turned out nicer than the prison where they'd been living. We were never meant to be here together.

Maybe she has left the school. Her parents could have decided to send her to be educated with the rest of the Germans. Which would be good, I remind myself. Her never coming back to my school is exactly what I should want. It's exactly what I thought I did want, until Margot put the bobby pin in my hair while I cried and cried about Ken, and for a brief sliver of time someone else was holding my fears.

Plink. Plink.

Chieko, knocking on the window. Wake-up time, line time, see how many minutes I can get away with making my

shower last when the limit is supposed to be three. The longest
I've succeeded yet is six. Today an old woman starts rattling
the wooden shower door after four. We all try to steal shower
time. It's the one place any of us can ever truly be alone.

*Maybe she got sick with whatever her mother had. Maybe
she swallowed too much dust, trying to help me in the storm.*

Chieko talks for a long time before she realizes I haven't
joined in. About how the monks giving Japanese lessons after
federal school hours are mean, and I'm lucky my parents
aren't making me and Toshiko go. About how there's another
sugar shortage, which means our rationing will change, about
how the pool is going to open soon. Chieko has adjusted to
all of this. She's never broken down. She has an older brother,
too, but he sleeps in the room next to her and she knows
where he is every night. She looks at me and thinks that I am
like her. I want to be. I wish I could just be like Chieko.

"So I think I will anyway," she says, as we brush our teeth
after our showers. "Do you?"

"Think I will what?" I say, trying to sound interested.

"Go to the judo match later. Are you paying attention at
all? Hey, do you want to come over tonight? My father got the
film they're showing on Saturday; he's going to test the reel."

"Do you think it's strange that we don't watch with the
Germans?" I ask.

"What do you mean? We have our own projector. They
have their own projector."

"I don't know. I just—like that Margot girl. If we wanted

to go to the Saturday movie with her one night, could we invite her to the late showing when we had the reel? Or go to the earlier showing at the German recreation hall?"

"Marg—" Chieko's face screws up while she tries to place who I'm talking about. "I told you, if you want to see a movie twice, you can come to my house when we test the projector; you don't have to go to the German screening. You're so funny sometimes."

Geometry, social studies. Guards come in while we study; they've done this every day, whispered a few words with the teacher and glanced at us sitting in our desks.

Miss Goodwin passes me a note. My father forgot his lunch. *Correction,* I think: My father forgot the concept of packing his own lunch because it was something my mother always did, but now she has a job, too. Could I go to the mess hall and get him something during my own lunch break, the note asks, and bring it to the gate? It's the second time this has happened this week.

Margot could be gone, not just from school, but completely gone from the camp, and I wouldn't know.

Crystal City is like the snow globe my father once got: a whole city in a bubble. You can feel momentarily fine inside it, until you want something on the outside and you realize your entire world, and everything you are allowed to do, or see, or buy, or read, or eat, or look at must exist inside the fence with you. If Margot was on the other side of the fence, even two feet, she would no longer exist in my world.

Home economics. We girls learn to baste a hem. I am terrible at basting my hem.

Physical education.

Margot.

She's there: sitting in her seat when I get back from playing volleyball, her notebook already open while Miss Goodwin tells her to stay after class for the assignments she missed. I'm still sweaty from the match, my hair clinging to the back of my neck.

When she sees me she tentatively smiles. "Hi."

Hi, I say, but in my head. Before I can say anything out loud, Chieko arrives behind me, and then the rest of the girls in my class. "She's back," one whispers.

I don't think she meant for Margot to hear it. But she did; her ears turn pink. When she looks toward me I can tell she knows I heard it, too, and she's wondering if I'll say something to defend her. I should. I should tell Linda to mind her own business. I should at least return Margot's hello, so she doesn't look crazy for offering it.

I don't, though. I can't in front of everyone. My tongue won't move. Talking here feels public and strange.

When I sit down, Margot averts her own eyes, her face fully red, and starts turning the pages of her book faster than she could possibly be reading them. My stomach fills with guilt, but I can't find a way to speak to her until the period is half over, when Chieko is at the blackboard doing a math problem, and the rest of the class is distracted.

"I'm sorry about your mother," I whisper out of the side of my mouth. "I wanted to—"

"You wanted to what?" she whispers back flatly.

"I wanted—"

The bell rings while I'm figuring out what I wanted to say. *Lunch.* I wanted to thank her? I wanted to make sure she doesn't tell anyone else what we talked about? I wanted to suggest we shouldn't talk again? Her steady gray eyes are waiting for me to finish.

The bell rings again and I'm too late. She's out of her seat and through the door, and I'm staring down at the note from Miss Goodwin. My father.

The mess hall isn't far away. I pick up beef stew and bread with oleo, the meal served today for the families who don't have kitchens yet. At the gate, the guard from the spinach field hasn't arrived to pick up the lunch, but there's another one standing just inside the fence.

"Hey, Colorado!"

"Mike," I say. He was here last time I brought lunch, too.

"Chewing gum?" He holds out his hand.

"Hmm, I don't know." I try to adjust my brain away from what I should've said to Margot and be here with Mike instead. "I'm more in the mood for a Mitchell Sweet from Hammond's."

He throws his hand across his chest, pretending to be offended. "An arrow through my heart," he says. "You reject my gum *and* you imply that Hammond's is better than Baur's? This was the last pack from the store in town. Should I give it to someone else? There's an old German man here from Colorado Springs who I could talk to instead."

Hammond's. Baur's. A Mitchell Sweet with caramel and marshmallow. Mike is the only person I've met inside the fence who also exists back home.

"No, I'll take it, I'll take it." I hold out my palm.

"Are you sure?" He playfully snatches his hand back. "Because this old German man—" Mike breaks off and his smile disappears. Another guard has arrived. Mike stands up straighter, clasping his hands officially in front of him. "After-noon, Officer."

The other guard watches us, hovering a few feet away instead of climbing up the tower to take his post. "Does this detainee need any assistance, Officer?" he finally asks loudly. "Anything I can help with, since I'm sure you'd like to be off on your lunch break?"

"Miss Tanaka has been instructed to deliver lunch for her father. She has permission to wait until someone comes to pick it up, and I have been assigned to open the gate."

The older guard, still suspicious, finally huffs up the lad-der. Mike puffs his cheeks in an imitation of his colleague. "He gets grumpy because he wants all my attention for him-self," he whispers, then looks over my shoulder. "Oh, your father is here."

Two figures approach the fence. My father, in shirtsleeves

and worn pants covered in dirt. A bandanna around his neck.
I didn't think he'd be here. Last time I just passed the food
to an employee. But here he is, escorted by a guard, dressed
worse than he ever would have dressed to go to work at home.
He wouldn't have dressed like this to take out the garbage.

"Haru-chan!" He smiles when he sees me waiting.

"I got your note. I brought the food." I hand the pail to
Mike, who unlocks the gate and hands it to the other guard,
who inspects the contents before handing it to my father. The
exchange complete, I nod and start to turn.

"Why don't you stay?" he calls. "There is enough food
that we can share."

"I have to get back to school. I took up my lunch hour
running to the mess for you."

"Did you eat while you were there?" I shake my head no.
"So, more reason to stay." He opens the pail and pushes a slice
of bread through the fence links. "You have a few minutes. And
I have to wait here until the guard finishes his lunch anyway."

His guard has produced his own lunch pail and is eating
a sandwich while talking with Mike. I don't want to stay, but
I can't figure out a way to be so deliberately disobedient as to
leave my father standing here, eating alone behind a fence.

Except, I realize, he isn't inside the fence. Not right now.

"Look what happened," I say. "What side of the fence
we're each on. Somehow I'm the one in prison now. You're on
the outside."

"Haruko."

"I was joking."

"Can't we have a pleasant lunch together?"

"Of course we can, Otousan," I say, but I am being impolite through my politeness. My father has never required formal honorifics and it comes out of my mouth sounding mocking.

He sighs. "Haruko, what is wrong?"

I roll the leftover bit of my bread into a ball. Why am being I so rude to him? Why am I living up to the Nisei stereotypes published in the *Rafu Shimpo* back home, the angry letters from old Issei men complaining that we second-generation girls have no respect for our elders.

"I know you are not happy to be here," he says. "I don't think there is any person in this camp who would not prefer to be somewhere else, but the way you are behaving toward me..." He shakes his head. "Is there something you want to talk about?"

Yes. There are a dozen things I would like to talk about. Why is he *letting* me be so rude? Where is the lecture on *shitsuke* that I should be getting about using good manners? My father might be less strict than most of my friends' parents, but still I used to get that lecture in Denver: if I was late coming home, if I was giggling in the middle of church.

Is he letting me be rude because he feels guilty I'm here? *Because he thinks I know something?*

I would like to talk about the things I haven't allowed myself to say out loud until I said them to Margot. The things hiding in the back of my brain that I didn't even realize I felt.

"Haruko?" he asks again.

"Why didn't you protest when they said they were going to take you?" I blurt out.

He closes his eyes and sighs. "We talked about this."

"Tell me again."

"What would have been the point? If the government decided it had evidence against me, then the government had made its decision."

"You could have tried."

"Did that work with any of the other families who are here?" he asks. "No matter how they tried to fight it, did you see it work? *Shikata ga nai.*" *It cannot be helped.*

My father still doesn't know everything that we went through. How my mother spent a frantic month trying to give away all our possessions to neighbors and friends. "For safe-keeping, temporary," she said, as she handed away her grand-mother's tea set, my roller skates, our good dishes. It was easier to give things away at the beginning. When people realized what my father had been accused of, they were afraid to associate with us. Every Japanese person who lived on the West Coast had already been relocated, forcibly removed from their homes. The only thing keeping those of us in Colorado safe was the fact that the government wasn't evacuating noncoastal states. If my father had been taken, that meant nobody was safe after all.

My father was not with my mother and me when our hair salon posted a sign on the door: NO JAPANESE, or when a car drove past and the window rolled down and the driver threw a bottle of soda at us that splashed all over our clothes. We were so humiliated. I was so serene. "It's okay, Mama, probably an accident," I said. I didn't tell her that the English-speaking driver had yelled, *Yellow bitch!* before he drove off.

"Why are you asking now?" my father says again.

I am asking now because there are terrible things that I have not been able to stop worrying about. I am asking because something happened on the day they took him. Something he almost told me, but didn't.

"Why are we here, Papa? Why are we *really* here?"

He quickly glances over to Mike and the other guard before lowering his voice to a hiss. "You know that they did not need a reason to take any of us. Stop asking questions, Haruko."

And that is what worries me. They didn't need a reason. The government didn't need a reason for doing any of this. People were taken because of the artwork they had on their walls, the martial arts they practiced for their exercise. People were taken because of Executive Order 9066, which said the government could invent military zones and relocate anyone it wanted. The government could have taken us because of that, and then we would have gone to a camp run by the War Relocation Authority, which is where the West Coast Japanese went. But they didn't do that with us. They said they were taking us because my father was passing messages to hotel guests. They put us in a camp run by the Department of Justice, which was meant not just for Japanese people but specifically for enemy aliens.

It's such a specific charge.

"I just want to know the truth," I say, desperately, too loud. Mike has looked up because even with his bad ear, he heard me. I lower my voice again. "You looked at me, on the day they came to take you. I want to know—"

"Thank you for bringing my lunch," my father interrupts. "Now go back to school. Your questions are not helping."

"But would you tell me?" I ask. Nearby, the guard who brought my father keeps checking his watch. It's time for them to leave; he'll come over any minute.

"Tell you what? There is nothing to tell."

"But if there were something?" I say frantically. The guard has finished his sandwich; he's starting to walk over.

Reassure me, I want to say. Reassure me that I have nothing to worry about, that I don't need to be angry with you anymore.

"This conversation is incredibly disrespectful," my father says stiffly, and here is the *shitsuke* lecture, which I deserve, because I don't usually press things this much. "I am ashamed that you have not learned better manners.

"But if you want the real answer to your question, it is no. Of course I wouldn't. You are my daughter. My job is to protect you. Of course I wouldn't tell you things that are dangerous."

NINE

HARUKO

THE UNION STORE AFTER SCHOOL. THE UNION STORE BECAUSE THIS is where I am supposed to take Toshiko, to use our parents' cardboard tokens so she can buy a new pair of shoes. Where I will not think about what my father told me at lunch. Because he managed to say exactly the right thing and also exactly the wrong.

"I'll come, too," Chieko offers, but I wave her off because I don't think I can pretend to be fine in front of her.

Toshiko chooses her shoes quickly; there are only two options in her size.

"Do you want the mail while you're here?" asks the clerk, a chatty woman my mother's age. "I saw a few things with your family's name on them."

Outside the store, while I wait for Toshiko to change into the new shoes, which she wants to walk home in, I flip through the small stack: a catalog, some official-looking things for my parents, a letter whose return sender I recognize as one of Toshiko's teachers from back home. And a piece of V-mail. *V-mail.*

"Did we get anything good?" Toshiko asks.

"You got something from Miss Nina."

While Toshiko squeals and begins to open her letter, I slip the one from Ken into my pocket. I don't know why I'm not telling her about it; it's selfish and unfair. But she won't be looking for another letter from him so soon, not when we just received one a few days ago. And I don't want to read another letter from Ken in front of my family. I don't want a repeat of everyone else acting so happy, nobody else thinking something is wrong.

"Do you want to go straight home, or do you want to go to the community center?" Toshiko asks. "We could listen to records."

I don't want to go to the community center. I want to read the letter from Ken.

And what I really want is to read the letter with Margot.

The thought comes quickly before I can stop it. We hadn't spoken again in school, but now I'm standing here with a letter from my brother, and who else can I read it with? My father, who I don't trust? Chieko, who, if I start to cry again, will tell everyone? *Poor Haruko, be gentle with her, she is going through a rough time.* It would get back to my family in hours.

I want to read the letter with a person I barely know, because she is the only person I have been honest with since everything changed.

"You should go to the community center if you want," I tell Toshiko, before I can second-guess myself. "I ran out of school too fast. I need to go back and—and get some papers and things. I'll see you for dinner later."

It hasn't been more than twenty minutes since the last bell, but when I get back to the school, our classroom is empty. Miss Goodwin must've already finished explaining the assignments to Margot and the hallways are dark and quiet. I try to swallow my disappointment, to convince myself that it's lucky she's already left. What was I even thinking?

The door to the girls' bathroom opens as I walk down the hall.

Margot sees me and freezes. Then she quickly lowers her eyes, gathering her pile of books from outside the lavatory.

"I'm sorry," I say, as she stands, thinking too late I should have helped with her books.

"For what?"

"For earlier today. Ignoring you. I didn't know how to...I had a lot on my mind."

"Were you waiting for me?" She looks over my shoulder to see if I'm alone.

"I came back to find you."

She shakes her head, pressing her books tightly to her chest. "I shouldn't have talked to you. You told me it was

97

easier for you if we didn't talk at school. It's probably easier for me, too."

She brushes past, head down. I can't tell whether she's telling the truth, or upset with me, or trying to get away from me. She'll barely even look at me.

"How is your mother?" I ask, before she can reach the door.

Margot stops and slowly turns. "She's fine. Please thank your mother for offering the tea, even if we didn't take it."

She must read my confusion. "I thought that's how you knew she'd been sick," Margot explains. "Your mother was one of her doctors."

"Miss Goodwin said your mother was sick. I didn't know she'd gone to the hospital. Is she okay?"

"She's just pregnant and she's . . . she's been unwell before." Margot looks back over her shoulder toward the door. "Is that everything? I told you, thank you for your apology. But I have homework to catch up on so I should probably go home now."

She reaches for the handle.

"Hold on!"

Margot pauses.

"Will you come with me to the icehouse again?" I ask.

"When?"

"Right now, just for a minute."

"Why?" she asks warily.

"Because."

"Because why?" Now she seems genuinely curious.

I scramble for an answer. "You could borrow my notes for the classes you missed while you were out."

I don't think she believes me.

She's biting her lip, making a calculation I can't figure out, but in this moment I need her to say yes. I don't have anyone else to go to. I need her to say yes.

Because the last time we were there, you told me I could share secrets with you because you didn't have anyone to tell. Because it turns out I don't think I have anyone to tell, either, anyone but you. Because you were right the first time. I am alone.

I let Margot leave first. By the time I get to the icehouse, she's laid out the blankets again, but not where they were last time. Now they're far from the entrance, tucked behind some of the largest ice blocks so nobody who opened the door would see her at first. I don't myself until she waves her arm. There's also a thermos of water and another oil lamp, the kind they sell at our Union Store and probably in the German commissary.

"I've come here a few other times," Margot explains, when I point to the thermos. "It's nice to have a quiet place."

"I take long showers for the quiet," I say, relieved for something to immediately talk about. "I can usually get a couple of extra minutes before someone starts yelling at me to hurry up."

"My mother and I started doing our laundry at midnight so we wouldn't have the crowds," says Margot.

"But everyone does their laundry late at night."

"Because my mother and I started it," she says simply. "Do you want to give me your notes?"

By the lamplight we go over the homework, and I'm trying to be normal with her, to treat her like any other school friend in order to make up for ignoring her in the classroom. But she barely laughs at the jokes I try to make, and it's obvious after a few minutes that she didn't need help on the homework. I still can't figure out why she agreed to come, or if it was stupid to ask her. And I can't figure out how, now that I know her mother was in the hospital, and Margot probably wants to get home, to bring up that I invited her here because I wanted a favor.

"Are you sure you understand the guidelines for the Milton paper?" I ask when she's finished copying my notes, though I've already explained them twice and she understood them the first time.

"Haruko." She shifts a little on her blanket. "Why else did you ask me here?"

"What do you mean?" My voice is fake and high-pitched.

Margot focuses on her pile of papers, smoothing them down, making sure each page aligns with the one below. "I appreciate your help with school. But you don't have to be nice to me if you're worried about me repeating the things you said about your family. I won't."

"I know you won't," I say, though it's exactly what I worried about a few mornings ago. "I'm not worried about that."

"Then...then I guess I don't understand what I'm doing here." She looks up. Her irises have flecks of blue I didn't notice before, just around the pupils. Margot doesn't make eye contact often. Her eyes are deep and opaque and I still have no idea what she's thinking at all.

When I don't answer, she starts to stand, brushing off her skirt. "I guess I'll see you tomorrow."

"Wait." I'm louder and more desperate than I meant to be. She stops, and I hear annoyance in her voice for the first time.

"Haruko, what do you *want*? You don't have to be my friend. We don't have to do this."

Instead of saying anything else, I stand, too, taking Ken's letter out of my pocket and handing it to her.

She looks at the return address. "It's from your brother?"

"It came this afternoon. I haven't read it yet."

"Why not?"

"Would you read it? Out loud, to me?"

Margot turns the letter over in her hands but still doesn't open it. "Why do you want me to read it?"

I don't know why a letter from Ken fills me with such dread. I am dying to hear from him. Dying for a long, chatty, ridiculous letter full of the bad jokes that would tell me everything is okay.

"Please," I say. "I can't read it alone."

Margot finally reaches into the envelope.

"It's just one page," she says, pulling out a thin white sheet that I can see is covered in a tiny version of his sloppy cursive. "Are you sure?" she asks one more time, waiting for me to nod before she sits again and starts reading aloud.

101

"*Dear Everyone,*" Margot says. It's startling to hear Ken's words come out in her voice.

"*Well, family, the big news here is that yours truly is officially not over his fear of snakes! I was putting on my ol' boots this morning, and discovered that a nasty lil critter had gotten there first. I screamed something awful, but now I double-check my boots, triple-check them, even, before I put them on every morning!*

"*The other big news is that we had a fella come out here last week with a camera who said he was working on a newsreel about us. He filmed me for about twenty minutes doing a crossword puzzle because he said he was impressed by how 'realistic' I looked. Ha! I hope I get to be a movie star!*"

"That's a lie," I interrupt.

Margot looks up from the letter. "What is?"

"I'm sorry, I just—Ken would never want to be a movie star. I don't even think he would joke about it. He made fun of me whenever I used my wages to buy film magazines. Go on, though. Keep reading."

She pauses like she wants to say something, but then skims to find her place in the letter again. "*Do you remember Mrs. Minemoto from the post office?*" she reads. "*Her son is in the 442nd. Boy is it good to get to spend some real time with my old friend!*"

"Lie," I say again. "He hated Steve Minemoto. Hated him. He never told my parents that, because Steve was such a bootlicker that everyone's parents liked him."

"*—And reminisce about all the fun we used to have—*"

"Lie."

"—*Especially how we both miss the ice cream socials that the Japan League used to have for kids.*"

"*Lie.*"

Nobody liked those ice cream socials. The punch was awful. Every month our parents would send us, and every month a group of us would sneak out early and go walking instead, or drive out to Red Rocks before gas was rationed. Steve Minemoto didn't come with us, and if he was at the ice cream socials we never would have known. We didn't stay long enough to see him there.

Margot glances up. "Some people don't express themselves well, especially in letters," she says.

"Ken does. Ken used to leave notes for me behind the register at the soda fountain where we worked after school."

"Well, maybe he hated Steve Minemoto in Denver, but by the time he got to wherever he is, he was excited to see a face that reminded him of home."

Would I have been happy to see Evelyn Minemoto, Steve's boring younger sister, if I had arrived in Crystal City and found her waiting for me? I can't imagine it. Maybe I would have been, but as hard as I try, I can't imagine it.

"Or," Margot continues, "have you thought that maybe he's just putting on a brave face? To give your family one less thing to worry about?"

Of course that's what I've thought. Of course that's what I'm thinking. But wouldn't Ken know I'd rather hear a terrible truth than an innocent lie? Wouldn't anybody rather that?

"Can you keep reading?"

"Say, Mama, a couple of us were arguing about the proper time to make mochi *at New Year's. I told them that you always made it the night before."*

It's not right, none of it is. I'm trying to find Ken in those sentences, but I can't. I'm trying to picture him writing those words, but in my mind the only way he would is if he was being forced. In my mind, he is writing those words because the enemy is standing over him, telling him, *Write a happy American letter. No, happier. No, more American.*

That fear is ridiculous, of course; if Ken were captured, his letters wouldn't arrive by V-mail. If Ken were captured, we probably wouldn't get letters at all.

Margot sees my exasperation. "I don't know your brother. I'm just trying to point out that there are lots of reasons the letter might not sound like him. And not all of them necessarily mean something terrible has happened."

The way Margot is asking these methodical, rational questions is irritating, but they are also, I realize, exactly the points Ken himself would drily raise, if he were here reading his own lying letter. *Maybe my letter is absurd because I didn't want to deal with our parents' questions,* he would say. This whole conversation with Margot is making memories of him flood back. *Maybe you should pull the twig out of your hair, Haruko, since we were all supposed to have been eating sundaes, not climbing around a bunch of rocks.*

Margot looks down at the letter again. "I don't think I should keep going," she says.

"No, I want you to."

"It seems like it's upsetting you and it's none of my business."

"I want you to keep going."

She looks at me again and this time I don't let her look away. "Please," I say. "I won't interrupt anymore."

Finally, Margot sighs and clears her throat and searches for her place.

"It's killing me to say all of this to you."

"*Go on*," I tell her. "I said I want to hear it."

She shakes her head, stricken. "No, that's what the letter says. That's the next line in the letter." She points at the paper to illustrate her point and then reads the line again:

"*It's killing me to say all of this to you, to pretend everything is fine, when what I really want to do is tell you how sorry I am that—*" Margot breaks off.

"That what? How sorry he is that what? What does he say next?"

My throat is full of lead. This is the first sentence I've heard or read in either of my brother's recent letters that sounds like it was written by Ken. It sounds terrifying—the first real sentence and it sounds terrifying.

Instead of continuing, Margot tries to hand the letter back, her face ashen. "I'm sorry," she says.

"Finish reading, just finish. Let's get to the end."

"I can't, that's it." She holds the paper closer to the lamp, scanning the back and the margins, as if searching for a missing paragraph. "That's all there is in the letter."

"What do you mean? It ends there?"

I snatch the paper away, racing to the bottom, where all I find are black lines. Straight black lines, and then below them, my brother's signature.

Love, Ken

It's been censored. Someone has crossed through the rest.

I hold the letter up, trying to see if any of Ken's words made it through the thick black ink. The dot of an *i*. The curving tail of a lowercase *g*. Nothing.

"I'm sorry," Margot is saying, her voice emotional. "I'm sorry, I should have scanned to the bottom before I started reading so I could warn you."

I'm still looking at my brother's handwriting. What could he have been trying to say? Was it something for me? Written in cursive, was it a secret message he knew only I'd read?

I wonder when the letter was censored. Were his words scratched out across an ocean, weeks ago, or were they scratched out a hundred yards away by a camp employee who sees me every day and counts me when I stand in a row?

The letter feels damp in my hands; my palms have broken out into a sweat. It's just two lines crossed out, not more than a sentence before Ken's signature. What could he have apologized for in one sentence? What did he have to be sorry for?

"Do you want some privacy?" Margot asks.

"I want my brother."

And now I'm crying again, because it seems like that's all I do in front of Margot. Quietly, she takes a handkerchief out of her skirt pocket and hands it to me.

"Distract me?" I ask. "Tell me about something else."

"What do you mean?"

"You listened to me pour my heart out twice, and I barely know about you."

She shakes her head. "That's all right."

"No," I insist. "I'm asking. I want you to."

"It's getting late."

"But you've barely told me anything and it feels…unequal."

"But that was your choice." The pitch in her voice raises a little. She's grabbed at the work blanket underneath her. "And I told you why my father was taken. I already told you my story."

"Not really," I press on. "You told me facts. You didn't tell me what it did to your family." I can see that I'm upsetting her, but I can't figure out why. Isn't this what friends would do, even secret friends? I've told her things I haven't told anyone else. Doesn't she see how that would make me feel grateful, but also exposed?

"I don't want to talk about what it did to my family."

"You said that—"

"I don't want to *talk* about what it did to my family. My family is *fine*. We are here and we are *fine*."

She scrambles to her feet, her face flushed, and I close my mouth, stunned. I wanted her to tell me something, but this doesn't look like vulnerability, it looks like fear.

"I'm—I'm sorry," I stammer. "I didn't know it would upset you so much. That wasn't fair of me."

Margot is looking into the oil lamp, the flame flickering off the curved walls and blocks of ice. "What does being fair mean to you?" she asks, frustrated. "I don't know if the rules in this camp are the same as outside. We're not even allowed to have chemistry books."

"Sometimes talking helps."

Her eyes flash. "And sometimes it doesn't."

"I really didn't mean to upset you."

Her breathing slows, and she reaches over to adjust the lamp. We both watch the flame on the walls.

"I didn't mean to get angry," Margot says, composing herself. "But I would do almost anything to protect my family, even things that didn't make sense. And I am sure your brother...I'm sure he is the same way. Trying to protect you. I'm sure that even if you can't see him in those letters, he's doing what he thinks is best. Everyone here is doing what they think is best for each other."

She looks toward the door, and then back to her notes piled on the floor. "It's almost dinnertime."

"Can I come back here tomorrow?" I ask, surprising myself. "We have an extra pillow. I could bring that. It would be more comfortable to sit on."

She bites her lip, thinking. "If you want to."

"The pillow, and maybe some food," I offer. "And, Margot, what's best would be for Ken to be honest with me. You can't just—you can't decide what's best for someone else. Don't you agree?"

"I don't know," she says, gathering her things. "I think people end up doing things for reasons we don't understand."

HARUKO

I should have seen it. I should have guessed by that conversation that the events that were going to ruin my life had already begun to occur, and I didn't even know it, and they weren't the ones I thought they would be. It's never what you think it will be.

MARGOT

Nothing had begun to occur. Sometimes people will do inexplicable things to protect the people they love. That was all I was trying to say.

TEN

MARGOT

September 21, 1944
Diameter of the swimming pool: 100 yards
Water required to fill a circular swimming pool with
    a diameter of 100 yards: 1,250,000 gallons
Bathing suit styles that have appeared in the General
    and Union Stores in the past two weeks in
    anticipation of the swimming pool opening: 5
Bathing suit styles that Haruko says are not
    "hideous": 0

"I HAVE SOMETHING FOR YOU," HARUKO SAYS. "BUT I CAN'T GIVE IT
to you unless you come with me now."

"I can't come with you now," I mumble, even though I'm

dying to know what she's talking about. "I have to do something for my parents before the lunch hour is over."

We're alone in the classroom. I didn't realize Haruko was orchestrating it when she sighed loudly and said, "I guess it's our row's turn to clean the blackboards." But this morning, *our row* meant just the two of us: Chieko and the other girl are both on Yell Squad and had permission to leave early and rehearse for the celebration later. It also wasn't actually our row's turn to do anything, but no other students were going to correct Haruko, not today, when they wanted to run home for their bathing suits. Now we're alone and wiping the blackboard with wet cloths and buckets.

"This is for your parents," Haruko tells me. "Your mother, at least. It'll be quick. But you have to come with me—he's meeting me at the gate on the Japanese side; that's where he's stationed today."

"Haruko, then I definitely can't come with you," I say, leaving aside the fact that I don't know who *he* could be. "You know I don't go there."

"I've thought of that," she says triumphantly. "We're going to say it's for our teacher. That we were selected to pick up a gift for Miss Goodwin. It won't be strange for you to be there if it's for school, and I heard that her birthday really is next week."

I'm smiling, of course I'm smiling, her triumph and excitement are contagious. But Haruko is talking about a public act in a place I don't belong. The federal school is supposed to be neutral and I am already out of place. It turns out only twenty-four German families ignored Mr. Kruse's recommendation and sent their children here, and none of the others are in my year.

"Do you really want us to walk through camp together?" I ask, pulling Haruko to reality. "When nobody else knows we talk after school? When we barely look at each other all day?"

"You know that's your decision as much as mine now," she responds quietly, scrubbing the same section of blackboard for a long time.

I say nothing because she's right and she isn't. It's still easier for her not to spend time with me at school. But it's also easier for *me* to not talk to her there, rather than risk having other people see us being friendly and convince her I'm too odd to spend time with. And it's easier for me not to have her at my house, where my father might be in the kind of mood where he says something about the Americans. So, it's a decision we both made. But it's her decision because she's embarrassed by me, and it's my decision because I'm embarrassed by me, too.

Still, in spite of all this, I have a friend. As long as I am careful, as long as I don't open up too much and ruin everything. I have a friend who hid from a storm with me in the icehouse seventeen days ago, and then kept coming back. She brought dried plums. I brought an extra pair of socks for mittens. She brought a skirt she was sewing. I brought a button for it. She hummed something while she sewed it on, and I remembered the tune the rest of the day.

"Margot?" She flicks water on me from her bucket. "Margot?"

"I think it's better if we don't," I tell her finally.

Her face falls. "I just wanted to do something for you. You never talk about yourself, you let me talk all the time, you told me about the icehouse. I wanted to pay you back."

"How?" My legs are wet. Listening to her, I hadn't noticed I was holding the sopping rag against my dress.

"It's nothing big," she says quickly. "The guard that I'm— Mike?—he's nice to me. I asked if the next time he was in town he could look for some tea that was more like what you said your mother wanted than what we have in our store. It took him a couple of weeks but he found two kinds and I don't know which is better. And I can't—I had to use the American dollars that I brought with me, and I couldn't put aside more than for one box. Mike is going to bring both kinds, and then return the one that's wrong."

She looks embarrassed at her lack of money, but I don't have any at all. My family used all our American dollars within two months of coming here, to order necessities from catalogs. Now we get the standard four dollars a month in tokens, to be used for incidentals, and we ration them carefully.

Haruko wants to use all her extra money for me. My mother hasn't been sick in a few weeks, but that's not the point. Haruko told her guard friend about me. She planned a surprise.

"You're smiling," she says.

"I do smile sometimes."

"You're actually smiling instead of telling me that it will actually take more than a minute because of the distance to the eastern gate, which you somehow will have memorized."

"Well. It *will* take more than a minute. It will take six minutes to walk there."

"That's a yes?"

Haruko needs the icehouse so there is a place where she can be who she really is, I think. And talk about the things she is afraid of without upsetting her parents. I need it because I am grateful for a place where I am *not* myself.

I don't know what we would look like outside the icehouse, if we would make sense at all. I want for it to work. I would like so badly for it to work.

"Yes," I agree now. "It's a yes."

"Does it look like your side?" She tilts her head, watching me as we walk down a street in the Japanese neighborhood. "Are the houses different or anything?"

"You've seen our side. The day we met." There are a few people outdoors, women sweeping the stoops of their tar-paper huts, but so far they've looked only slightly curious about my presence.

"I saw the German school before the dust storm came, that's all," she says. "What does your house look like?"

"Like these."

"What *else*? Margot, I'm just asking you to describe a house. It's one room? What about the outside?"

"There are planter boxes outside that my father built. He built a little porch, too, so my mother could sit outside. And he's going to make a bassinet. So we can rock the baby to sleep." My mother suggested it last night, something else to keep him busy, and my father agreed, and we all had a happy evening.

"That sounds nice," Haruko says. "Your father sounds really nice. Maybe I'll meet him one day."

"He is nice," I tell her, ignoring the second part of what she said and looking around at two Japanese boys tossing a baseball, a mother and daughter hanging clothing on the line.

"How did he meet your mother?"

"At a dance," I say, because I don't mind talking about the happy times. "My mother didn't want to go. She doesn't like dancing. She didn't give away her dancing shoes from that night until we came here, though; then she said she had to because she knew there wouldn't be enough space."

"I bet your family will be assigned bigger quarters when the baby comes—we get the two rooms because there are four of us," Haruko says. "See if you can get one close to the east side of your camp. I always think that those must look out into the orchard. It would be nice, to look out at trees and not at a fence."

We come to a small, unmarked building that Haruko tells me is the Union Store, which looks like the General Store's twin: the same structure used for houses, but with a screen door and a bigger wooden porch than houses are allowed to have. The guard tower where she's meeting Mike is less than fifty yards away.

There are more people standing outside the Japanese store than I've ever seen outside ours. Haruko hesitates as we get closer; it must be out of the ordinary here, too. Some of them are looking at me. It might be my imagination, but I don't feel like their curious looks are as benign as those of the other people we passed.

"It's fine," Haruko says, determined. "The milkman is German; he's here all the time. And there's Mike already." She points to a young guard with blond hair. He raises his hand. "Are you okay to wait here? I'll be right back."

I wave her off, but almost immediately wish I hadn't. The people outside the Union Store are all my grandparents' age, talking to each other animatedly, and now I'm certain at least some of their whispers are about me. I try to look purposeful, to make it clear I'm waiting for Haruko. I wish she would hurry. In the distance Mike opens a bag he's carrying, and I see them discussing the contents.

"Are you lost, miss?" One of the old men on the porch looks at me meaningfully, and the others fall silent, too.

"It's—it's for school," I stammer. "We had to pick up

something for school." I should go over to Haruko. I should have suggested that; it would be better than me standing here by myself.

"This might not be the best time for you to be here," the man says. His voice isn't rude, but it is pointed. He glances back to another older man. Only then do I notice how everyone else seems to be orienting themselves around that other man. He's holding a small rectangle of paper and his face looks gray. "Just for now, you might want to leave," the first man says.

"I have to wait for my friend."

"Perhaps you might ask her to hurry."

I gesture at the distance and am filled with relief when I see Haruko already walking back toward me, proudly waving two canisters of tea. She gives me them when she gets back, oblivious to the tense air. "This one has peppermint, which you said was important, but I didn't know if it was more important than Saint-John's-wort, which it doesn't have. Here, the ingredients are on the side."

I don't want to ruin this gift for her, so I try to ignore the people on the porch and concentrate on the ingredients she's pointing to.

"This seems fine," I say, after scanning the first can.

"No, but the other might be better. Read that one, too."

"This is good, really. Go give the other back to Mike," I tell her, wanting to leave. I glance back to the store and then lower my voice. "That man told me I shouldn't be here. I'm making people uncomfortable."

Now she looks over to the group clustered on the porch. "I don't know any of them," she says. "But I'll explain you're here with me."

"Let's just leave."

"No." She looks worried. "It's better for me to tell them it's for school, before some other gossip spreads halfway around camp."

I watch as Haruko speaks to the older men in Japanese, keeping her eyes low, nodding toward me and shaking her head. I watch as one of the men hands her the paper they were all looking at before, a telegram. Her lips move as she reads it, and they quiver a little when she hands it back. She says a few more things to them, then comes back to me.

"Let's go," she says, turning back in the direction we came from. We still have both canisters of tea.

"What happened?" I ask, trying to keep up with her. "Don't you have to give one of those back?"

"I'll find him in a few minutes," she says tightly, picking up speed.

"The point of you asking me to come was so he could return one today. Did you get in trouble? What did those people say?"

"Mr. Ito's grandson. They got a telegram. He's missing in action."

"Ken."

I know that's what she must be thinking.

She's shaking her head. "His grandson wasn't in the 442nd. He was only a quarter Japanese. He was somewhere else. But they told me—"

"That they didn't want to see a German person."

"Not right now. Just not right now."

"What else did they tell you?"

"What do you mean?" she asks, but her question has a hitch in it.

I stop. We're almost to the edge of the Japanese neighborhood. "The man said something else to you. After you read the telegram. What else did he say?"

Haruko is forced to stop, too. "He told me that I might want to think about us being friends. That school was one thing, but it wasn't wise for us to be friends."

"Oh," I say, watching Haruko play with the label on one of the canisters.

"I made you come," Haruko says. "And you were right, I shouldn't have."

"We'll know not to do it again," I say.

Haruko nods, but she still looks troubled.

"Unless," I say, fearing the worst but making myself continue. "Unless you think it's better to stop seeing each other in private, too."

"No, no, I don't want that." She looks back in the direction of the Union Store, now invisible. Her voice cracks. "Margot, what if it had been—"

"It wasn't Ken."

"It wasn't the 442nd today but it could have been."

"Why don't you go back?" I suggest. "Go back and see if you have a letter from him. It will make you feel better."

I watch her run, back toward her camp, wishing I could go after her, knowing that won't happen.

Apfelkuchen. That's the errand I was supposed to run during my lunch hour. I have tea for my mother now, and she also told me this morning that she had been craving apple cake, the kind that our neighbor in Fort Dodge used to make.

They sell it at the camp bakery for two red cardboard tokens. I'll buy it even though it's more than I should spend. Now I'll be able to give her tea and cake at the same time.

"Margot!" a voice calls when I walk up to the bakery.

"Heidi?"

She's sitting on the steps out front, drawing something in colored pencil. Immediately, I look around to see if Mr. Kruse is nearby.

"Are you going to the swimming pool?" she asks. "I'm making a sign. My mama said there was a big celebration for the opening, and that I could get a cake. I'm going to get the same kind of cake I got when I turned seven last month. I just have to finish this."

"I have tokens to buy cake, too. And then after I check on my own mama, I'm also going to the swimming pool. I'll look for you there."

Inside, two girls my age stand at the counter. I recognize them both. One of them, Lena, was on my train, and she was friendly to me until it became clear that my family was going to speak in English and skip meetings. She's wearing an apron; this must be her part-time job. The girls were laughing when I opened the door, but when they see me they stop.

"Can I order a slice of cake?" I ask, and Lena silently goes to cut it.

Less than an hour ago I felt horribly out of place on the Japanese side of camp. Now I'm where I belong and I still don't belong. The other girl, Adali, makes uncomfortable conversation with me, about how Mrs. Fischer has just put *Pfeffernüsse* in the oven, if I want to wait for them to come out. About how it looks like my school is also getting out early for the pool opening. We're both saved from talking longer by the sound of the door chime.

I think it will be Heidi, but it's not; it's my father, pushing open the door, waving when he sees me.

"Is everything all right?" I ask immediately, walking over to the entrance. He was supposed to be home with my mother until I came for lunch.

"The patient is sleeping," he says. "She was reading a sentence out loud and then her head was on her chest."

"Oh." I look back toward the counter, where the girls are

pretending not to listen in. "Should I tell them we don't want the cake after all?"

He shakes his head. "No, get it. Actually, I was thinking you and I could eat here and let your mother have the hour to sleep. Or at the mess hall if you prefer, but it's cow tongue today."

We order more *Apfelkuchen*, and when the *Pfeffernüsse* come out of the oven, my father insists we get those, too. They're too soft; they should have been allowed to cool, but the pepper and molasses are the right kind of spicy.

"Mrs. Fischer is a wizard," he says to Lena when she brings them to our table. "Please pass our compliments."

"She said this is the last batch for a while. No more molasses in prison camps."

My muscles tense and I wait for my father to get angry, but instead he laughs and tells her she'd better bring us extra, then.

"You seem happy," I say cautiously.

"I'm having lunch with my daughter. Doesn't it make you happy?"

I can't remember the last time I didn't worry about my father getting upset about something. I can barely remember the last time we sat together like this, just the two of us, and had an easy conversation. It's been months. It's been eleven months and twelve days, when we repaired a rotted board in the barn and he told me he had a feeling it was going to be a girl, a sister, but not to say anything to Mutti. The next day the FBI came.

"The lake was in Germany," he says, when we are both on our second piece of cake.

"What?"

"Earlier. When you were talking about the Lammey boys seeing you in the lake."

"Earlier, when Mutti was in the hospital?" I say. It's been two weeks since that conversation. He must have swimming on the brain because everyone does.

"You said you were afraid the Lammey boys were going to see you practicing in your underthings. But the Lammey boys weren't there. You learned how to swim in Fasaneriesee, the lake by your grandparents' house, when we took you back to meet them."

I didn't remember that. I barely have any memories of Germany. My parents hadn't planned on taking me so young, but Vati's father got sick and they wanted him to see me before he died.

My father reaches into his pocket and fumbles around before pulling out a folded handkerchief. He slides it across the table and nods for me to open it. Inside is a delicate golden bar with a blue porcelain bloom: a cornflower, the national flower of Germany.

"It was my mother's brooch. Your mother and I were going to give it to you for your birthday, but we decided not to wait."

"What's it for?"

"Put it on," he encourages me, fastening it for me under the collar of my dress. "You look lovely."

"I look the same; it's just a pin." My face reddens. "I don't mean it's just a pin. I mean..."

"I'm very proud of you, Margot. I know this hasn't been easy for you. But I have never heard you complain."

"It's all right," I mumble. "I know it's not forever."

"I wanted to give you something that reminded you that you're not from here. This is where you are right now. But it's not *who* you are."

My face burns from the compliment, which is exactly what I needed after earlier today when the people at the Union Store thought that was exactly who I am. "I know it's not forever," I repeat. "And I know things will all be okay when we go home. Mr. Lammey will realize that he can't lease our land to someone else. He'll—"

My father drops his head, looking down at the table. His face has darkened.

"What's wrong?"

He looks up again and tries to smile. "We don't need to talk about it now."

"You heard back, didn't you?" My stomach falls. "He's already leased the land."

My father reaches across the little table in the middle of the bakery and puts his hand over mine.

"The house isn't there anymore, Margot," he says quietly.

In the background, Lena is arranging trays of bread by the register. The metal scrapes as she slides each one onto its shelf.

"What do you mean, the house is not there anymore? You mean someone else is living there right now."

"When Mr. Lammey wrote back, he told me he'd heard noises in the middle of the night. Someone had painted swastikas on the barn and burned the house to the ground."

I am still having trouble understanding what my father is telling me.

Gone. All gone. The books I couldn't fit in my suitcase. The radio we were told wouldn't be allowed. The flames must have been huge and smoky. The last room my father finished before he was taken was the bedroom that was going to belong to the baby my father thought was going to be a girl. Some of the wood was still green. That room doesn't exist anymore. That baby doesn't exist anymore.

"Who did it?" I whisper. "Did they catch them?"

In a small town like Fort Dodge, we know almost everyone.

"Margot," my father says. From the sound of his voice, it's not the first time he's said my name. I look up. "I wasn't going to tell you, at least not like this. I didn't think there was a need for you to know yet. Are you okay? It will be okay."

He leans over the table, over the crumbs of cookies. He is calm. Too calm. I don't know how he is so calm; he is never that way.

Lena is pretending not to listen, but I know she is. Finally, she comes over, shifting her weight back and forth. I want to be angry with her for spying, but when I look up, she is bashful and embarrassed.

"I'm sorry," she says. "Do you want anything else, or can I close the bakery? It's just—I only work here on my lunch hour to fill in for Mrs. Fischer while she's on her break, but she said I could leave to get to the swimming pool."

I push my chair back with enough force that the table rocks on its legs. Lena steadies it, and then my father catches me, by the hand. I wave my other hand to show them that I'm fine, this is all fine.

"Remember, none of this has to do with you," he tells me. "It isn't your fault."

"Is this why you gave me the pin?" I ask. Was my grandmother's brooch a reward meant to soften the fact that our house is gone?

My family needs that house to have something to go back to. We need to have something to go back to so that we can have something to look forward to. We need to have something to look forward to so we don't lose our minds and we can all stay together.

"No," Vati says. "That was because I'm proud of who you've been. And it was an apology for how difficult I have made things for you and your mother recently. I haven't been thinking straight, but I am going to take care of our family, and it is all going to be okay."

"What do you mean it's all going to be okay? How can you *say* that?"

"When I first learned, I was as upset as you are," Vati says. "But I've had time to think. I have a plan. You don't need to worry anymore. Do you see how I'm not worrying? You should hurry or you'll miss the pool opening. You love swimming."

I love swimming. It will be fine. He is wrapping up the cake and the leftover *Pfeffernüsse* for me to run home to my mother. Eight *Pfeffernüsse*. Nine. It will be fine. I am trying to keep Crystal City in its box.

ELEVEN

MARGOT

THE FEDERAL HIGH YELL SQUAD IS GOING TO DO CHEERS. THE football team will also be there, in uniform. Haruko says this is ridiculous, that the football players are wearing their uniforms only to justify the fact that they have uniforms when they'll never play any real games. She says this theatrically, after I get back from dropping off the tea next to my sleeping mother. She says it to some of the other girls, but I can tell it's me she is trying to make laugh. Not because of what happened with my father, she doesn't know about that. Because of what happened earlier, with the tea.

We're walking together now. The whole school, both elementary and upper levels, for the first glimpse any of us have had of the pool with water in it.

There's already a crowd of adults waiting when the students arrive. Most of the camp has come out for this, either carrying bath towels or in their nicest clothes for the official opening ceremony. A length of ribbon has been tied between two posts at the pool's entry; platters of food are being laid out, and a photographer takes pictures of all the littlest kids lined up in their bathing suits. German and Japanese women together are arranging stacks of plates. A young German mother admires the cups that an older Japanese woman has brought to lay out with a bowl of punch. I've never seen committees from both groups working on something. This is the only holiday the camp has ever had to celebrate together.

The pool is big and round, black like a lake. Wooden diving platforms float in the middle; a rope divides the shallow from the deep end. The water is circled by a concrete deck where people can lay out their towels.

"Look," Haruko says to Chieko and to her sister, Toshiko. She points to a sign on one of the fence posts. Next month they're offering lifeguard training for detainees.

"I wonder who will guard the pool until then?" Toshiko says.

"Probably him." Haruko points to a skinny dark-haired lifeguard. A camp guard, stripped of his rifle and wearing red swimming trunks instead.

My house is gone, but my father says it's going to be all right.

Mr. Mercer says he has two announcements. First: A field

trip outside the fence has been arranged for tomorrow, for the upper-level students of the federal school. A special Friday treat. Miss Goodwin smiles. She must have arranged it. And second: Tonight's evening roll call is canceled so we can enjoy the festivities. He makes a speech about how the detainees who built the pool should be proud of their hard work, and how it will provide a respite from the heat. Before he cuts the ribbon, he signals with his hand, and a small group carrying musical instruments starts to play "When the Saints Go Marching In." This must have been a compromise. I am sure that some of the camp wanted them to play the American national anthem, and others protested.

I try to listen to the band. But after a few bars, I hear another song, coming from outside the pool gates but getting closer, competing with the sound of the trombone and trumpets.

"What in the world—?" Haruko starts to say. For a minute people politely ignore the other noise, until a few walk to the edge of the concrete deck to see what's going on.

I shade my eyes: Whatever the noise is, it's coming from the opposite side of the pool but there's a glare on the water.

It's a small parade of men, marching around the periphery. One of them is holding a flag and waving it. It's black and white against a red background.

I know immediately what's happened. The Bund has won its negotiations, the ones they have been having for weeks. To celebrate the opening of the pool, they have been allowed to display a Nazi swastika. They brought their own song, too. The "Deutschlandlied," sung by this straggling group. That's what the noise was. No, wait, I am wrong. The men have sung the first verse of the German national anthem, but instead of the second verse, which is about nice things like music and wine, they are singing about the swastika.

"This isn't the real anthem," I say.

"What song is it?" Chieko asks, her curiosity winning out over disgust. "What do the words mean?"

I shake my head. I don't want to think about the words. I don't want the work of translating them into English and I don't want any of my classmates to know how awful they are.

The camp band that had been playing "When the Saints Go Marching In" has stopped. A few feet away, a woman in a housedress wipes her floury hands on her apron; it's Mrs. Fischer, come from the bakery to see what the commotion is. To our left, another German woman kneels to whisper something to her little boy. Then she looks over to me with anger in her eyes. She turns back to the parade and, while I watch, she spits in the direction of the marching men, into the dirt.

I'm grateful for that woman's spit. It tells me I am not crazy. There's still right and still wrong. Most of us prisoners know the difference. Frederick Kruse was only elected to his position because the votes were too spread out among the saner candidates. He got a plurality, not a majority. It was a fluke. It wouldn't happen if we held the election again. Most of us know the difference.

Suddenly, someone grabs my hand. I know without looking that it's Haruko. I've never felt her hand before this, but
in the middle of this crowd of people, in front of everyone,
Haruko has reached for my hand and she doesn't let go. She
laces her soft fingers between my bony, knuckly ones and
squeezes tightly. Startled, I look over to her. She is staring
straight ahead, unblinking, toward the parade. The "Horst
Wessel Lied" is loud in the background. And the feeling of
her hand is what's keeping me upright when this song is making me want to sink to the ground.

We both stand there, our clasped hands hidden by the
folds of her pink gingham dress.

The small parade gets closer and louder, finishing its circle around the swimming pool and turning to march down a
street in front of the beer garden. Now that they're at their
closest point to us, I can make out some of the faces. The
blond pockmarked man who can fix electric fans. Mrs. Fischer's potbellied husband, who Mrs. Fischer does not wave to as
he passes, who she instead regards with a stony stare.

I thought Mr. Kruse would be the man waving the flag,
but when I spot him at the front, he doesn't have anything
in his hands. His job is to marshal the other walkers, cueing
everyone with the next line of the song. As they reach the
fourth verse, everyone's hands raise in a Hitler salute, like I
knew they would.

"What the words mean..." I start to say out loud, to
Chieko, but really to Haruko. "The words are telling people

to clear the way for the Brownshirts. To cheer for Hitler's banners, flying all over the streets. Because the banners represent...because they represent..."

"What do they represent?" Haruko asks.

As the parade comes almost to us, I can see that it's the man next to Mr. Kruse who is actually carrying the swastika, on a polished flagpole. And I can also see that man is my father.

TWELVE

MARGOT

WE HAD BROUGHT OUR SWIMMING SUITS TODAY. I PACKED MINE
this morning with our oldest bath towel, to make sure I
wouldn't forget it during lunch. Vati watched me do it. Our
whole conversation in the bakery, he knew I'd been planning to
come here. He must have known he was planning to come, too.

"What do the banners represent?" Haruko asks again,
turning to look at me now. "You started to say—because they
represent what?"

Dimly, I realize Haruko is asking me to finish a sentence
it feels like I started a century ago, about the lyrics of the
"Horst Wessel Lied."

"That's my father."

"Where?"

She scans the crowd. Not the small crowd of Nazis, but the crowd of regular people who have come for the opening. She doesn't think my father could be with the other crowd.

"I have to go." I can't let her see me fall apart. She's still holding my hand. She would never have held my hand to comfort me if she knew which side my father was on.

"They'll go away again. Look, they're already leaving," she says, pointing to the Nazis, who have finally come to the end of their song and are dispersing. The camp's musicians haven't started playing again yet; they're looking at one another, wondering if they should.

Chieko noticed Haruko and I are talking; any minute she'll ask what about.

"I have to go," I tell Haruko. "I'm sorry."

I don't know how I get home. I don't know if I run fast or slow, because I don't remember any of the route. One minute I'm standing at the swimming pool. The next I'm standing in front of my house and I'm panting. Panting, so that must mean I ran fast.

Inside my mother is resting. She starts to sit up to ask me what happened; from our house you would have been able to hear the sound of the march. I cut her off before she can say a word.

"Did you know? Did you know he was there and he was going to—?"

"Did I know he was going to what?" Her eyes get sharp and then soft. My mother is so quick at figuring out the meanings between unspoken things. She didn't know, her expression tells me. But she suspected.

"We have to go find him." She struggles to her feet, finding her housecoat to pull on over her dress. "We have to bring him back from—he's probably at the beer garden. I bet that's where they would all go."

"I'll go find him. You stay here. I'll bring him home."

"Margot, I'm not going to let you deal with this mess alone."

I'd thought my father was calm when he told me about our house burning down. But it *wasn't* calm that I saw when he told me he was going to care for our family. It was delusion. The way he planned to fix our burned-down house was to go and march with the Nazis. *I haven't been thinking straight*, he said. *I have a plan*. Why didn't I notice those were odd things to say? I was so relieved to see him relaxed that I didn't ask what his plan was.

More music. My mother and I both hear the German anthem, hummed by my father as he walks up the path. He stops when he sees us in the doorway.

"So you're waiting for me," he says.

"Where have you been, Jakob?"

"How could you?" I whisper before he can answer my mother. He has to know that I saw him at the pool.

The curtain flickers in the house next door, the one that shares a flimsy wall with ours. I barely know these neighbors, but I know them enough to know they would be horrified by what my father has done. My mother must realize this, too; she backs into the house again, shutting the door behind my father when he follows.

My father takes his time. He splashes water on his face. He takes his outer shirt off, examining a hole in the elbow. Stalling. "Before you both get upset, let's calmly talk through this." He hangs the shirt on the back of a chair.

"This is not a thing that can be *talked through*," Mutti hisses.

"Ina, I couldn't keep sitting here, with nothing to work on, with no way to contribute. You understand that, right? I couldn't keep being useless. This doesn't mean I agree with everything they stand for. Just with a few premises." He turns to me. "Do you see what I'm saying, Margot?"

No. No, that's not right. I wanted the explanation to be different. I hoped he would tell us that he was spying, maybe, or that this was a scientific experiment.

"You shouldn't agree with *anything*," I say. "Their whole... their whole..." I search for the word Vati used. "Their whole premise is hateful."

"When did you decide this?" My mother stands behind me in her dressing gown. "This morning when you said you were going for a walk? This afternoon when you said that maybe you would go look at the new swimming pool after all? Earlier than that? You must have known what we would think of this, or you wouldn't have kept it a secret."

My father holds up a hand. "I don't have to think they

are right in every single matter in order to think that their other points hold water. You can't deny that we've been discriminated against here. Organizing ourselves into a group is a smart strategy."

"Was it just for the job, then?" I try to wrap my head around what he's saying. "Was it so Mr. Kruse would put you on the next crew?"

"No, it wasn't!" He points at me, excited that I've asked this question. "Listen, I'll explain. We thought America was so great?" He laughs, sweeping his hand around our small room. "The America that brought us *here*? It is obvious the country only cares about its own citizens. So what is so wrong with Germany wanting to have a policy that puts its citizens first, too? What is so wrong with wanting to join an organization that will dedicate itself to me and my family? I don't have to be a Nazi to see that. Your mother and I came here and gave this country everything—"

"Do not bring me into this," Mutti interrupts. "Don't you dare."

"We *did*," he insists, turning to her. "We decided we would come here and we would learn how many original colonies there were, and who wrote the Declaration of Independence. And for what? So they could decide we would never be American enough for them, and put us in here?"

I'm trying to put my thoughts in order. I want to have a discussion where we lay out evidence and he sees that I'm right because I have more correct points in my column. But

I already know my father is right about one thing: Logically, there is no defense for us being here.

I have always known this. No matter how many shipments of new detainees I count and swimming pool volumes I calculate, there is never an answer at the end of my calculations.

My father never would have become a Nazi if they let him stay home with our family.

Or would he? Did he really just go to that first meeting as a favor? I'm having such a hard time remembering who my father was before. But he can't have partial credit for this. Marching with a Nazi swastika is not like algebra, where you can get the wrong answer but be right some of the time. This is all wrong.

"I don't understand," I say again. "I don't understand why you had to carry that flag."

"Because he is weak," my mother spits. I've never heard her like this. My father whips his head around.

"Don't you call me that." His voice gets lower and quieter until his last word is barely more than a whisper. "Don't you ever call me that."

"I will call you what it is the truth to call you. You have become a weak man. Bad things have happened to you? Bad things have happened to me. They have happened to this whole family. To thousands of people. You lost your job? Thousands of men lost their jobs. You are in here? So is Margot. *So am I.* Is it right? Of course it is not right. When the war is over and we leave here I will go to my grave making sure the United States knows it is not right."

"I am not saying that it hasn't been terrible for you," Vati says. "I am doing this *for* you. I am doing this for *us*. I am making the choice that will put our family first."

"You're making the choice to support Adolf Hitler," Mutti says. "A man who has assumed power through manipulation and lies and hate. That is despicable."

"Shut up, Ina," my father says softly. "Shut up right now. Adolf Hitler doesn't have anything to do with this."

My mother lets out a sharp laugh. "Yes! Yes, there is no Hitler here! And do you know why that is, in some ways, the stupidest thing of your little endeavor? That is the stupidest part, because it means that none of what you are doing *is even real*. If you were marching your ugly little flag around in Germany, singing your ugly little anthem, you would probably be doing it while preparing to go off and fight in a war. You would be on the wrong side of it, the evil side of it, but at least you would be risking your life for the idiot thing you believed in. But you are not in Germany. You are not being bombed. You are living in a camp where your food and clothes and beer are provided by the government you now profess to hate."

"Shut up."

"So you and Frederick Kruse, marching around the little camp? That is not standing up for something. That's two desperate little boys waving a bit of cloth, pretending to be brave when in fact they are pathetic."

"Shut up!" my father says again. He's not speaking softly anymore. He pushes back his chair so fast it topples, landing with a *crack* against the floor. He raises his hand.

The way he flung her hand away at the hospital. The way he was angry because he thought we were not respecting him as the head of the house. The way we have tiptoed around him for months.

"No!" I yell, lunging toward him.

I'm afraid he'll do it. For the first time, I'm actually afraid of my father and what he could do. I reach for his hand and he pulls away from me, and then I'm off balance and spilling to the ground. My mother rushes toward me, but she's forgotten about the fallen chair. Her foot twists around the rung, and instead of shooting her hands out in front of herself for support the way I did, she's keeping them wrapped around her midsection, protecting her belly.

"Mutti," I cry out, but I can't get there in time, I am frozen in horror as the side of her face slams into an upturned chair leg, as her lip splits open. I reach out at the same time my father calls, "Ina!" and my mother's body splays out on the floor.

"Oh God, Ina, are you all right?" he says. "It was an accident, I didn't mean—"

"Stay away from me." She thrusts one arm up, blocking him. "For God's sake, stay away, Jakob."

"I promise—" he starts to beg.

"I don't care about your promises!" There's blood on her tooth and her mouth.

She pants on the ground while I rub her back, and then, after a minute, she reaches to her lip, wincing. She motions for me to grab her hand and help her to her knees. Her skirt is twisted around her hips, her blond hair undone from its bun. She faces my father. "This is your bravery? You're going to hit your pregnant wife?"

"Ina—" my father starts again, but he doesn't get anything else out before his words turn to sobs. His own knees buckle. "Ina, Ina," he says, and then my whole family is on the rough wooden floor of our hut on the day I was supposed to go swimming.

My family is not fine. We haven't been fine for a while. Haruko has spent her time here trying to figure out what her father might be hiding from her. I've spent mine ignoring what's happening in front of my own face. For the first time I am really seeing it, how broken we are. As if it's not even happening to me.

"Don't move, don't move, Mutti. I'll have a neighbor go for the doctor," I say.

"I don't want the doctor yet," my mother says, watching my crumpled father still sobbing in front of her. "Give me some time alone with your father. Leave, Margot."

"I don't want to—"

"Leave for an hour. Go get some ice for my face. Your father and I need to talk."

Numbly, I fumble for the door handle behind me. I wrench it open and stumble down onto our wooden steps. Without really thinking about what I'm doing, I walk briskly past the little dirt plots in front of the little tar-paper houses of the camp. Eight tar-paper houses. Two with curtains. Keep Crystal City in a box. Past the clotheslines hung with shirts and faded dresses drying in the sun.

THIRTEEN

HARUKO

BY THE TIME I GET TO THE ICEHOUSE FROM THE SWIMMING POOL, Margot is already there, her knees drawn up and her arms around them. She doesn't seem to notice she's shivering as she stares toward the wall.

She also doesn't acknowledge me when I climb over the ice blocks to get to our spot. "I didn't know if you'd be here," I say, when it's clear she won't speak first.

I'd waited to see if she'd come back. Long enough to see the Nazi marchers disperse and the rest of the crowd look confused and uneasy, until Mr. Mercer announced we should move on with the festivities and Chieko cheered with Yell Squad.

I tried to swim, but it was hard to focus once I realized

what had happened. The man holding the flag had looked after Margot as she ran away, and then somehow I knew. It wasn't in the swimming pool crowd that Margot had spotted her father.

She still hasn't said anything. Her teeth chatter.

"It was too crowded to swim much," I say.

Nothing.

"My sister flipped off the diving platform and almost lost her bathing suit."

Nothing.

"So your father, would he hate me?" I don't try to control the bite in my voice. "I can't remember. Are Japanese people an inferior race, or are we—what was it Hitler called us in his pact—honorary Aryans?"

"Don't ask me that," she whispers, closing her eyes.

"I bet it won't last very long, though. Once we're done helping you by distracting the Americans, he'll turn on us, too."

"What do you mean, when *you* are done helping *me*? We don't live over there. Neither of us is fighting."

"That's what I told the old people at the Union Store earlier today, but your father seems to disagree. Your father seems to think you're very, very German. I guess that's why you never tell me anything about your family. Is that why you never want to answer my questions?"

"I told you, he didn't—he wasn't—" she says. "I don't know what happened to my father." She finally opens her eyes and they are dull and bloodshot. "I wish you could have known him before we came here. Today he told me that our house in Iowa is gone. And even if it wasn't, our landlord wouldn't let us come back. For my father, it's like our family became the enemy overnight."

Margot's excuses are infuriating because she is talking like there was no choice, like what her father did and became was inevitable. It wasn't inevitable. They can't make us become animals.

"I'm so sorry," I spit out, "that your father had to wake up and realize that you had become an enemy overnight. But at least you didn't have to wake up and realize that other Americans had thought of you as an enemy all along."

"I don't understand what you mean."

I mean that the reason this imprisonment is hard for Margot's father is because they didn't know yet that this country was unfair. They got to be—I think of another word I didn't know the Japanese translation for when the FBI man made me say it to my mother—*assimilated. We are worried your father has not fully assimilated into the United States. Tell your mother that. Did you tell her? Ask her if she understands.*

The West Coast Japanese had already given the government their shortwave radios, and they had already agreed to their curfew, eight PM to six AM, but it wasn't enough, it was never enough. It was so easy for the government to make those rules. You can't hate someone all of a sudden. It takes practice. It takes a long time.

"I already told you that all the Japanese people on the West Coast had to report for assembly," I tell her. "The government drew a line, and if you lived on the wrong side of it then you were rounded up and sent to assembly camps in old racetracks and carnival grounds, and you slept in stables—the ones meant for horses—until the permanent relocation camps were ready. And then those people had to go to wherever the government said. To Wyoming, or Idaho, or—"

Or Colorado. There was a relocation camp in Colorado. For West Coast Issei, located a few hours from home. Camp Amache. We learned about it in church; we made care packages for the people who were being sent there, toothbrushes and handkerchiefs and magazines, and delivered them at the train station one Saturday morning. I handed a package to an old woman and she told me how the stables had been converted to "apartments" but she thought they still smelled like hay and manure. How she was afraid she still smelled like hay and manure. How I felt so sorry for her. I have told Margot all of this before. I told her this one time at the icehouse, and she didn't share anything in return, because she never did.

I want to grab her by the shoulders and shake her, and I don't know if I'm more angry because of what her father is, or because she hid it from me. I trusted her with my secrets.

"I'm sorry," Margot says.

"Sorry for what? For letting me think your father was different? For not having to go to a transit camp first and sleep in a horse stable?"

Her jaw clenches a little. "We did have to go to a transit camp."

"You what? You *never* mentioned anything like that."

"We *did*, Haruko. For four months. On Ellis Island."

The absurdity of what she's said makes me think I must have misheard. "Margot, what are you *talking* about? Ellis Island? Like, the Statue of Liberty?"

"Did you know that it's not a national park anymore? It had been one. People think that national parks are all wild places like Yellowstone. But actually places like the Lincoln Memorial are part of the National Park Service, too. But Ellis Island isn't a park anymore."

"It's—"

"It's a camp," she says.

I take a step closer, a piece of my anger replaced by confusion. "It's a camp?"

"I'd been once before. When I was little. My grandpa was sick and we went to Germany. When we took the ship back it docked in New York. There were vendors selling shaved ice. It's funny, I barely remember Germany but I remember the Statue of Liberty and the shaved ice. When Mutti and I went there this time to wait for our Crystal City papers, we weren't on the island with the statue. We went to a big warehouse with rows of cots. There wasn't any privacy. Not partitions or...or stables, I guess. In the beginning, you tried keeping your nightgown on while you put your skirt on underneath. After a few weeks, it didn't matter. There was no point."

Margot looks up at me. She tries to smile. Her face—her gray eyes, and her crooked nose—her face is so open and so fragile. For the first time, I feel like a door inside her has opened. I take another step closer, and then kneel in front of her.

"Most of the prisoners there weren't from Iowa like Mutti and me," Margot continues. "They were from New York. One girl had lived in one of the tall buildings right on the water. She said she could see her apartment window from Ellis Island. I didn't really believe her; I could barely make out the building, but she said she could. At night, when they turned all the lights out, she would cry. After a month, she would also pull out her hair. Her scalp bled.

"Somehow I had talked myself into thinking that was related to my mother waking up with blood on her cot," Margot says. "That the girl from New York had woken up and gone and bled on my mother's sheets. Even though it made no sense. Even though there was too much blood. My mother woke up and her mattress was covered in blood. She woke me up and we called for a doctor. The guard came, as quickly as he could, I think, and brought a nurse with him. They took her to the medical center. I thought the guard was being concerned, but when I tried to follow, he told me to get back in bed. He wasn't helping her. He was guarding her. To make sure she didn't try to escape. To make sure it hadn't all been a ruse."

Her eyes fill with tears and then the tears are spilling over her cheeks, and she's still talking, she's still looking into me as her words are coming out as hiccups. The brave way she's trying to talk through it makes something course through me, something tender and strong and unfamiliar, and I don't want her to have to do this for me, and I also don't want her to stop.

"You don't have to," I tell her. "We can talk about something else."

"No, I need to finish," she says. "I need to finish because it happened. Because the baby is why we had decided to follow my father to begin with." She swallows. "I used to just think my mother got sick."

"When did you think that?"

"Three other times. I was too young; I thought there were times when she got sick and needed to be in bed. This was the one that went the furthest. This was the one that was supposed to be the miracle. That's why my mother and I decided to come here. So that we could be together. Even if it was behind barbed wire. We voted, we all agreed unanimously that my mother and I would come. I chose this place, for that reason. Only it turned out it wasn't a good reason, because when my mother came back from the medical center on Ellis Island she wasn't pregnant anymore. She was tired, and she'd stopped talking, and she was not pregnant anymore."

"And then you came here," I whisper.

"We had to by then. It was too late to go home, after all. And then my mother was...gone. For months. I don't know how to explain it. She was there, but she wasn't there. But when we came to Crystal City she got pregnant again. Now *this* baby is the miracle. And my family is together. The way we had planned it all along. We were together, and that's what we'd said was important."

Finally, she stops with her long horrible story and looks at me, searching for something.

"It was a mistake," she says finally. "I can now see that it was a mistake for us to come."

She hasn't moved since the beginning. She's still sitting on the ice block; her arms are still wrapped around her knees and she's still shaking.

"You need a blanket," I say. I find one bunched in the corner, shake it out, and wrap it around Margot's shoulders, rubbing up and down the way my mother used to when Ken and Toshiko and I were small and we would step out of the bathtub freezing and wet.

Rub rub rub. Hum a tuneless song.

"I'm warm enough now," Margot says.

"Your lips are still blue."

"But I'm warm enough now."

"Oh. Right." I stop rubbing her shoulders, but then it feels like my hands are hanging uselessly at my sides and I don't know what to do with them, like all of a sudden I've realized for the first time that I have hands and they don't work.

My heart is clattering inside my chest. I feel like Margot must be able to hear it. I can—it's pulsing in my ears—I'm thinking about everything she's been hiding, and how much it must have cost her to hide it.

"I should go," she says. "My mother. I'm supposed to bring her ice."

"Do you want to go?"

"I should."

But she doesn't go, and neither do I, and I am looking at her for the first time and seeing who she really is.

"Haruko. I didn't tell you everything before because—"

"It doesn't matter."

"It does," she says. "I didn't tell you because I was afraid if I told you everything, I couldn't handle it. And neither could you."

"I could."

"Are my lips really blue?"

"A little."

"They don't feel cold."

"They're cold compared to mine. See?"

I press my index and middle finger to my own mouth, which suddenly feels hot and swollen, and hold them there for a minute, and then I take those same fingers and press them against Margot's. Her lips are chapped. She closes her eyes. I feel her breathing, and then I feel her stop and hold her breath. I feel my pulse, very faintly, in the tips of my fingers, pressing against the cool of Margot's lips, and slowing so that every beat crashes in my ears.

I feel—

"Hello?"

The icehouse door has opened. It's not the only time it's

happened since we've been coming here, but it's the only time we haven't noticed it in time to turn off our lamp and hide. A detainee, a cheerful-looking older man, carrying a bucket to chip some ice off into.

"You girls having a picnic?" he says, noting our blankets as he sets about gathering his ice. "Smart way to beat the heat. Don't know why I never thought of coming in here and doing the same thing for an afternoon."

As soon as the door opened, I had removed my fingers from Margot's lips. I had done so by smearing them across her face, so that anyone who saw would think I had been helping her remove a smudge, kill a mosquito, something innocent and explicable.

"You girls go to the pool opening?" the man asks, chipping away at his ice. "It was something, wouldn't you say?"

Margot's eyes are wild.

"I was leaving," she yelps, loud enough for the man to hear. He's still puttering around behind us. "I should get back to my family."

"Me too," I say exaggeratedly. "Homework." I'm still shaking from whatever just happened. *What just happened?* "Why don't you go ahead? I'll clean up here."

When she leaves, I fold the blankets with unsteady hands. I put out the oil lamps and tuck them in the corner, while making polite conversation with the older man, who tells me he has a granddaughter my age.

When he leaves, too, I sit on my pile of folded blankets,

trying to calm myself, trying to collect my thoughts. I suddenly feel like I have never been here in the icehouse before.

I have no idea what just happened.

Something pointy is digging into my thigh, from inside my pocket. The corner of an envelope. I forgot. I almost forgot.

That's what I had gone back to do, earlier today after we got the tea, after I walked Margot to the border of the Japanese neighborhood. Check the mail to make sure there wasn't a telegram saying Ken was missing in action. There wasn't. But there was a letter.

Alone in the icehouse, I take the envelope out of my pocket, and then take the letter out of the envelope. One page. One side of one page. Whatever Ken is lying about, at least it will be short, and I cannot believe I feel relieved to be reading this right now, to have something to focus on.

Dear Family, Ken writes.

And then he writes nothing. Or he writes everything. The point is that I can't see what Ken has written because it has all been censored, all of it, inked over by thick black lines. Line after line, paragraph after paragraph.

I'd been afraid of all the terrible things Ken could tell me in a letter. That he'd had to shoot someone. That he was missing an arm. An ear. I thought nothing could be harder than hearing lies about what he was going through, but I was wrong. What is harder is having to imagine what your brother is going through, and knowing that whatever terrible things you might imagine, the truth might actually be worse.

HARUKO

I don't regret that, that afternoon in the icehouse. It will sound strange to say, but out of all the things I could and should and do regret, that afternoon is not one of them.

FOURTEEN

MARGOT

IT'S DARK BY THE TIME I GET HOME.

I don't know how long it's been since I left. It could have been an hour. It could have been three. I am thinking of the way Haruko pressed her fingers against my mouth. I am embarrassed to be thinking about this instead of worrying about my mother. About my breaking family. But for the smallest of seconds, it felt like all of that disappeared because all of the blood in my body had moved to where the lavender girl was touching my lips.

In the gray of the night I can still make out the silhouette of the sad little planter boxes that won't grow flowers.

My mother and father sit at the table. My mother holds a wet cloth to the left side of her face. Her blond hair sticks to her forehead. They've been waiting.

"I brought more ice." I hand the ice-filled handkerchief to Mutti, exchanging it for the used one she has pressed against her face. She accepts the trade but makes sure to tilt her head away so I can't see how badly she's hurt.

"Margot, we're glad you're back," my father says. His voice is raw. I wonder how long he cried after I left. How long they both did. He gestures to the empty chair across the table. One of the rungs is broken off, it's the chair he threw to the floor earlier. "There is something we'd like to discuss."

I know the emotion I'm feeling is hate, but it's hard to recognize it as that, feeling it toward someone I love. How can he offer me a seat, like he is conducting a business meeting? I look at my mother, waiting for her guidance, but she won't meet my gaze. I want to tell her we could run. We could run from here right now.

"Margot," my father says again.

"Margot, sit," says my mother.

I want there to be a way to run from my father but also bring him along. Get us all away. Finally, I pull out my chair.

"Thank you," he says. "I want you to know that what happened between your mother and me is complicated. We are both under a lot of stress. Everyone here is."

"You were going to hit her," I say. *"He was going to hit you,"* I say to my mother.

"I have apologized to your mother," my father says. "It was a horrible accident that will never happen again, and I mean that." He clears his throat. "And we have made a few decisions. That we think will make things easier on the whole family."

Can married couples in Crystal City separate? Would they send my mother and me to live in another hut? *Thirty-seven houses.* Because of my numbers, the way I have tracked all the shipments, I know that there are exactly thirty-seven unoccupied huts at this time.

"What are the decisions?"

"We have decided," my father says, "that you will no longer be going to the American school."

"What do you mean? Mutti, what does he mean?" I ask, but she still won't make eye contact. "I like the American school."

"We've decided that if the German school is good enough for other German children in the camp, it is also good enough for you."

No, no, no. I'm shaking my head back and forth. He keeps saying that: *we.* I want my mother to jump in again, like she did the last time he talked about the two of them as a unit. *Don't bring me into this,* she said.

But this time all she does is to readjust the ice cloth on her face. A few shards spill onto the table. My father sees, and immediately takes the cloth, carefully refolding it. He's always been a good caretaker. When I was young and sick to my stomach, I always wanted him, instead of my mother, to hold my hair back.

"The German school doesn't have advanced courses," I

protest. "The person they have teaching math is a plumber, not a teacher."

My father knows all of this. They're the same reasons he gave when we talked about what school I should go to. "And it's not certified. If I go to the German school, then I might have to repeat a grade when we go home. I'll need an accredited diploma from the federal school to get into a university."

Across the table, my mother bites her lip. For the first time, she looks up, but not at me. She and my father exchange a glance. I don't know yet what's coming, but I can tell it will be bad news. He puts his hand over the one of hers that is not holding her face. It's a gesture that says he is taking care of things.

My mother opens her mouth like she is finally about to say something, but at first all that comes out is a dry cough that reminds me, somehow, of a broken bird.

"You have to understand, Margot," she begins. My father raises one finger and clears his throat, telling her that she does not need to speak. He will take care of this, too.

"That is the other thing," my father says. "We have decided that the federal school will no longer suit your needs because we will not be going back to Iowa."

"Where will we go?" I ask, but I already know the answer and I can already hear the blood rushing in my ears.

"We're going to our real home, on the next ship. We're applying to be repatriated on the next available ship to Germany."

FIFTEEN

MARGOT

September 22, 1944
Bottles of Grapette required for a field trip outside a
    fence: 36
Hard-boiled eggs: 72
Prison guards: 2

FIELD TRIP DAY. IT'S WRITTEN ON THE BLACKBOARD IN LETTERS
that someone has drawn a wreath of flowers around: *Field
Trip Day*. The day we will all meet to leave the fence. To
help us develop a sense of camaraderie and a sense of school
pride.

It is my last day at Federal High School. My father let me

come today for the field trip mostly because I needed to clean out my desk.

"Tell him you need to finish the math unit," Haruko says when I tell her about last night, as everyone else watches two boys throw the baseball they've brought along for the trip. "Tell him you need to take the next test."

"Would you tell that to your family?" I ask. "Would you really tell that to mine, after what happened?"

She closes her mouth because she knows the answer is no, to both questions.

"I can't think about it now," I say, because thinking about it is making my eyes sting, in plain sight of everyone else. "Any ship departures are probably months away; they might not be organized at all. I can't—"

"Watch out!"

I barely have time to duck before the baseball flies over my head. Haruko quickly wipes her own eyes. "Maybe *you* should watch out," she calls to the boy, and then, to me, quietly, "Okay. We won't think about it now. There's lots of time for it not to happen."

I've seen her get emotional so many times, but never like this, because of me. But I can't ask her about that. Even if we weren't surrounded by our entire class, I wouldn't have the words.

We all go out to the flagpole, for one last count before leaving. Some of the girls are in pants, with kerchiefs over their hair; a few of the boys have ball gloves in addition to the baseballs; someone has a guitar. We also have a pair of guards to accompany us for the whole day. They look happy for the assignment, but they are still carrying guns.

A pretend-fun day. That's what Haruko suggests we think about today as we exit the school. Pretend-fun. Not a day when things are actually better, because we know that's not true. But a day when we pretend things are better. That I am not about to be sent to a different school. That Haruko's brother is not sending censored letters she can't read. That my father is not trying to get us repatriated to Germany. That Haruko's father was not giving her worrisome answers to questions. That my mother's lip is not swollen.

We're going to walk about half a mile, Miss Goodwin says, and then we'll be in a nice spot for a picnic.

As the gate opens and I walk past the fence, the most unexpected thing happens: I laugh.

Because I can see the horizon and there are no fences on it. Because we can walk in a long, straight line without running into a guard tower. Haruko gives me a curious look.

There's a stream outside the camp, beyond the line of vision from inside. It's not pretty, but it's one I've never seen before. I'd been aching so much to look at something new. There are new trees. A new road, with new paving.

"It looks the same," Chieko says to Haruko. She sounds disappointed. "When my bus got here it was nighttime; I've never seen outside. But it looks exactly the same."

"It doesn't look the same," Haruko says. "There's no fence."

They are both right. The landscape outside the fence is so similar to the landscape inside the fence. Except out here, there's a sky, long and uninterrupted. I look at Haruko and smile, giddy, because she understands it, what the real differences are.

We walk through the small, dusty downtown of Crystal City. In front of the post office, a woman holding the hands of two young children looks confused when she sees the group of us, an unexpected addition to her small town. She smiles at first, and then, when she realizes who we must be, grabs her children's hands more tightly.

"She thinks we're going to kidnap her children in the street?" Chieko whispers.

"Or that our enemy anti-Americanism is contagious," Linda says back.

"Good *morning*," Chieko greets the woman with elaborate politeness.

Even this, the sidelong glances of Crystal City residents, doesn't bother me as much as it could, because they can't change the fact that for one day, at least, we are not in the camp.

We stop at a spot along the stream, where the banks are thick with mesquite trees and low enough that we can wade into the water. Mess hall workers have sent along wax-paper parcels with cold fried chicken and hardboiled eggs. The boys who brought the baseball are organizing a game. "We need outfielders. Do any of you girls know how to throw?" one of them asks the cluster of us, and Chieko, Linda, and some of the other girls volunteer. Haruko quickly raises her eyebrows at me, and I shake my head.

"I'm too starving for baseball," she tells the boy. "I'll come cheer after I eat."

When everyone else has gone farther up the banks, where the land is flat enough for a game, I let Haruko make her way down through the mesquites, and then follow a few minutes later. She's sitting on a low rock, her shoes and socks already off.

"You should be there." She points to another rock and I realize what she means: If we were in the icehouse, that's where my hay bale would be. Now that we're away from everyone, I think I hear a shyness in her voice I've never heard before, but maybe that's my imagination. It must be my imagination. She peels me an egg by rolling it between her palms until the shell cracks into tiny pieces. The sky is such a pale blue it's almost white.

"I wonder if the students at the German school get field trips outside the fence," I say.

"I wish we didn't have to go back to camp at all," Haruko says fiercely. "I wish we could turn in the other direction and keep walking to—what's the biggest city near us? San Antonio?"

"It is. But we'd keep walking in the same direction to get to San Antonio. We were already walking east."

"Is that where we'll go after the war? San Antonio?"

"After the war?" I repeat. "I think after the war they let people go where they want to, probably. I don't think we all will go to the same place."

"I don't mean, *we all*. I mean you and me. Where are we going to go after this is finished? I could get a job at a soda counter," Haruko continues. "I'm good at it. You've never had a lime rickey as good as the ones I make."

"I've never had a lime rickey at all."

My face flushes hot. She's mentioned an *after*. She's mentioned a *we*. I never would have let myself dream of a world so big. A world where I am far away from Frederick Kruse and what happened in my Victory Hut. There will be an after. This war won't last forever. There will be a time when we will have a whole other life.

"I'll make one for you. It's limes, and sugar, and soda water—it tastes better than I'm describing it—and that will be my job. Becoming the star clerk at a soda fountain, and then the manager, and then maybe I'll buy it. What will you do?"

"I'm not sure," I say slowly. My rule is to try to accept the actual words people are saying, but I don't know what to do when the actual words seem more like a dream than reality. "I want to go to college. But I could figure out how to keep the books at your soda fountain. Or I'm a pretty good farm-hand. I know how to fix the basic things that go wrong with equipment."

"No, keep the books. You'll have a little office in the

back, and then when it's time for the fountain to close, we'll grab slices of pie from the display case, and we'll take them home and eat them while listening to the radio and drinking evening cocktails."

"Won't you . . . won't you go back to Colorado after this is all over?"

She looks at me. "Do you want to go back to where you're from?"

I always thought I did. But right now I don't want anything as much as I want to think about the fact that we are both on the outside of the fence. "Tell me about our apartment."

"It will have a screen door to keep out bugs. There will be real beds, not cots. Oh, do you know what else we'll have?"

"A shower," I say automatically. "A private shower with a private toilet."

"And hot water and no lines to wait in. And a refrigerator instead of an icebox."

"And there won't be any countings," I say, letting myself get caught in the fantasy.

"Right, no roll call. If I come home and you are already there, I'll say, *One, two*. And then I'll be done counting all of the residents."

"One, two," I repeat.

"We could do it right now. We could run away. We'd start by—" Haruko says, and now she's giggling. "We'd start by stealing the lunches. While everyone else is playing baseball,

I'll grab the baskets and start running." She waits for me to add something to the story.

"We'd...we'd follow the train tracks to make sure we're going in the right direction?"

"We'd tell anyone who asks that we're university students whose car broke down. Maybe they'll give us a ride."

"Would they believe we're university students?" I ask.

"Betty Asamo gets to leave Crystal City when she turns eighteen next month, and go to secretary school. Did you know that was allowed? Because she's a citizen and she has her parents' permission. A church mission sponsored her in Austin."

"I don't turn eighteen for more than a year. I'm only sixteen, remember?"

"Shhh," Haruko says. "I'm hitchhiking to San Antonio. I'm walking if I need to."

We couldn't, obviously. We're a hundred miles from San Antonio. But we're young and healthy. Could we do twenty miles a day? Fifteen, maybe. The chicken and the eggs would go bad but the apples would be fine, and the bottles of Grapette that were in the cooler. It's still so hot when the sun is overhead, but if we slept during the day and walked at night...

"Margot?" Haruko has stopped laughing while I've been lost in thought. She's looking at her lap, folding the wax paper from her chicken into neat little pleats. "When the man came into the icehouse yesterday."

I freeze. "Yes?"

"Just before he came in. Right before. Do you know what I'm talking about?"

My chest thuds. I would never have brought this up. So many things happened yesterday that I wondered this morning if I'd made some of them up. If grief and anger caused me to misremember things or misunderstand them.

Of course I remember when the man came into the icehouse yesterday. Of course I remember that, and what was happening just before then. Every detail of it. My mouth is dry, and I can't tell if what I'm feeling is longing or fear.

"Margot?"

"I remember," I say quietly.

"I wondered whether—"

"Haruko?"

For a minute, I think it must have been me who said Haruko's name. But it's not. It's Miss Goodwin, who is calling my name, too. "Has anyone seen Haruko Tanaka?" Miss Goodwin yells out. "She might have been with Margot Krukow; I don't see Margot, either?"

My stomach twists. Someone has seen us together. Someone has told her we're plotting to escape. *Someone has told her about the icehouse.*

When she calls again, I realize she doesn't know we were talking about running away, or even that we were together at all. She just doesn't see us, and she wants to make sure we didn't wander off.

The thick bushes along the bank shake and then part as Miss Goodwin steps through, frantic.

Beside me, Haruko slowly stands, brushing the grass off her skirt. "We're here," she says, her voice cracking. "We're both here."

Miss Goodwin's face relaxes, but just a small amount, and only then do I notice two guards standing behind her. Not the ones who came with us. The guards who came with us had rolled up their uniform sleeves and were helping keep score of the ball game. Different guards. Buttoned-up, sweaty at the temples and breathing like they sprinted all the way from camp.

Haruko and I start toward them. It's my mother. What else could it be? Why else would two guards be dispatched from their duties to interrupt a school picnic? But when we get over to Miss Goodwin, it's Haruko she turns to and not me.

"Go get your things, and these men will escort you back to camp," she says. "Just you, Miss Tanaka. Miss Krukow will stay here with the rest of us."

Haruko's eyes are panicked. "What do they—"

"I don't know."

"Am I going to—"

"I really don't know, sweetheart," Miss Goodwin says. "But I think you should hurry."

SIXTEEN

HARUKO

THE GUARDS DON'T KNOW ANYTHING. THE GUARDS ARE USELESS. The guards told me, when I asked, that they didn't know why they'd been asked to come and get me, only that they were told to do it quickly. Now that we're heading back they are walking slow, and I can't believe I'm wanting them to speed up, to get me back to the fence as soon as possible. My throat is tight and I can barely breathe. *Something happened to my mother. Something happened to Toshiko.*

But when we get to the administration building, my family is waiting outside. I let go of a fraction of tension, because the presence of my family means there are at least three terrible things I will not learn have happened when we go inside the building.

Waiting with them is Mr. Mercer, the camp director, but from my mother's wild-eyed look, he hasn't told them anything, either. She's wearing her white coat from the hospital. Usually she changes out of it before she comes home, so they must have called her straight from work. "Did they tell you anything?" she whispers in my ear as I join them. "Us, either," she says when I shake my head no. My father looks gray and nauseated. Toshiko grabs my hand before Mr. Mercer leads us inside.

"Right in here, please." He holds the door open for my mother, and the rest of us file in behind, silent except for the shuffling of our feet. We've come into a room that makes my heart break for a moment, because of how normal it is. Two armchairs covered in floral fabric facing a matching sofa, with a coffee table and a vase of flowers between them. A *sofa*. I had almost forgotten such furniture existed. My first thought is that it will get dusty in here, that Crystal City is no place for soft squishy sofas.

This must be a room of bad news. Why else would they offer us water or coffee, tell us it will only be a minute. Why would they do all that unless it was to make us comfortable before they ripped out our hearts?

It will only be a minute, I automatically translate for my mother.

The war is over and America lost, I tell myself first, but that makes no sense, because why would they pull each family into a room to tell them one by one? My family is being

173

separated, each of us sent to a different camp. My father's father back in Japan, the one I've never met, has had a stroke and died.

The reason I am thinking of all these ridiculous possibilities is obvious: All of them are better than the most likely reason my whole family would have been brought here. Because my brother is dead. Because my brother went off to fight in the war, and somebody shot and killed him, and the United States government wants us to be comfortable when we learn the news.

My parents have had the same thought that I have. My father grinds his teeth—I can hear across the coffee table the scrape of enamel—and my mother keeps reaching up to dab her eyes with a handkerchief. Toshiko and I clasp each other's hands harder.

Ken is dead. Ken is dead. Ken is dead.

I'm still thinking this, exactly this, when the door swings open, and Ken is standing in the middle of the frame.

Pinch yourself in dreams. I heard that once, that if you think you might be dreaming, you are supposed to pinch yourself, because you can't feel pain when you're sleeping. I'm pinching myself and it hurts.

Toshiko screams, and my father bursts into tears, and my mother rushes over to Ken, but then instead of hugging him, immediately starts to smooth back his hair, and adjust his collar, none of which really need fixing because even though the last time we saw Ken he was an absentminded teenager whose shirt was always half-tucked and whose buttons were always loose, now he is a soldier with the US Army with not a hair or thread out of place.

There's another soldier with him, a white man, a commanding officer, I think. I don't know anything about how the military works but this man is older and his uniform looks a little more official.

I try to hug my brother, but when my arms wrap around his right shoulder, he winces. "Careful."

"Are you hurt?" my mother asks. Her poking and prodding changes from motherly to medical; she maneuvers his limbs, lifting his arms up and down. "Does that hurt?"

"I'm just scratched," he says. "Lucky. The right side of my upper body was numb for a week; I couldn't feel a thing. They thought there might be permanent nerve damage so they put me on a plane. As soon as I stepped off it, my shoulder started to hurt. Which is actually a good thing, in medical terms, they said. If it hurts it means I'm recovering."

"The doctors over there probably don't know anything," my mother says, while Toshiko says, "I bet the other guy is worse than you."

"I bet you didn't stay around too long to find out," my father says to Ken, and then we all laugh and laugh like it's the funniest joke we've ever heard.

Ken is alive. Ken is standing here in front of us, with all his arms and legs intact.

"You seem shorter," Toshiko says.

"It's because you got taller." She beams.

While we're hugging and greeting and debating whether it's Ken or Toshiko who changed the most, we almost don't hear the door opening and the camp guard clearing his throat, joining the little circle that my family has made.

"The secretary is going to bring in some coffee and cookies," he says, addressing my parents. "I'm told you've been granted permission to use this room for up to two hours before Ken and Sergeant Oakes go back to their hotel."

"What do you mean up to two hours?" I say.

"His *hotel?*" my mother asks after Toshiko translates. She can barely hide the horror from her face as she and my father exchange glances.

"I'm told it's really just a local woman who rents out a couple rooms," Ken says, after a beat. "But it will be fine enough for me. They said I can come back here tomorrow to see you again."

"I'm sure the hotel is very nice," my mother says awkwardly, as the guard settles in the corner.

But of course until the mention of this hotel, my whole family thought that Ken would come back to our hut. Now we see the camp director intends for us to have our entire reunion in public, with a guard leaning against the door.

We all stand frozen in a tableau, suddenly aware we're being observed. I open my mouth to protest the idea of Ken staying at a hotel, but close it almost immediately when I can't think of how to start my sentence. My mother stiffly folds her skirt underneath her legs as she sits down on the sofa and gestures for the rest of us to do the same.

"It's not fair—" Toshiko begins, but my mother silences her with a look. Toshiko stops talking, but her mouth is still angry.

"Thank you," my mother says in her best English when the secretary brings in the coffee tray. My mother directs it to be set on the table. I'm proud of her in this moment, for finding a way to make it seem like she is the hostess, like she invited us to tea and the secretary and soldier are no more than staff.

"Ken," she says, handing my brother a cup, which he takes with his left hand. "Please tell us how you are."

"Oh, I'm swell," Ken says. "Probably not worth all the fuss to send me home, but I don't mind hitching a ride if it means a chance to see you all."

"We're so happy," my father says, accepting his own cup. "We're so happy to see you."

None of us are behaving naturally. It's like we're in a play about a son who comes home from war, like we can't remember how we're supposed to be around each other. Toshiko is drinking her coffee with her pinkie finger raised, which I've never seen her do. I've never heard Ken say *swell* in his life. It's like *fellas* from his letters—a word that the brother I know would roll his eyes at.

He's thin. He has tired lines around his mouth. He sets

down his coffee and his cup clinks loudly, which I wouldn't be able to hear except that our conversation is so stilted and halting.

Suddenly, I'm glad the guard is here because I can blame my family's awkwardness on him. What I'm really afraid of is that if the guard weren't here, things would feel just as false.

"Once you are processed, you won't have to stay in a hotel," my mother says. "They assign bigger houses to families of five. We'll be able to get a house with another room that you can sleep in for some privacy. I'm sure they just need to process the paperwork."

"I'm sure they won't go to the trouble," Ken says, "as I'll be heading back in a few days."

He says it so casually that it takes a minute to sink in. My mother's hand trembles midair as she reaches to refill my father's cup, and my own cup screeches against its saucer.

"What do you mean you'll be heading back?" my father asks, his voice even.

"Since it seems like my shoulder is better," Ken says. "Can't have an able-bodied man here when he's needed over there. I'll get a few days' R & R, then it's back on a plane for me."

My mother looks at my father, and then, almost imperceptibly, at the guard, who is now examining the band of his wristwatch with such elaborate studiousness that I'm sure he's listening to us. I have no idea if he speaks Japanese. I'll assume he does and can understand everything we're saying.

This time, not even Toshiko says it's not fair. How can

she, in front of the guard? How can any of us do anything except pretend that we think it's wonderful that my brother is going back to war? That now that we finally have him with us again, now that we have been able to touch him and hug him, we absolutely want to put him back on a plane to God only knows where, where he might be killed. We must pretend that. We are serene. We are good Americans. We are behind the barbed wire, but we are still such good Americans.

"Well then," my mother begins, but her voice cracks and she starts over. "Well then. We will have to make the most of the time that we do have, won't we?"

We talk about movies. How we watch them outside the community center. How my brother, wherever he is stationed, has seen a few movies, too. We talk about food: how he gets better food than the average American because the country is saving its sugar rations for the boys in uniform to have Hershey's bars. How we get decent food, too, for a different reason: because the United States government has to feed us well in case Japan is watching. They want to treat us as well as they hope Japan is treating its American prisoners of war.

We are careful, so careful, not to talk about anything that actually matters. Not to ask Ken where he's been, or how his unit is doing, or anything else that might make it sound like we are trying to figure out if Japan can win the war.

In the corner, the door opens. It's the sergeant who came with Ken, whose name I already can't remember. He gently clears his throat. We all pretend we can't hear, because we know what it means, but eventually he interrupts. "Private Tanaka," he says, "it's time to go."

Behind him in the doorway, Mr. Mercer appears again, looking as jovial as he did when he first led us in here. I suddenly realize that when he didn't tell us why we were called to this room—that when it never occurred to him to say, *Don't worry, this is good news not bad news*—he thought he was doing us a favor. Arranging a special surprise. He had no idea that we might, at this point, find the idea of surprises to be horrifying.

"Did everyone have a pleasant visit?" he asks. He turns to Toshiko and me. "You girls must be very proud of your big brother."

Toshiko and I nod mutely. It's our father who answers out loud.

"Mr. Mercer. We have very much enjoyed our visit, but I am sure you can appreciate that two hours is not enough time to visit with a son we haven't seen in months. I ask that Ken might come and stay with us while he is in Crystal City. My wife and I have missed him so much, and so have his sisters."

Mr. Mercer's face reddens, but he keeps the same cheerful expression. "That's...ahh, that's not protocol."

"We can make space for him." My father presses on while the rest of my family stands behind him. Toshiko is crossing her fingers, which I know is stupid but then I cross mine, too. "We won't need to request extra food. He can have my rations. But it would be very important. To our morale. To the morale of the whole camp, I think, to see one of our own sons here, coming back in his uniform."

He says all of this in English, of course, but my mother must understand at least the basics. She's grabbed my shoulder and is holding it so tightly I can feel her fingernails through the cloth of my dress.

Mr. Mercer's smile falters. "Y'all know I wish I could," he says carefully. "Y'all know if it was up to me, you could have your visit in private and Ken could stay as long as he liked. But unfortunately I don't make all the rules."

Of course you make the rules! I want to scream at him. How dare he act so bashful. How dare he pretend he doesn't have power, when he has all the power? When my father is begging him to let Ken come and sleep in the same house as his own family. When my whole family's life has been torn apart, and my brother risks his own life every day, and Mr. Mercer's job is guarding a bunch of women and children in Texas.

"Please," my mother says. She enunciates her English words very carefully. "Please. Ken stays with us."

Mr. Mercer thinks, tapping his finger against his chin.

"I'll tell you what," he says finally. "Ken is the first soldier we've had come and visit Crystal City, and we're still trying to figure out the right protocols here. But we absolutely appreciate his service to our country. I'm not supposed to do this, but how about this: If you promise to have Ken back by, say"—he stops to check his watch—"eight o'clock—then Ken can spend the afternoon with you all. Eight o'clock is when I was planning on leaving tonight, and I'll drive him to the hotel myself, on my way home."

He turns quickly to the sergeant, who gives an infinitesimal nod that this is acceptable, then expands his hands benevolently to us.

"Thank you," we all say, over and over, groveling, as if what he's given us is some unprecedented humanitarian gift, rather than the most basic act of human decency. "Thank you, you are too generous."

SEVENTEEN

HARUKO

PEOPLE PEER HUNGRILY AT US AS WE WALK WITH KEN THROUGH camp, my mother on one side and Toshiko on the other, my father and I behind. "My brother, visiting from the war," Toshiko calls out as we show Ken the Union Store and then the hospital, where the other doctors and nurses rush over to offer congratulations and to tell Ken how much they've heard about him.

"How boring that must have been for you," he tells everyone. "I'm so sorry." And then the women laugh and slap him on the shoulder.

We only have to introduce him a few times; camp gossip takes care of the rest. A few people I've never met come to ask Ken if he knows their nephews or neighbors in the 442nd, and by the time we get back to our cottage, our front step is already lined with bowls of rice and vegetables neighbors have stopped by to donate. Made by families who live in the huts with kitchens, so that we can eat in our own house, too, instead of going to the mess hall.

It's a little after three PM, an odd time for a meal, but since people have given us food we decide to eat it, pulling over a trunk for my sister and me to sit on like a bench.

My mother has only just served the food when there's a knock at our door, a neighbor wanting to congratulate us. This happens two more times, and on the fourth knock my father sends me to answer the door. "Haruko, please tell the neighbors we will bring Ken to meet them later this evening," my father says. "And perhaps you could ask this visitor to spread the news so we don't keep being interrupted?"

But this time it's not a neighbor. Margot is still wearing the clothes from the field trip earlier this afternoon, the hem of her skirt dirty from where we sat on the bank of the stream. Her face looks frantic and then, when she sees me, filled with relief.

"I'm sorry I just showed up," she says immediately. "I didn't know what to...you didn't come back and I...One of the assistants at the hospital told me this was your house."

I cannot believe that she came to find me here, not after what happened the last time she was on this side of camp—the embarrassing looks and the people asking her to leave. But she came here in spite of all that, for me. "It's good news—"

I start to say, and then there are footsteps behind me, a hand on my shoulder.

"Margot, this is my brother. This is Ken."

Her face turns from concern to elation; she takes Ken's outstretched hand and shakes it.

"I'm so, so glad to meet you," she says. "Your letters, all of the things Haruko's told me. I feel like I know you."

"My sister showed you my letters?"

"I didn't introduce you," I interject. "This is Margot. She's my friend."

My mother appears beside Ken to find out what is taking us so long. It's only when she looks past me, out into the street, that I see what she must be seeing: Several of our neighbors peering from behind their curtains or loitering in their yards in a way I've never seen them do. A lot of it is because they want to see Ken, but some of it is because a girl with blond hair has run up the street and knocked on our door.

"Mama, this is Margot. We go to school together," I explain in Japanese. "Or, we did, until today. We were working together on a project. She came to tell me some things I needed."

"Margot." My mother looks as though she is trying to place where she knows Margot from. "I hope your mother is well. Has her morning sickness abated? Everything else is good?"

Margot waits for me to translate. "I think her morning sickness is better. Haruko helped—I mean, my mother has some tea that will be helpful, I think."

"Very good," my mother says in English, looking back and forth between us, before turning to me again. "People were so kind to bring us food. We don't want to let it get cold, and I am sure your brother is hungry."

"I'll find you later," I tell Margot, even though what I really want to do is invite her inside. "To talk about homework."

After we finish dinner, my mother rinses out the containers that people brought the food over in. "We could play cards," she offers. "Or, Kenichi, are you tired? You could lie down for a little while on one of the girls' beds. We have some books I could give you to read. Or, Haruko has a friend whose father has a nice film projector. Or maybe we could—"

"Why don't Ken and I return the bowls?" I say spontaneously. "Papa has been at work since this morning; you are all probably tired. We can return them and give you a rest."

"No, no, we can wait." My mother looks stricken at the idea of us leaving and the family not being together. "People will understand if we don't return them today."

But I'm already grabbing Ken's hand. "I want to. And I didn't get to show Ken the school before. He said he wanted to see that, didn't you?"

Ken barely hesitates before nodding, like in the old days: *Mama, Ken and I have to stay after school because we volunteered to help with a clothing drive. Isn't that right, Ken? They'll probably keep us late.* "We can be back soon. Still lots of time for us all to spend together."

Toshiko opens her mouth like she wants to come, but she

doesn't ask. We never invited her along when we were sneaking out in Colorado, either; she was too young. My mother watches us leave, and then stands at the doorway until we turn off our road, trying to follow Ken with her eyes.

It ends up taking just ten minutes to return the bowls. "Let's keep walking, though," I say. "I don't feel like going back yet, do you? I'll show you the school like I told Mama I would."

Ken shrugs. "Whatever you want."

"Because if you'd rather not walk to the school, I guess we could find a quiet place to sit for a little—"

"Whatever you want, Haruko."

Now that we are away from our parents, Ken changes. At first I think it's in my imagination but it's not. Even though we talk and talk, Ken is not really talking. He answers my questions, and he laughs when I laugh. But it's always a beat too late, like he is waiting for me to tell him when the joke is, or like he doesn't really understand what a joke is. His shoulders droop, and so do the corners of his mouth. *He's tired*, I tell myself. *He's just tired, because he's traveled a long distance, but he's here, and he's all right, you can see for yourself.*

We keep walking. We pass a guard tower, and Mike is working. I steer Ken over in Mike's direction and call up a greeting.

"This is my brother. Visiting from the 442nd. I'm showing him around."

Mike nods and performs a jaunty salute. "A fellow man in uniform. Glad to know you."

Ken doesn't say anything. He looks at Mike, whose fingertips are still at his forehead, for what feels like a long time. Mike glances at me, wondering if he did something wrong.

I stare at my brother. Finally, he raises his own arm—the wounded one, the one that made him cry out when I hugged too hard—to return the salute.

"So, where's my chewing gum?" I ask Mike after the awkward pause, wanting Ken to join in, to have this afternoon be fun.

"You caught me unaware. I'm out."

When we leave the guard tower I glance sideways at Ken to see if I can tell what he's thinking.

"You have interesting friends."

"Mike is from Colorado, too. He gives me chewing gum. He always has extra. For me and Toshiko both."

Ken stops. "I actually wasn't talking about Mike. Who is Margot?"

"I told you. She's my friend from school."

"She's read all of my letters. Do most people have friends here who are German?"

"Some do." My face flushes as I babble on. "Do you know who Margot would remind you of? That girl who used to come into the soda fountain, and then spend the whole time sitting at the counter with her nose in a book, and in the beginning we thought something must be wrong with her because she was so—"

Ken is shaking his head back and forth.

"Can we not?" he says quietly.

"Can we not what?"

"Can you not ask me to talk and laugh?"

"I wasn't trying to make you talk and laugh. I was trying to show you around and—"

"I can do that in front of Mama and Papa, but when we're not around them, can you just . . . let me rest?"

"Sure. Of—of course," I stammer. "You don't have to talk. I was trying to give you a break from the family."

But it turns out it is hard to say nothing to a person. Especially when it is a person you are used to saying everything to. Ken and I have always had something to say to each other, and if we were quiet, it was comfortable quiet. This silence with Ken doesn't feel comforting, it feels like a hole.

We passed the school a long time ago. We've been making a square around the periphery of the camp. Now we're coming up to the big, circular pool, where I can already hear kids laughing.

"Do you want to go swimming?" I ask him. "I told Mama that we'd be an hour; we have time."

"Not really," he says.

"Come on, it opened yesterday."

Really, I am embarrassed to admit to myself, it's that I don't want to be alone with my brother. What kind of sister am I? I've spent the past month angry at Ken's letters because I felt like they were hiding something. And now I have him here, and I'm doing exactly what I didn't want him to do. I'm so cheerful I'm making myself sick.

"They sell men's bathing trunks in the Union Store. I have tokens, I can buy a pair for you."

I pull him to the store, where I make a big show of pretending to care whether he purchases the blue swimming suit or the black one, and then to the pool where I make a big show of choosing a shady patch on the concrete, where we're far enough away from other people to not be bothered. It's mostly smaller kids, but both Japanese and German. And their Japanese and German mothers are talking to one another while their children swim, and that doesn't seem strange at all.

This could be a place where I could come with Margot. Where nobody is hiding and everyone is supposed to be here.

"Haruko?" Ken asks. I've been staring at the pool without moving.

"It's nothing."

I dangle my legs in the water, making splashes to entertain Ken, but he stays on the deck, still wearing the shirt he borrowed from Papa so his uniform wouldn't get mussed around camp.

"Are you modest all of a sudden?" I ask when I walk back, wringing out the wet edge of my skirt. "How are you supposed to swim if you don't take off your shirt?"

"I don't want to swim, Haruko."

"You don't have to swim, just get a little sun."

I tug on the hemline of his shirt until he obliges, wincing

as he pulls the top over his head. He crumples the T-shirt next to him.

I thought he would be more muscular, strong and tan like the GIs we used to see in magazines. Instead he is thin, so much thinner than I remember him looking before. I can nearly count his ribs. His torso and arms are covered in bruises. And his wounded shoulder is covered by a big piece of white gauze.

"Happy?" he says.

Oh, Ken. "Does it still hurt?"

"What? My shoulder?" As if I could be talking about anything else. "It's not serious," he says.

"It looks serious."

"It's not. I promise."

"You can't promise, you're not a doctor."

Ken sighs. "If it were just my shoulder I don't think they would have given me leave."

"What do you mean—is something else hurt?" I ask.

He smiles the saddest, most ghostlike smile I have ever seen. "My brain," he says, lightly touching his index finger to his temple. "Battle fatigue. Combat illness. They said I'm sick in the head."

"No you're not!" I say automatically.

"Would I make it up?"

"You need to rest so your shoulder can heal. That's all."

"Haruko. The government doesn't send soldiers home

because they have minor flesh wounds. People are shot all the time there. They go to a hospital tent and rest until they are better. They send people home if there's something more broken. And there is for me. Something more broken than everyone else."

"What do you mean? What happened?" I ask.

"It's not one thing that happened."

"What are the different things that happened?"

"I don't want to talk about it," he says shortly. "They had me meet with head doctors. A psychiatrist. He examined me. He said I will be fine."

"Did he say they can treat it?"

"I am treating it now. R & R. They said I needed a few days away from the front, and I would be fine, everything would be back to normal. They told me to go see a movie. Dance with a pretty girl."

I watch the breeze ripple across his skinny arms, raising goose pimples, making the soft hairs on his forearms stand on end. A toddler runs past us, faster than he should on a pool deck, and his mother swats at his rear end.

"Where is *back*, Ken? When you say that after a few days they'll send you back, where are you going?"

He glances at me and shakes his head. "You know I can't."

"Why not?"

"I'm not supposed to tell you."

"But what does it matter?" I wheedle. "Tell me where you're going."

"*Loose lips might sink ships*," he says, parroting back the poster that we used to see all the time in Colorado, a picture of a military cargo ship sinking into the ocean because some unknowing American had accidentally gossiped in front of a spy.

"*An enemy's ear might be near*," I say back automatically, the text of another poster. That poster, of a big black-and-white ear, used to hang right across the street from the hotel. Underneath *An enemy's ear might be near*, it said, *Stop all loose talk to strangers*. It always seemed a little too silly to be effective. Ken and I used to make jokes: *An enemy's feet might be just down the street. An enemy's spleen might be close but unseen.*

We did it until our father told us it was inappropriate. That Nisei children couldn't make jokes to deal with the dark mood, because people might not know we were joking. Ken signed up for the 442nd shortly after, when he turned eighteen, and I bet nobody thought he was joking then.

"An enemy's gallbladder is very, very badder," Ken says.

I burst out laughing. "That doesn't make sense."

Ken laughs, too, and it's an old-Ken laugh that makes my heart leap. This feels like being with my brother again. My real one, not the one who sends overly cheerful letters, or who says his brain is sick.

"I know it doesn't make sense, but I thought of it a while ago when I was on guard duty. It was a long night, and I was doing anything I could to keep my mind occupied. I wanted to tell you, but I was pretty sure if I put it in a letter they would think it was some kind of secret code and censor it out anyway. You should have seen me at the time, though. This tall Japanese-looking guy, in an American GI uniform, laughing to himself like a crazy person about gallbladders, pacing up and down this little cobblestoned street."

"So you were in a place with a cobblestoned street!" I say.

I don't know why I want to know so badly where my brother has been, except that it feels safer, somehow, if I can picture him writing from a place, not just from a void in my imagination.

"Nice try. They all have cobblestoned streets," he says wryly. "Being hundreds of years old, and all."

"Not Italy," I tell him. "If you were stationed in Italy, instead of walking on cobblestoned streets, you could be stationed on a gondola."

He laughs again. But this time it takes him longer and he won't look at me. "Let's talk about something else," he says.

"It's Italy! It is, I can tell by the way you're not looking at me."

"I didn't say that," he says quickly. "I didn't say anything."

"I know you didn't say anything. I guessed. Because I am your sister and I am a genius."

He's supposed to laugh at that now, too, and maybe punch me in the arm or try to push me into the pool.

He doesn't, though. He just buries his head in his hands, scraping his fingers through his hair. "I'm stupid. I'm so stupid. I don't know why I said that. I don't know how it just slipped out." His face is twisted and he's breathing heavier, too.

"It's just a *country*, Ken," I try to reassure him. "The only thing you told me—and you didn't *tell* me, really—is the name of a country. And who cares about that? Everybody already knows that Nisei soldiers wouldn't be allowed to go to the Pacific front, so that only leaves Europe, and Europe is small. Right? I only guessed Italy because my marks were so bad in geography that Italy and France are the only countries I know. Except for Germany. Now I know Germany. Because of, you know, Hitler."

"It's not a joke, Haruko," he says, agitated. "Things have unintended consequences. Even silly things. There might not be any silly things anymore. I shouldn't have told you that. I shouldn't be telling anything to anyone."

The splashing in the background is distracting, and I want to scream at everyone to shut up, just shut up. I reach for Ken's good shoulder, but barely touch him before he shrugs my hand off. He shakes his head in what looks like a warning. It looks like the same kind of warning I have seen before.

"Ken," I say.

"What?"

"I need to ask you something. I need you to take it seriously."

"What, Haruko?"

"Ken, do you think Papa had unintended consequences?"

"What are you talking about?"

The question I have been afraid to ask. The question I tried to ask my father the day I brought his lunch to the fence.

"When they took him, did you ever wonder if there was a reason for it?"

"A reason for it?"

"Some way that he actually did something. That he actually was passing messages between guests."

It's such a specific accusation. It always has been. It's always been such a specific accusation.

"Think of it. Maybe he didn't even know he was doing it. Maybe someone just came to the front desk and said, *I have an envelope to leave for my colleague.* Papa would have passed it on, you know he would have."

Ken flinches, the smallest flinch. "God, Haruko, what are you talking about? What has our father ever done in his entire life that would make you ask something like that?"

"Ken, the day they took him, he thought about telling me something. You were already gone, you didn't see. But something odd happened. The FBI were in our house, and he thought about telling me something but he didn't."

"You have no idea what you're saying."

"I can't explain it, but I know what I saw."

"And what if you saw something?" Ken explodes. "What would that matter? You are already here and these questions could hurt our family. Why are you still asking them?"

"Because I want to understand what happened," I say, just as angry. "And right now I don't understand *anything.* You sent us these letters that don't even sound like you, and then the ones that maybe would sound like you were censored. They came to us with these black lines through them. And now I don't know whether that's because the censors don't understand your dumb sense of humor, or because you're sick, but do you have any idea how terrifying that was for me? I *worry* about you. All the time, I worry. So please tell me, Ken. Tell me anything. Tell me what it's like over there. I won't tell anyone else, I promise. Is it bad?"

He doesn't answer, so I poke him. I meant to lay my hand on his arm, but at the last minute I become his little sister again and I do what I always did when I wanted him to pay attention to me, what Toshiko does when she wants me to pay attention to her, jabbing at his arm with my index finger. "Is it bad?" I ask again, more quietly.

He reaches down and catches my finger mid-poke. "Over there—it's the worst thing I've ever seen," he says slowly. "I've seen the worst things I could have imagined. Do you understand?"

I nod, even though what he's told me isn't possibly enough for me to understand.

"But I'm doing my best to serve well," he says. "So that I can come home and you can get out."

"We're okay here. You don't have to worry about us."

"You are not okay," Ken says, more fiercely than I expected him to. "Don't let yourself think you are okay. Don't let yourself think this is normal. It's not."

"I'm not saying it's *normal*. The whole country is not normal. We are at war."

"No. I am at war. *I* am in the war. You are in a prison. That's not normal."

He turns away from me, watching the little kids do cannonballs off the diving platform and into the pool. Every time one of them hits the water, the sound makes him flinch. "Have you ever heard of Manzanar?" he asks a few minutes later.

"It's a camp, right? Back in California?"

Before I ever heard of Crystal City I had heard of Manzanar, maybe in a newspaper, maybe through the Japan League. The name sounded like another fairy-tale place, even more than Crystal City. A lost place that time forgot. Xanadu. Camelot. Manzanar.

"Do you know about what happened there?" Ken says. "Do you know about the Manzanar uprising?"

"No."

"The Manzanar uprising is what some newspapers are calling something that happened there. Some detainees thought the white cafeteria workers were skimming off goods and selling them on the black market. There was a riot, and it ended with the guards firing into a crowd—"

"I don't want to hear about that."

"With a machine gun—"

"I don't want to *hear* about that," I say louder.

"Guards fired into the crowd with a machine gun," Ken says, louder than me. "Two people died. *Two people died.*"

"That wouldn't happen here," I say. "I don't think the guards here would do that."

"Why wouldn't that happen here?" Ken asks. "Manzanar was a camp, like this one."

"It *wasn't* like this one. This is a family camp. That's what they said it was, a family camp, and there are schools, and stores, and—and a football team."

"Do you think the other camps don't have families?" Ken asks. "Do you think that all the Japanese children in the entire United States are here in Crystal City? Maybe they treat you better because you're *enemy aliens* and they think Japan might be watching, but you shouldn't think you're that special."

I look at my brother. "Why are we talking about this? Why do you want to make us have this conversation? You just said: You will go back to war, and I will have to stay here. Why are you telling me things like this when I have to stay here?"

Nothing about this reunion has gone the way I pictured it would, all the times I pictured him coming back. We're not happy. We're not carefree. Ken is sick and I am scared and we're talking about things that only serve to confirm that sick and scared are the right things to be.

"Because," Ken says. "I don't want you to ever forget where you are. You are a prisoner here. I don't care if you have a new friend, or if there's a school newspaper, or if there are books in the library, or if there are community picnics. Or if there's a football team everyone comes out to cheer for. At the end of the day you're a prisoner in the only way that matters. If our family wanted to leave, they wouldn't let you."

EIGHTEEN

MARGOT

VATI AND A MAN I BARELY KNOW ARE SITTING AT OUR TABLE
when I get back from running to Haruko's house. It's Mr.
Mueller, the pockmarked man who fixes appliances around
camp. I've only ever seen him with Mr. Kruse. But now it's
just him. He and my father both have wet towels draped over
the backs of their necks to keep away the heat and they're
drinking ice water.

"—told them we were trying to make marmalade, and they
believed it," Mr. Mueller is saying. He's laughing hard, almost
wheezing. "*Scheisse*, it's a good thing it was as bad as it was. The
parts were too mangled for them to see what it really was."

He slaps his hand on the table and wipes tears from his
eyes.

My father laughs, too, but his laugh doesn't seem comfortable. Frederick Kruse is not a good man, but he hides it well. He's courteous and polite, like most of Vati's friends at home were. Mr. Mueller is vulgar, swearing in German and leaving his shirt unbuttoned low. I can't recall seeing my father spend time with someone like him.

"Technically speaking, the concepts behind a distillery and behind a bomb are not so different," Vati says tightly. "When it blew up, you're lucky they believed you were making marmalade. They could have assumed you were making a bomb."

"No kidding?" Mr. Mueller finishes his water. "Didn't want to get anyone killed, just drunk."

The distilleries. They're talking about the illicit homemade alcohol distilleries around camp. One must have exploded.

I slide around the table toward my half of the room. I don't want to be here for this. I'll get my books and go to the icehouse. Except Haruko won't be there. She's with her brother now. I could head back to the school, except I don't go to that school anymore, I realize. Today was my last day.

"How are you, Margot?" Mr. Mueller asks, as I open my trunk to search for my notebook. "Your father tells me you will be starting at the German school on Monday. I'll have to introduce you to my sons. You'll like Barrett: He's very smart, not an ass like me."

"You were worried you wouldn't have friends at the new school," my father says. "Barrett plans to attend university in Munich when the Muellers go back."

"Where's Mutti?"

He nods to the door leading to the communal kitchen. I bet she's been in there since Mr. Mueller arrived. Her split lip from last night was a bruise by the time she woke up this morning, gray and lilac and traveling halfway up her face. She hadn't wanted to leave the house because of it. Vati made a show of telling her to rest, that he would stay with her, do all the cooking and cleaning.

Mr. Mueller doesn't wait long for me to say anything about his sons before he turns back to my father. My notebook isn't anywhere in my trunk. I get on my hands and knees to search under the bed.

"Anyhow, all of that brings me to why I am here today," Mr. Mueller says. "Frederick would obviously prefer that our stills don't keep exploding. This was the second one. Luckily the *dummkopf* guards never found out about the first. Do you have any thoughts on how to solve this problem?"

"I'm not really a drinking man."

"I'd say it's more of a mechanical problem than an alcohol problem."

"I'm not a mechanic, either. I don't know that I can be of any particular help."

"Oh, just give it a try. If you had to guess." Mr. Mueller's glass has been empty for a few minutes and my father hasn't offered him more water. It makes the hopeful part of me believe Vati is ready for him to leave.

But then instead of declining again, or rising to signal the end of the conversation, Vati rubs the side of his head. It's what he does when he's thinking; I have seen him make the gesture a hundred times. "Well. It seems like there is probably just some kind of leak, and the vapors are catching on fire?" he says. "Again, I don't have any experience."

"But you're an engineer. Frederick says you completed graduate school back in Berlin. He thought you might be at least willing to take a look."

Now I can see the gears whirring in my father's head, the way they always do when he has a new project, a new way to be useful. I used to love seeing his face light up like that. It's not fair for him to do these things that make him look like his old self, when he's not.

"Do you have any more parts?" Vati asks Mr. Mueller. "I can't imagine you buy what you need for this sort of project at the General Store."

"You'd be surprised at how creative we can be. For the stuff we can't gin up on our own, there's a man who is with us—Wilhelm Boehner; good man, I'll introduce you—who has one of the laborer jobs outside the fence. His contact gets the parts to a little storage shed. It's where workers store their equipment."

"Guards don't go inside?"

"Never. Wilhelm brings them back piece by piece. They never suspect a thing."

My father sighs. "I suppose I could try, at least. While I'm waiting for a different job. Building alcohol distilleries is not particularly what I am interested in doing."

"We'll pay you in product." Mr. Mueller winks. "You're not a drinking man, but others are."

It's just what my mother was saying. Petty criminals. Acting like they are brave spies, with their *contacts* and their smuggling of equipment. When really they are just bored men trying to make illicit alcohol to get drunk inside the camp.

Only a few months ago, the mention of Frederick Kruse's name made my father angry. Now he has become one of the lackeys.

"Let's go to the beer hall," Mr. Mueller says. He nods at his empty glass. "I could do with something a little stronger than this now, in fact."

Another reason the distilleries are idiotic. You can buy beer with cardboard tokens already.

"I can come along for the stroll," Vati says.

I go through the door that leads to the kitchen. My mother has opened the icebox, leaning into it to feel the cool air on her face. When I come in she starts to turn away before realizing it's me.

"I know I'm not supposed to," she says, nodding toward the open icebox. "I know it melts everyone's things."

"We can always get more ice. Leave it open if it makes you feel better," I tell her. "Vati's gone now. They left."

My mother nods. Even with the icebox door open, it's hot in here, several degrees warmer than our main room. My mother's dress clings to her. In the past few weeks, her belly has truly begun to show. A smooth, round bump protrudes from underneath the loose cotton.

"Is that man his friend now?" I ask. "Is he going to be here a lot?"

"I don't know, Margot."

"Is he coming back for dinner tonight?"

"I don't *know*, Margot. I don't know who his friends will be now." She bangs the icebox door closed.

"How are you feeling?"

"You should try speaking in German at home now," she replies, in German, instead of answering my question. "Your conversational skills are fine, but I wonder if we need to go over terminology for a school setting. If I can remember myself. It's been a while since I had an advanced math course in German."

"A plumber is teaching the math classes," I say to her in English. "I'm not sure how advanced they'll be."

Mutti sets her mouth in a firm line, but I think I see exhaustion under it. "Smart people find ways to succeed in circumstances that are less than desirable."

"Do they build distilleries?"

"We should be glad they are talking about building distilleries. It's a foolish thing to focus on. You and I both need to hope they never find something bigger to care about."

She puts her hand on the door of the icebox and hesitates before finally deciding to open it again, putting her face back in toward the cold.

"You could move out for a little while," I say. "You could request another hut here."

"And after?" She raises an eyebrow. "What would you and I do after?"

"We could work." I try to picture my mother and me in our own house. But when I think of living somewhere else, what I keep picturing is the apartment that Haruko described to me in San Antonio, with a screen door and a private bathroom. The one that we were talking about when we were interrupted on the banks of the stream, before I could figure out how much of what we were saying was real.

She closes the icebox. "Margot, I have not had a job besides being your father's wife since coming to this country. I am not an American citizen. Who would hire me after the war? When all the American soldiers are coming home from fighting in Germany, who would look at my job application and say, instead of hiring this twenty-two-year-old man who has served his country in the war, let me hire this forty-one-year-old pregnant German woman with no work experience who spent the war in an enemy alien internment camp?"

My mother places a gentle hand on her stomach. "I need your father. I want this baby."

"Then we need to convince him to let us go home," I beg. "To take our names off the list for Germany. We have friends in Iowa. People who can help him start over there. Do you really want to go back to Germany? You don't, do you?"

My parents were young when they left there after the

Great War because their country had become poor. My mother's parents are still there, but they are old, and since my father's parents died, I've never heard my parents mention a single other family member or friend. We barely get letters from there. They left that life behind.

My mother looks at me. "We can't go home," she says. "Look at your father now. Do you think he would fit in at home? Do you think we could have a happy life there?"

I try to picture Vati back in Iowa. At the feed store. At the general store, trading jokes with Mr. Lammey. At a party in someone's home, talking about local politics or whose crops are doing well this year.

Most of Vati's friends weren't sent to camps. Haruko was right the first time we talked. It was not like with the Japanese, where entire communities were sent away. With us it was like a scalpel: a German here, a German there, while the rest of the Germans and the rest of the town went about their business.

Our friends at home went to Europe to fight. Or they are spending the war collecting scrap metal or raising victory gardens. I think those are things that are still happening outside these walls. Sewing quilts. Buying war bonds. Supporting the war effort in a world that is the same as the one we are living in, but completely different.

I try to picture Vati going back into their world. He's too angry. He believes things about America now that he would not get away with saying. But the thing is that he believes those things because he is stuck *here*.

"He would get better," I say stubbornly. "Once he's away from this."

Mutti shakes her head. "You can't picture him there. I can't picture him there. Sometimes people are too broken to start over." She swallows. "Listen to me, Margot. I don't want this, either. But I don't know what else to do. The people at home have sent their husbands and sons to risk their lives and die in the war. Can you imagine your father going back to Iowa and praising Germany? They would kill him."

This time, she stops me before I can say anything. "It's true, they would," she continues. "When we get out of here, we will find a new way to start over. You can do it. I was not much older than you when I came to America. It was hard, but I managed. But if we went back to Fort Dodge and your father said out loud the kinds of things he was saying after the swimming pool, everyone we know would want to kill him. And I would die of shame."

NINETEEN

MARGOT

September 23, 1944
Times I have gone to the icehouse in one morning to see
whether Haruko might be there: 3
Times she has been there: 0

THE NEXT DAY I HEAR VATI WAKE EARLY ACROSS THE ROOM, AND
before I can decide whether I want to acknowledge him he's
already gone. Mutti has an appointment at the hospital. A
routine one, she says, to check on the baby. I go with her, but
it's the blond doctor and not Haruko's mother who conducts
the exam.

So maybe Ken is still there, and the family is still spending time together. Or maybe Haruko doesn't want to see me.

Maybe after her brother's visit she is feeling foolish about the conversation we had yesterday, about indoor plumbing in our make-believe house in San Antonio. In the icehouse, the blankets and the lanterns stay folded and placed exactly where we last left them.

On Monday, I start at the German school. It's different. It's smaller, eight of us are in my class. It's formal. When we arrive at our desks in the morning, we're expected to stand next to them until the teacher gives us permission to sit. We learn botany. We learn geography, but German geography; and history, but German history. The curriculum is useless to me. None of it will prepare me for the future I want.

The other students here are from families that have applied to be repatriated. At school they talk about it excitedly, repeating things their parents have told them about Germany. Later at lunch a few of them find me privately, and ask what the federal school was like. Did we have pep rallies, they want to know. They say their old schools in New Jersey or Massachusetts had pep rallies.

After school, I'm walking past the main gates, a long route to the icehouse, when I hear my name.

"It's Margot, right?"

I shield my eyes. "Ken?"

Haruko's brother is in uniform, not the wrinkled shirt he was wearing when I knocked on her door. It makes him look older and more formal. I immediately look around, but I don't see Haruko nearby; Ken is alone by the gate. "Are you leaving?" I ask.

"If the car ever gets here. That's my escort, trying to figure out where it is." He nods to where another man in uniform stands by the guard tower, speaking into a Handie-Talkie.

"Is—"

"She and Toshiko went back to school already. I made them. I told the whole family that it would be . . . easier."

I want to ask how his visit was. And how Haruko is. I want to ask him to do his impression of the governor of Colorado's secretary. But maybe he would think that was strange. He probably doesn't know I know about that. "I bet they were really happy to see you. I bet Haruko wishes you could stay longer."

He shrugs. "I think she does and she doesn't. I don't know if I was making her happy by the end of the visit."

"Sometimes it's hard in here, to be the people we used to be."

That sentence comes out before I can really think about it. Am I saying, *we*, meaning Haruko and me? Or we, meaning all of us?

"To survive," I explain. "Sometimes to survive you have to pretend that you have always lived here. That you wanted to live here."

He stares at me. "You don't seem like my sister's other friends."

"Oh."

"That probably sounded rude. I didn't mean it to."

"It's okay," I say. "Haruko told me once that you were not like her other friends, either."

"What did she say I was like?"

"She didn't mean it to be rude then, either."

"She trusts you," he says. "Haruko was really popular at home, but I don't know if she really had any people who—she is . . . something different with you."

"What do you mean?" I take a step closer.

Ken looks out through the fence. In the distance I can see a jeep puffing in the dust, probably the car sent to pick him up. The other man in uniform puts down his Handie-Talkie and goes to the gate to flag it down.

"Margot. Will you do something for me?"

Ken doesn't wait for me to answer. He looks back and forth between the car and me, and then, seeing his escort isn't watching, reaches into his breast pocket. "I have another letter for my sister."

"You didn't mail it?"

He hesitates. "It's not the kind of letter I can put in the mail."

"Why didn't you just tell her whatever is inside?"

The jeep is getting closer; Ken talks quickly. "It's not something I want to tell her. Not yet, I'm not ready yet. I was going to leave it under her pillow, but I knew she'd just open it, so then I thought I'd scrap it entirely, but—the letter is in case I don't get a chance later." He stares at me. "Do you understand what I'm saying? In case I don't get a chance."

"I understand."

He hands me the envelope. Sealed, because it hasn't been through the censors like the other mail we get. No return address saying it's come via the War Department. Just *Haruko*, in the middle of the envelope.

"Don't give it to her unless you have to. Okay?" he says.

"I promise."

The big Crystal City gates are creaking open, and the escort motions for Ken to come out. He straightens his posture, transforming into a soldier in front of me. When he gets almost to the car, he turns around again. "Make her a scavenger hunt on her birthday," he calls out. "She pretends she hates them but she doesn't."

He gets in the car, and I watch as it disappears down the dirt road.

By the time I get to the federal school, where Ken said Haruko went, she's already come out of the building, past the flagpole. She's alone. I check to make sure, but we're in such a public space that I hesitate in going over to her until I realize she's already running toward me.

"I went to the icehouse," she says immediately. "Twice. I almost left a note but I didn't want anyone else to find it."

"I went, too. I thought about going to your house again, but I'd already gone there once."

"I thought about trying to find your house, too, but…"

She trails off, but she didn't need to finish the sentence. After what she has seen and heard about my father, why would she want to come to my house?

"Ken is leaving today," she says. "He told us he didn't want anyone to wait with him, but I shouldn't have left him—I was going there now."

"He's gone already."

"How do you know?"

Should I tell Haruko that I saw him? One day Haruko and I might read his letter together in the icehouse. But only in the worst possible circumstances. So is there any point in telling her the letter exists? Or in telling her that I talked to her brother at all?

"I passed the gate and there was a jeep driving away. Nobody else was outside."

Her head drops. "I shouldn't have left him," she says again. "Why would I let him just leave?"

It's been three days since we've seen each other but it feels like twenty, and I can't stop wondering what Ken would have said about us, and I am awkward again like the first time we talked. "Do you want to go there now? The icehouse?"

We both turn and start walking back in the direction that I've just come from.

"Was it nice to see your brother?" I ask, at the same time as she says, "How is the new school?"

"My father is trying to make moonshine," I blurt out,

because it seems like the kind of thing that might make her laugh. "They have secret hidden distilleries."

"Moonshine?" she repeats. "Like, Al Capone, 1920s gangster?"

"They blew up a distillery. Apparently making moonshine involves the same materials as building a bomb."

We've reached the wall of the school, right in the nook of the U shape. Haruko stops, lost in thought.

"It wasn't what I expected it would be," she says.

"What wasn't?"

"The visit. He wasn't what I expected, and the conversation wasn't what I expected."

He knows it didn't go like you wanted, I want to say. *He feels bad about that.* "In what way? Did he explain his letters?"

"Sort of. He explained that he was sick." I want to ask more about what she means by *sick,* but Haruko is biting the inside of her cheek like she still has something else to say. "Do you think—do you think that the government thinks they're doing the right thing?" she says.

"They have to, right? At least some of them. Why are you asking?"

"I can't stop thinking about something Ken said. He said—I can't even remember what he said. Ken talked about how letting myself be happy here was dangerous, because it wasn't true. He made me feel like Crystal City might explode at any minute."

"It might. The treacherous distilleries."

She smiles. "I'm not explaining it well. It's not like I haven't always known where we were. But somehow, until I talked to Ken, I didn't realize what it meant that we were all *here*." She shakes her head. "I don't know what I'm talking about."

"I do," I whisper. "I really do know what you mean."

We're standing against the side of the school, and though nobody has walked by yet, they could anytime. Having this conversation outside, when the sun is so high that we barely cast any shadows at all, makes these words bleaker.

She's thinking about Ken, and I am thinking about Ken's letter in my pocket. And the fact that it only took a few months for my family to turn into the opposite version of what my family had always been. I didn't know that was the number I should have been recording in my notebook the whole time. The only number that ever mattered. The number of days for my father to lose himself.

"It feels like it is going to be impossible for all of us to come out right," I say.

"Not *right*, exactly," Haruko says. "More like whole. It feels like it is getting more and more impossible for all of us to come out of this and still be whole."

She shakes her head quickly, resetting her thoughts. "I was thinking we should get a chaise longue in our apartment in San Antonio, right?"

"A chaise longue?" I try to keep up with the conversation.

"It's sort of like a combination between a sofa and a bed.

They're really comfortable. I was thinking that when I leave here, I want all my furniture to be really comfortable."

She leans back against the brick wall, wrinkling her nose. I have a sudden urge to touch her nose, her hair, to go with her to the icehouse where it's dark and private. There is throbbing, deep in the pit of my stomach.

"San Antonio is where the Alamo is, isn't it?" she asks.

"It's a museum now."

"Good. We should make a list of all the things we want to do. Starting with the Alamo. Then jobs. Then an apartment. Then chaise longues."

She tilts her head. I think she's going to say something else, but instead she cups a hand over her ear.

"What's that noise?"

"I don't hear anything," I say, but then I do hear a noise. It's faint and far away; I can't make out what it is.

Haruko steps away from the building, peering around the corner.

"It's coming from by the pool," she says. "Some kids messing around."

I follow her out into the clearing. Away from the building, I can hear the noise better, too. She is right. It is coming from the direction of the pool. But it's not kids messing around. It's someone screaming.

MARGOT

I know you're collecting stories from the war. What did you call them? Personal histories? You were collecting personal histories from the war, and Haruko told you about me, and you came for my story, too, and then you'll—I don't know what you'll do with them.

I'm not sure if Haruko told you that from then on it was awful.

From then on, there is nothing about this story I like.

TWENTY

HARUKO

MARGOT IS A FASTER RUNNER THAN I AM. SHE GETS THERE FIRST, and she puts her arm out, stopping me. At first I think it's to keep me from crashing into her, but it's to prevent me from seeing what she's already realized has happened.

The crowd at the pool is three-deep, some people in street clothes but most of them in bathing suits. Hair scraped back from their blotchy, exerted faces, arms wrapped around their goose-bumped waists.

"Let's not go any closer," Margot says.

"Why not?"

"Let's just not."

But when I start to move, she follows me. I push through

the crowd in their damp towels until I'm close enough to see what's happened.

The lifeguard—the one who I know is really a camp guard, but wearing a bathing suit instead of his uniform—is a skinny man with suntanned skin. He's pulling something out of the pool.

It is a dead animal. A stray dog that jumped in the pool looking to cool off. It is a wad of clothes—a prank played on someone who will now have to walk home wet and cold. These are things I tell myself because you can make yourself believe almost anything, really, if you try hard enough and if you want badly enough to ignore the truth.

It's only when the lifeguard has laid the object down on the ground that I see there is another object already there, next to it. Somehow seeing the two of them together, as a set, is what makes me realize the white and the red colors I'm noticing are bathing suits. And somehow it's only when I realize they are bathing suits that I also realize the two objects are little girls.

Two little girls, pulled out of the pool, limp as rag dolls. *Toshiko.*

It's not Toshiko. I can see that now, they're both too small to be Toshiko. But they could have been, Toshiko in her red bathing suit that used to belong to me. The lifeguard smooths the black hair away from the face of the girl in the white bathing suit, the one he's just pulled out of the pool. He turns her on her stomach and spreads her arms out into the shape of a T, and then he straddles her tiny body and begins to apply pressure to her back, compressions that begin at the middle and stroke up toward her lungs in a steady rhythm. *Out goes the bad air, in comes the good air,* remembers a numb part of my brain. Artificial respiration. You can also time it by counting Mississippis, we learned at my YWCA class. One Mississippi. Press. Two Mississippi. Press. The guard's bony frame moves up and down.

"My father said the bottom of the pool needed to be painted white." Margot's voice next to me is low and angry. "He said it was too dark for swimmers to tell when the water was getting deeper."

The girls have goose bumps on their legs; they need blankets.

"One of them slipped under the lane line into the deep end," the boy next to me whispers. "The other tried to help her. I always thought that if people were drowning they would call for help. But the girls weren't calling for help at all, they just kept bobbing under the water. I thought it was a game. I think the lifeguard didn't realize what was happening, either; at first no one realized what was happening, then someone else had to yell at him to save them."

Save her, I think, we all collectively think, pressed against one another's clammy skin. Thirteen Mississippis. The lifeguard has been joined by a Japanese woman in a white coat who slips in and efficiently drops to her knees. It's my mother in her hospital uniform. She barks a quick order to the lifeguard and immediately begins to work on the other girl, who has light brown braids, a little German girl.

And then someone else comes: A round-faced woman flying toward the pool deck in a housedress and slippers.

"Where is she? Where is she?" she yells out, elbowing her way toward the lifeguard and the two little girls. "Ruriko!" As she pushes through the crowd she calls out her daughter's name, the daughter who is still receiving chest compressions from the lifeguard, endless Mississippis. A wave of nausea passes through my stomach. It's Mrs. Ginoza, who arrived with me on the same train, who organized all of us to walk to the camp on that first day when the bus was broken down. "Ruriko, you're all right, I'm here," she wails.

"Stop," my mother says to her without looking up or breaking her count. "Madame, you cannot interfere while the lifeguard is trying to help your daughter." She must recognize that it's Mrs. Ginoza, but her voice is clinical.

"She's going to be all right?" Mrs. Ginoza says. "She knows how to swim, her uncle taught her back home, she could hold her breath a long time. She's going to be all right." She lurches forward again.

This time my mother looks up. "Somebody keep her away," she instructs shortly. A fat woman with a towel wrapped under her armpits reaches out to Mrs. Ginoza, folding her in closely, making clucking sounds, preventing her from running back over to Ruriko.

"Ruriko wasn't supposed to be at the pool today," Mrs.

Ginoza babbles to the fat woman, to nobody and all of us. "Today she was going to play hopscotch. With her friend, she said. Other people heard her tell me that, too, my neighbors all heard."

In the crowd, I see a few people nodding that yes, they had heard Ruriko say she was going to play hopscotch, and then more people are nodding, and then I am nodding, too. Like if enough of us agree the girls were never supposed to be at the pool, then we can go back in time and make it so they never drowned.

It's only now that I notice someone in the crowd who isn't doing any of that. A brittle, birdlike German woman standing a few feet from Mrs. Ginoza. She has weathered skin drawn tight around her cheekbones, and she's in traditional German clothes, with her hair pulled into a braid crown like some of the conservative German women do. She watches my mother and the lifeguard with her arms wrapped tightly around her thin body, swaying in place, her eyes glassy and unfocused.

"Her mother," Margot whispers next to me. "Oh God. Oh God, no."

Twenty-nine Mississippis. Thirty. Thirty-one.

Something has twisted in Margot's voice. It's filled not only with horror, but with dread. I want to ask Margot if she knows the small, brittle woman. But I can't pull away from the scene in front of me, from my mother, so professional, not even noticing that her white coat is now covered in water and splotches of dust.

The artificial respiration isn't working, I can tell from here. Ruriko's mouth hangs open, slack like a fish. The other girl's lips are cold and purple. Mrs. Ginoza is crying.

My mother whispers something to the lifeguard. He looks panicked for a second, shaking his head and trying to go back to his compressions. My mother puts her hand on his arm, gently but firmly, and tells him something with her eyes.

And slowly, in a way that makes this seem like a dream, he stops. They both sit back on their heels. The girls' bodies are still on the ground. My mother reaches out and gently rolls them over. They are small enough she can do it by herself. Then she closes the girls' eyes.

A million Mississippis. Mississippis to infinity.

"No! No, my daughter. Keep going. You have to keep going." Mrs. Ginoza starts to collapse, and the woman in the towel holds her up under the arms, all the while making the same cooing noises.

"They're stopping. They're stopping instead of saving her."

"Shhh," the fat woman says. "Shhhh."

"Ginoza-san," my mother says, calmly but with compassion at the devastated woman in front of her. The mother of the German girl is standing a few feet away, but I don't think my mother realizes who she is. "Ginoza-san, we tried for several minutes to revive your daughter. We were not successful. I am so sorry. There is nothing more to be done."

The fat woman lets go of Mrs. Ginoza, and she runs over

to her daughter at last, collapsing to her knees, gathering Ruriko's body to her chest. The little girl's hair is still wet; it tangles between her mother's fingers in long, stringy pieces. For a minute, in the crowd there is stunned silence and muffled sobbing. We are not going to cry louder than Mrs. Ginoza. We are not going to draw attention to ourselves by pretending in any way that our horror belongs on the same level as the mothers'.

And then in the middle of this silence, the lifeguard, wild-eyed, rises from the ground. My mother reaches up, as if to try to stop him, but he doesn't seem to see her. He's looking around at all of us uncertainly, and when his eyes land on Mrs. Ginoza he takes a hesitant step toward her. "It wasn't my fault," he says. "I want you to know that—"

She isn't paying attention to him; she is crying too hard. "Did you hear me?" he asks. "It wasn't my fault."

"Shut up," a voice says, but it's not Mrs. Ginoza, it's the fat woman who was holding her up. "Shut up with your excuses. Why weren't you watching them?"

The lifeguard turns to her, uncertainly. He wasn't expecting to be addressed by another person. He raises his palms. "I couldn't get there in time."

"You should have been *watching* them."

"Listen. This could have happened anywhere," the lifeguard protests.

"Yes, it could have." Now another woman has joined in, a woman with blue veiny legs poking out from under her bath towel. "It could have happened when this family was home in Los Angeles instead of in this prison, but it didn't happen there, did it? She's not at home, is she?"

"No, she's not," calls someone else.

We're packed together densely on the concrete pool deck, and there's no room to go anywhere. An angry buzz rises in the crowd. Because he hasn't apologized. Because he hasn't fallen to his knees in front of Mrs. Ginoza and the other mother and begged for forgiveness. Their daughters are dead and all this lifeguard has done is try to say that it's not his fault.

"You should have been watching them," the man behind me says, and then it's something everyone is saying, like they were all saying the girls were supposed to be playing hopscotch, and over all of it is the sound of Mrs. Ginoza wailing.

I look at Margot, who looks to me at the same time. *Should we leave?* her face is asking. *Is it a bad idea for us to be here?*

I can't, I tell her. My mother is still there, in the middle of the clearing.

I stare at Mama hard, until at last she looks up, melting in relief at seeing me. She shakes her head a little and then looks meaningfully toward the pool's gate.

Go, Mama mouths, and I'm about to, when another figure comes through the pool gate, dressed in olive drab, with a shock of blond hair.

Mike. My body fills with relief. He'll know what to do,

how to calm everyone down. I try to catch his attention when he passes but he doesn't see me as he works through the circle to where the lifeguard is still standing in his swimming trunks. Mike puts his hand on the lifeguard's shoulder and leans in while they quietly consult. He doesn't talk to my mother; she's still on the ground with the girls.

He clears his throat and raises his hands, about to make an announcement. When his eyes travel across the crowd, I think he finally sees me. I give him a small nod of encouragement just in case, but I can't tell if the nod in response is directly to me.

Mike will make the lifeguard apologize. He will tell us all that the lifeguard will be fired; he'll at least take him away so that people can grieve on their own.

He clears his throat. "Folks, this is a terrible thing that happened," he says, in the official voice he usually only uses when other guards are around. "It sounds like the lifeguard had already given those girls several warnings to stay away from the deep end," Mike continues. "But they kept ignoring him. They waited until he was busy attending to something else before they snuck under the lane line."

A confused murmur rises in the crowd. This isn't the version I heard from the boy next to me. He didn't say it was the lifeguard's fault, exactly, but he did say it was the lifeguard's mistake, the mistake of everyone at the pool because nobody realized the girls were drowning. Mike's version makes it sound like the girls were deliberately disobedient.

"That's not what happened," the boy next to me calls out. "That's not what happened at all."

Mike opens his mouth in surprise; he glances quickly back at the lifeguard again and I can't see what passes between their faces.

"It—it is what happened," Mike continues. "I saw it myself from the guard tower. The lifeguard warned the girls several times. So all of you need to disperse now, so we can allow some stretchers to come through."

I saw it myself from the guard tower.

But could he have? Mike's tower does not have a real sight line to the swimming pool. It's too far away.

And he couldn't have heard the lifeguard warning the girls not to go in the deep end, like he says he did. Margot and I didn't hear him, from the school, near the tower. Mike is partially deaf. That's why he's here to begin with instead of fighting on the front lines with all the other boys his age.

"I'm telling you, that's not what happened. I was right there," says the boy next to me.

"Why don't you talk to more of us," someone else yells, "instead of just asking what your friend saw?"

"Mike," I call out before I can help it. My voice is a plea. His face snaps toward mine. It softens when he realizes it's me. *Why are you lying?* I mouth the words so others can't hear me. He needs to say that he was mistaken. That he doesn't know what happened.

But then his face hardens again. "Look, everyone needs to settle down and back up," he says, trying to control the crowd.

The crowd is restless. I'm jostled from behind. People shift their weight, edging forward.

"Back up!" Mike calls out. "Give us some room," he says.

I try to take a step back but I can't. There are too many people behind me, and people behind them, and not everyone has heard Mike's instruction.

"I said to *back up*," he repeats, but we can't move. There's nowhere for us to go; we're blocked between the pool and the fence. "I can't keep giving you warnings."

"We're trying to back up." My voice gets lost in the din.

"*Tell the truth*," the crowd yells. "*Say what really happened!*"

He reaches to his shoulder for his rifle. I have never seen a guard here draw a rifle. "I said to back up," he yells again. The lifeguard next to him looks terrified.

"He is lying," some people are still calling out, and others are yelling, "Calm down, calm down," even while their own voices get higher and louder. Mike looks scared, but he is the one with the gun.

Now we're all trying to move, but I can't tell where. Are we trying to run? To jump in the pool or climb the fence? Are we trying to charge at Mike, standing with his rifle above the lifeguard and my mother? There is a sharp metallic *click*.

A woman in the crowd screams, "He's going to shoot us!"

and then that travels through the crowd. A man who I know is a Methodist minister cries out, "O Father in heaven," and then to Mike he says, "It's all right, son. It's all right."

Next to me, Margot has grabbed my sleeve, the way she did that day in the dust storm, telling me we need to leave. But my mother is still there. *My mother is still there.*

This is Manzanar. This is what Ken told me would happen, and what I never wanted to believe. Our Manzanar is not coming because of camp employees selling food on the black market, but because of dead girls on the pavement beside the swimming pool. A guard will shoot into a crowd of unarmed people, and it's a guard I know, who I could have been friends with at home.

There are too many bodies, I can barely breathe. *"Oh!"* Next to me Margot's face freezes in pain and she doubles over.

"Are you all right?" I yell. "Margot, are you all right?"

"I'm fine, someone just—" She's gasping, someone must have jabbed her in the stomach.

"We need to leave."

"I'm trying, it's too crowded."

"Grab my hand, Margot. Not my sleeve, grab my *hand.*" Seeing her folded over and in pain fills me with a sudden visceral panic that I can barely explain. Like someone has hit me, too, and I need to get her out of here, and I will claw and elbow if I need to. "Do not let go."

"I'm not," she says, but she is, because everything is moving too fast and her fingers are sliding out of mine. "Margot!" I shriek.

"Just go!"

I'm closer to the gate, she's closer to Mike and the gun. I fight against the crowd until I am close enough to grab her hand again, and then I yank hard until she crashes toward me, and we're standing in the crowd with my arms around her and our hearts beating against each other's.

She opens her mouth to say something, but suddenly, the air is split by a whistle.

Three sharp blasts in a row. It's a lone figure, half a head taller than everyone else. Mr. Mercer. Behind the camp director are guards, four of them, carrying two stretchers.

My heart is still beating so fast, but the stretchers wake us up. They make us stop. Around us, the rush toward the gate is not as fervent. Because we are not animals. We need to let the stretchers through.

Mr. Mercer carries something folded, a pile of white sheets. He walks ahead of the stretchers. When he gets to the little clearing, he meets the eyes of Mrs. Ginoza, still huddled by Ruriko, and the eyes of the German mother, who hasn't yet come forward to her daughter.

After a few minutes, Mr. Mercer unfolds the sheet and hands one to Mrs. Ginoza, who wraps it around her daughter, and the other to my mother, who wraps the little German girl while her mother kneels nearby.

When that last piece of quiet agony is over, Mr. Mercer stands up. He gestures somewhere behind my head, and the men carrying stretchers appear.

My mother helps place the little German girl on the stretcher. As the two little girls are carried away, their mothers and mine following, Mr. Mercer finally turns to the lifeguard, huddled near him in a miserable heap.

"Go wait in my office, Jimmy," he says quietly. "Officer Branwell, put down your rifle. Hand it to me." Mike looks at him. I realize his last name is Branwell. This whole time, he only ever told me his first name. Mike keeps looking back and forth between Mr. Mercer and the rest of us. He's scared, I realize. He's scared to walk past all of us now that he no longer has a weapon.

Mr. Mercer clears his throat. "I'm so sorry," he says. "I don't even—I can't even—we'll investigate what happened here. I promise. I'll personally interview everyone here if I have to. And we'll close down the pool while we do it. It will be closed until further notice."

His voice cracks a little on the word *closed*, keening into a high falsetto. I think that it's this small, human sound that puts the tiniest fissure in my anger. I'm overtaken by sadness and hopelessness, and a sick kind of shock, at what happened and what almost followed it.

"Let's go," Margot says. "I need to get out of here. Let's go now."

Mike still hasn't left. He looks back at Mr. Mercer for guidance.

Mr. Mercer, now holding Mike's rifle in one hand, motions for Mike to go ahead. And resting one firm hand on Mike's

232

shoulder, he steers him through the crowd and back to the pool gate.

Mike looks up at me when he passes, but I can't even begin to imagine what he thinks I can give him. No matter how many pieces of gum he gave me, Mike made a terrible choice. He was allowed to make choices in the first place, while the rest of us are not. At the end of the day, Mike gets to leave.

Nobody clears a path for him and Mr. Mercer like they did for the stretchers. They make Mike worm his way through, turning sideways, muttering, "Excuse me," as he passes, brushing against our shoulders, tripping over our feet.

TWENTY-ONE

MARGOT

WE'RE SHAKING. ALL OF US, PROBABLY, EVERYONE WHO WAS AT that pool. Some of the people in the leaving crowd have tearstains down their cheeks, some of them are still talking angrily. Some are stunned.

"She was on my train," Haruko says again, as streams of people walk alongside us. We'd all started by following the van with the girls' bodies in it, and then when it moved out of sight, walking in the direction of its destination, the hospital. German and Japanese prisoners alike, all talking about what we'd seen. People who somehow missed the news keep coming over to this sad procession to find out what happened. "Her family was brought here because her father kept a portrait of the emperor in their study. Mrs. Ginoza told us that on the first day."

"Where should we go now?" I ask.

"She said they had put up the portrait to make her mother happy when she came to visit, and then they never took it down and didn't notice it after a while."

"We'll just go to the icehouse."

"I want to get to the hospital first. And Mike lied. Did you notice how he lied? He's always so nice to me."

"He's a guard."

"He could have incited a riot. He could have gotten you killed."

"Let's keep walking."

I know I'm being short with her, but what happened in the pool has filled me with dread and I want to get away from this mass of people.

As we come within sight of the hospital, we see a crowd already gathered, made up both of people who have just learned what happened, and of people who were at the swimming pool and didn't feel like they could go home. As we're passing, someone calls Haruko's name.

"Haruko! Haru-chan!" Dr. Tanaka jogs out of the employee entrance down the little path to meet us.

She asks something that I can tell is a question, and Haruko responds in Japanese, nodding, halfway through the sentence, in the direction we were planning to walk.

Dr. Tanaka shakes her head, nodding in a different direction, reaching up to smooth Haruko's hair behind her ears.

"She says she wants me to come home now," Haruko translates. "She says you should go home, too, that all mothers will want to hug their daughters tonight." Haruko looks back quickly at her mother and lowers her voice when she talks to me again. "I can try to get away. I'll find out if she has to go back to work."

"Go. Mutti will have heard what happened by now and she'll want to see me. Let's meet tonight if we can get away. Tomorrow if we can't."

I want her to stay. I want us to go back to an hour ago at the school. I want us to go back to four days ago when she told me my lips were blue and I had to feel her fingers to believe it. I want to think about what it meant that she grabbed me at the pool, that her face filled with terror when she thought something might happen to me.

I watch as she leaves with her mother, and then I try to figure out what I should do next.

What I didn't tell Haruko, because she wouldn't have immediately understood what it meant and I didn't have the time or privacy to explain, was that one of those girls was Heidi Kruse.

Heidi, sweet Heidi, with her sticklike brown braids, who clung to my hand when our bus got to Crystal City, asking me whether I thought her toys from home would be there.

I hate myself for not stopping to talk to her longer the last time I saw her, at the bakery.

I hate myself for not going over and holding her mother's hand at the swimming pool. I recognized her standing there; she had come by herself and she had nobody to talk to. I bet that, like the Japanese mother, she didn't even realize Heidi was going to be at the pool today. I can't imagine how Heidi and Ruriko would ever have become friends.

But I didn't go over. Things were happening so fast. She was all the way on the other side of the crowd. I didn't know if I'd be able to work my way through, or if she would have wanted me to. I didn't go over, even when she was taking off her own necklace and wrapping it around Heidi's neck. She picked up Heidi's head so gently to do it, making sure the necklace didn't get stuck on either one of her braids.

Mr. Kruse arrived, near the very end, after Heidi had already been placed on the stretcher. He put one arm around his fragile wife, and his other hand on top of the white sheet, on what was Heidi's arm or leg. She was so little on that stretcher. She barely took up half of it. Where her head was, a water stain spread beneath the sheet; her hair was still wet from the swimming pool.

As soon as I realized it was Heidi Kruse, my throat closed in sadness, but also in fear.

I think about what my mother said, about how we should be grateful that there were only distilleries to occupy Mr. Kruse's stupid followers with.

Be grateful there aren't serious things for them to get angry about.

TWENTY-TWO

MARGOT

September 26, 1944

Capacity of the German community center: 200

Number of people it takes to carry a tiny coffin: 4

BOTH FUNERALS, ON THE SAME DAY. THERE'S NO REASON TO POST-
pone them. Extended family doesn't need to be given the
opportunity to travel in. Most of the girls' families are either in
this prison camp, in another prison camp, or across an ocean.

The Lutheran minister conducts Heidi's service. Most
of the German families go to it, squeezing into our community center and around the doors outside when the building
reaches capacity. School is canceled and so are all but the necessary work shifts. On the Japanese side of camp, the Ginozas

are holding their own funeral with a Methodist pastor in their own community center. All day long, all through the camp, when I see people stopping into the General Store or the bakery, they are wearing dark colors.

Mr. Kruse is in a suit that looks like it is borrowed. He was a construction foreman back in his home state of New York. I seem to remember that. He might not have thought he'd need a suit here. Mrs. Kruse is in a black shirtwaist dress, shiny around the elbows from use and age. They sit in the front bench, poker straight.

"They have to be," Mutti whispers to me. "If something like that happens to you, every moment that you are not holding yourself up, you are falling down."

HARUKO

I WEAR MY BLACK DRESS AND A SPRITZ OF TABU PERFUME, AND when I spray some on Toshiko's wrist, too, I can tell she is thinking of two months ago when she asked me why I would ever pack such silly things and what I ever thought I could use them for.

Afterward there is a reception in the Japanese community center where we all take plates of food we don't eat and have awkward conversations.

I stand in the corner with some people from school, while the girls twist their handkerchiefs and talk about how sad it is. The boys tug at their shirt collars and look like they wish they knew how to stop the girls from crying. There aren't any guards, not at the service or at the reception. They must have been instructed to give us space. I haven't seen Mike at all since the pool.

I couldn't get to the icehouse last night. My mother didn't want us to leave the house. I don't know if Margot tried to go; I've seen her once today, from a distance. She was leaving the German General Store and I was leaving the sewing hut with a dress of Toshiko's: she only owned one dark enough to wear to a funeral, but she had grown too tall to wear it. I was assigned to lower the hem, putting to use my terrible sewing skills from my terrible home economics class.

I had waved to Margot. I started to jerk my head in the direction of the icehouse, but then her father came out of the store behind her and she shook her head that she couldn't. She quickly raised two fingers on her left hand instead: two PM. Could I come at two PM? I nodded, and then when her father looked up, I pretended that I'd been nodding to someone else.

After an hour in the reception, drinking watery punch, my father finds me and says it's time to go home.

"Could I stay and say goodbye to everyone?" I tell him I'll follow him in twenty minutes. It's almost two; I had been waiting and waiting for a chance when my leaving wouldn't be obvious. My father tells me to come home now, though. It won't take long, he says, but he and my mother want to talk.

MARGOT

WE SING HYMNS THAT MOST OF US KNOW BY ROTE. WE RECITE THE Apostles' Creed, we recite the Lord's Prayer.

I was afraid there would be a Nazi flag or a salute to Hitler, but there's not.

My mother is uncomfortable sitting for so long. She doesn't complain but I can tell from the way she grimaces in her seat. As soon as the service is over my father goes to talk to the Kruses and I move to walk my mother home. On the way out the door she stumbles over a loose stone. When I grab her arm to steady her, she yelps.

"The baby?" I ask.

"It's nothing." She pulls her wrist away.

"What's wrong with your arm?"

I take her arm again, gently this time, and roll up the sleeve of her dress. Midway up to her elbow are small bruises. Too big for my own fingers to have made just now.

"Mutti, what are these?" I ask.

She looks down. "Yesterday. When I heard what happened

at the pool. It was so terrible, I lost my balance for a minute. Your father had to catch me."

"Is that really what happened?"

"I thought I was going to faint again."

"Mutti. *Is that what happened?*"

"What are you asking, Margot?"

"You know what I'm asking." My voice rises, hysterical. "Mutti, you know what I'm asking."

Did my father help my mother because she lost her balance? Or did my father hurt my mother because this time I wasn't there? Even if it were the former, would I ever believe it again?

"Let's go home, Margot." The people coming out of the community center are starting to look at us. "There is nothing more to be done here. Stop getting upset, Margot. There is really nothing more you can do."

My father has finished talking with the Kruses. He walks over to us now, and I shrink back from him before I can help it, unable to think of anything but the bruises on my mother's arm. "It's settled, then," he tells my mother. She nods, she already knows what he is talking about.

"What's settled?" I ask.

"The Kruses," he says. "There's a repatriation ship leaving for Germany in two days. The Kruses had their names on the list to be on it. They can't leave yet, though. Mrs. Kruse won't leave without Heidi, and organizing that will be complicated.

"I said they could put us on the list instead. I said we would take their place."

〰

HARUKO

MY MOTHER IS ALREADY THERE BY THE TIME WE GET BACK; SHE'D LEFT the reception early to make the rounds of her patients. When we come in the door, she looks at my father, not me. "Did you tell her or did you wait for me?" she asks.

"Tell me what?" It can't be a letter from Ken yet, he only left yesterday, and even so, I was the one who checked the mail this morning. Maybe a letter from someone else. I can't imagine what other news my parents would have.

"We have good news," my mother says. "We have made arrangements for you to leave."

"Leave? Leave what?"

"The camp. In a few months, when you turn eighteen," she continues, looking to my father for support.

"Back to Denver," he says. "Mr. Mercer permitted us to contact the Japan League, and they found a family who is willing to accept you as a boarder. You remember the Watanabes; you met them a few times."

"A boarder?" I say, like the only thing I know how to do anymore is repeat words.

"They'll give you room and board in exchange for some light housework," my mother says. "Mostly being a mother's helper, assisting with the cooking and laundry. But you should have enough time for studying."

Slowly, what my parents are saying is beginning to sink in. "You're sending me home to do laundry?"

"And study. At the beginning of the semester, you'll enroll in a nursing program that accepts Japanese students."

"I don't want to be a nurse."

My mother sets her mouth into a weary line. "We are sending you home. And this is the arrangement we were able to make in order for that to happen. Mr. Mercer has to make sure your papers are in order, but he said he'll try to work quickly. We should be very grateful."

My voice rises. "When did you ask him to do this? Why did you ask him to do this?"

She looks at my father again and he is the one who answers. "We had him make the call right after it happened yesterday. After the swimming pool."

"It was too terrible," my mother explains. "We wanted our family to be together, but this is not a place to be young. This is not a place we want you starting your life as a young woman."

"It's not so bad here." I can feel myself starting to get frantic. "I can handle it here."

This is not the answer they were expecting me to give. It's also a lunatic answer because it is bad here. Worse than I imagined it, in some ways.

"It's good news," my father says. "We thought you would be happy."

Free. I could be back home, in a place where there are no fences. A place where I could pretend the last few months of my life never happened, and if I live long enough, that pretending might actually work.

They talk more about the details. "Are you listening?" they ask. "Haruko, are you sure you're paying attention?"

TWENTY-THREE

HARUKO

"YOU'VE DONE SO MUCH," I SAY SOFTLY. BECAUSE THE ICEHOUSE isn't an icehouse anymore. Margot has shoved around the hay bales and ice blocks to make a living room. Everything is covered in blankets, not just the work blankets that are usually in here, but blankets that Margot must have brought from her family's hut, and pillows that must usually be used for sleeping. Both oil lamps are lit at their brightest, and positioned around the shed in a way that makes it feel not like a shed but cozy, inviting. It's a house.

"You were a little late, so…" she starts. But I'm only twenty minutes late, and this must have taken an hour. "Look," Margot says. She runs over to one piece of furniture. It's two bales of hay pushed together, and a pillow along one.

"Is that a chaise longue?"

"I had never seen one before so I didn't know exactly what it was supposed to look like, but you said a combination of a sofa and a bed."

"It's exactly right."

"Sit on it. Tell me how it is, and then try the armchair next. Careful of splinters, under the blanket it's a packing crate."

"Are those—" I ask, pointing to something else, on her pretend coffee table. A bottle with flowers in it.

"From your mother's hat. You should take them."

"No, you should. You should keep them to remember me."

I blurt out the last bit and then realize I've said too much. Margot doesn't seem to notice, though. In fact, her eyes are red and she doesn't seem be focusing much at all. "What's wrong, Margot?"

"Nothing. How's the armchair?"

"It's perfect. Why don't you sit in it and tell me what's wrong?"

She shakes her head quickly. "There are two universities in San Antonio. St. Mary's and Our Lady of the Lake. Both of them admit girls, but both of them are also Catholic; I don't know if you need to be Catholic to go there."

"How did you learn about these universities?"

"The library. There's a set of encyclopedias, but fifteen years old, so it's hard to tell if the information is up to date. Also, in the 1940 census, the population of the city was 254,000 people and it's growing really fast. That's bigger than I thought, which is good, right? Lots of places with jobs." She paces around all her pretend furniture, talking faster and higher.

"Margot. Are you being serious?"

"What do you mean?"

"I mean—we talked about San Antonio but..." I pause. "Neither of us has actually ever been there."

"Been there *yet*. That's why I researched. That was the plan, right? We have a plan."

She is so hopeful, and I wish I could let her keep talking, or say, *Our Lady of the Lake sounds interesting, tell me about that*. But I can't, it's not fair.

"If I was going right after graduation, I should be applying now," she continues. "If we think the war will be over by then. But if I end up waiting, I can find a job and save up money."

"Margot, I need to tell you something," I say softly. "Come and sit with me."

"I wonder if there is a way to keep taking classes at Federal. I could still go to the German school in the day but I could do Federal work in the evenings."

"Come and—Margot." She's still pacing, touching the furniture, straightening tiny wrinkles. "*Margot*. My parents want me to leave."

She tilts her head, the same way I must have when I heard the news. "What do you mean? Leave where?"

"Leave here. In a couple of months. There's a family in

Colorado who will let me come stay with them and go to nursing school."

"You don't want to go to nursing school."

A nice family of five, I repeat, like my parents told me. *Light housework, Saturdays off. Share a bedroom but the little girl is a quiet sleeper. Can I drive a car? If not, they will teach me.*

"I guess the camp is trying to—to make it possible," I stammer on. "To place the American citizens who came here as voluntary prisoners, when they turn eighteen. Like—"

"Like Betty Asamo," she says. "Secretarial school."

"Like Betty."

"I don't turn eighteen for another year," she says.

"I know."

"What about opening our soda fountain?" she asks.

I shake my head helplessly. "I don't know."

"What about our apartment, and the private bathroom?"

"I don't *know.*"

"The whole point is we were supposed to be starting over together."

"I'm not saying I want to go, I'm saying—"

"But instead you're going to leave me. You can't leave me. You can't leave me alone to deal with all of—with all of—"

She suddenly falls to her knees, they buckle underneath and I run to her. I put one hand on her thin, shaking back, rubbing in circles, feeling her spine and her shuddering rib cage.

"We have to go together," she sobs. "I want to go with

you. If I ever didn't make that clear, I want to. I want us to go together. Do you?"

"This isn't my idea," I say, and what I'm really doing is pleading for forgiveness. "I didn't ask my parents to do this."

"But did you tell them you wouldn't go?" she demands.

"How could I tell them I wouldn't go?" I ask. "Shhhhh. Shhhh, it's okay."

"The same way I did!"

"The same way you did what, Margot? Shhhh."

She looks up at me through tear-filled lashes. "Today. My father told me we were going on the ship back to Germany in two days, I told him I couldn't go. He said I had to, but I said I wouldn't."

My hand freezes on her back, on the faded cotton between her sharp shoulder blades. "Margot," I say slowly. "Are you telling me that you are leaving in two days?"

"No, I'm telling you I'm *not* leaving in two days. That I was going to find a way to stay here."

"How?" My voice comes out sharper than I mean it to.

I thought there was more time. For both of us. I thought I would have a couple of *months* to figure out what to do about Denver, and now she is telling me that we only have two days before she gets on a ship to go to a country where we are not even allowed to send mail.

"I don't know yet," she admits.

"But you were trying to get me to stay here," I say slowly. "Even though you are leaving."

"That's not what I was doing. I am going to change my father's mind."

"How?"

"I *will*."

I want to believe her. I want us both to believe her. But the more times she repeats her plan, the more foolish and impossible it sounds.

"Margot, what are the signs that that was going to happen? What was going to change his mind in the next two days?"

"Something could change."

"Has he shown any signs?" I plead. "He's building exploding distilleries. He marched with the Nazi flag. He was about to hit your—"

"Shut up."

I reel back, taking my hand off her shoulder. "Don't tell me to shut up."

"Then don't *leave*."

Her voice is desperate, but I'm trying not to let myself be swayed by emotions. Margot wants *me* to stay, when she is about to get on a boat? She wants to subject me to the same loneliness that she is unwilling to bear herself?

"But *you're* going to leave, Margot. You're going back to Germany—"

"Not *back*, I'm not from there."

"You're going to Germany. And what am I supposed to do then? You're getting angry at me for planning to leave soon, but you were going to leave me. You were going to leave *me* alone here."

"Because they're deporting my family. Not because I get to go home. And I told you, I'm *trying*—"

"Margot, it doesn't make a difference where you are going or why. Our friendship was going to end anyway, the second one of us walked out the gates of this camp."

Margot cringes away from me as if she's been slapped. Her face fills with horror and then hurt.

"Our friendship was going to end anyway?" she spits out. "I didn't realize that you saw us as so... temporary."

"I didn't mean it like that."

"How did you mean it?" She rises to her feet, wiping tears away.

I only meant that we wouldn't be able to see each other every day. *I didn't mean it like our friendship wasn't valuable*, I want to say. *I didn't mean it like being trapped in a dust storm with you wasn't the only good thing that happened because I came here.*

But I also didn't think she'd be so angry with me, either, for pointing out the facts that are obvious in this situation. "For God's sake, Margot, aren't you a little happy for me?"

"Happy for—" She stalks across the icehouse, then whirls around to face me. "Happy for you? Because that's what I should be? I should let you tell me about a fantasy that is never going to happen? And then be happy for you when you leave to go home and I leave for a country I don't know at all?"

"That's not what I'm saying."

"I didn't realize this was just something to keep you busy until you got back to . . . to your real friends and your real life. I guess I misunderstood. What we were."

"What were we?" My hands are tingling, I am feeling this conversation in my whole body. I take a few steps closer.

"Margot, tell me what you think we were."

She freezes like a frightened deer, like my question has terrified her. She looks over her shoulder for an escape; for a second I think she'll run past me, out the door. But there isn't an escape, not from what we're talking about, not from what is welling in my chest. "You know," she whispers.

"I don't. Tell me."

"I can't."

"The last time we were in here, Margot," I prompt.

Color rises in her cheeks. "When the old man came in and interrupted us," she starts. "Before he came in."

"What else?"

I don't know exactly what I want her to say. But the man came in and interrupted us five days ago. Just five days ago, even though it feels like a lifetime. And whatever moment happened then felt so important. But it was also *one moment.* How can I be expected to make decisions about my whole life based on one moment? For a person I have known barely a month? For a feeling that was so fast and so strong, and that I can barely even describe?

I should tell her all of that now, but the words won't come out. I'm suddenly angry with her for making this harder. For even *existing*. If she didn't exist, this would be an easy choice for me. I should want to leave. I would want to leave if it weren't for her.

"Tell me," I say, taking another step closer. Because if I am going to stay here, and help Margot try to stay here, and turn down my chance to go home, then I need her to say why I am doing it.

"You know," she says again.

"I need you to say it."

"I *can't*."

She won't say it. My heart deflates, or maybe my heart shatters, because she won't put this into words.

She's leaving. I'm leaving. We're leaving. The situation is hopeless. What good would admitting anything out loud at this point do anyway?

"Are you sure?" I ask, and all she does is blink back tears.

I swallow the tears rising in my own throat. I make my voice come out harsh. "Then I have no idea what you're talking about. I guess you did misunderstand."

"Haruko—"

"I guess what happened five days ago is that you were giving me strange looks, and the old man came in and I thought I would die of embarrassment? Is that what happened?"

"You don't mean that," she says.

"I mean it," I insist, talking over my screaming brain. "It was so embarrassing. You left and I had to explain to him that we barely knew each other at all."

I can see the pain and humiliation I'm causing her. But I'm saying this because I'm angry that she missed her chance and because there are no more chances. Because anger is something that you can apologize for later, while hurt is something that you have to live through.

"I guess you did misunderstand," I say again. "I guess that when you're not used to having any friends, you can get desperate. It means something more to you than it does to the other person."

Her shoulders fall. Her whole body looks like it has fallen.

"You don't mean that," she repeats. She says it quietly, in such a genuine way, in such a hopeful, open way, in a way that gives me every opportunity to take it back. *You're right, I didn't mean it, I was saying these awful things because I am angry and scared.*

"You were here for months before me, and how many friends did you have? You had no friends. I pitied you."

And now what Margot is supposed to do is yell back. Tell me to go to hell. Tell me that I was the one who came crying to her that first time, needing someone to talk to, needing someone to read my letters. Shouldn't it be obvious to her that I was always the one who needed more? And now what I need is for her to say terrible things back to me, so we can get it all out of our systems and there is nothing left to do but hold each other and cry.

But she doesn't do what she's supposed to do. She doesn't overreact. She stares at me and I see that I've wounded something deep inside her.

"I guess it doesn't have to mean anything to either of us, does it?" she asks. "Not anymore."

"I never should have let you think we were friends," I tell her, the final, awful words flying out of my mouth. "I wish I was leaving tomorrow so I wouldn't have to see your Nazi family again."

Margot rushes around the room, gathering her blankets, trying to leave before she starts to cry again.

Wait, is what I should say. *I didn't mean it. Let me explain.* But I don't say anything. Because it's better to hang on to my anger as long as I can before it turns to grief.

It's better to leave it until tomorrow, when I'm calmer. It's better to sit here on this pretend chaise longue in the pretend living room that is the closest thing to a real life we will ever have.

There is dust in my throat and I'm all talked out.

HARUKO

*We didn't leave it until tomorrow, of course. We
didn't leave it until any other time, because that
night was the last time we ever spoke.*

MARGOT

Haruko meant that night was the last time we ever spoke out loud. I have spent every night since then talking to Haruko and wishing I could hear anything back.

TWENTY-FOUR

MARGOT

FREDERICK KRUSE IS IN MY HOUSE. FREDERICK KRUSE, THE MAN I have been thinking about in one way or another since I first heard about him in my father's letters almost a year ago. Only now he looks smaller than I could ever imagine a human man looking. Shriveled, like his life has been sucked out of him through his eye sockets.

Which it was. The second he saw Heidi on the deck of the pool. The one piece of humanity I was always sure about in Mr. Kruse was how much he loved his daughter.

He's sitting between my father and Mr. Mueller now, slumped in a way that makes me think it is only the back of the chair helping him stay upright. If it weren't for that, he would be on the floor.

"Mr. Kruse," I say automatically, as my heart finds an even deeper level of hurt, thinking of Heidi. "I'm so sorry for your loss."

My father glances up at me and his eyes dart to the door. He wants me to leave. "I didn't mean to disturb you," I mumble, backing toward the exit.

Crystal City doesn't feel like it's in its box anymore. It has overtaken all of us. I can only feel pain, my own and everyone else's. It is so acute that it feels like an object, something that has weight and dimensions.

I guess you did misunderstand, she said.

I want to believe it was just a fight. People have them. People get over them. Or so I have heard. I never fought with anyone before coming here. And now all that happens here is fights, which get worse and worse and never better.

And she fought by picking at the softest parts of me. The things I hate most about myself. *Your Nazi family.*

My Nazi father, who is my greatest shame. And Haruko knew that. And she said it anyway.

"Go, but don't be gone too long," my father tells me as I back toward the door. "We need you to come back and pack."

"Pack?"

"You don't have too many things, do you?"

In the middle of all of this I somehow forgot that this was the cause of the fight in the first place. It wasn't that both of us are trapped here in Crystal City, but that both of us are leaving, and we were fighting about who got to go first.

That's not true. We were fighting about the fact that I thought something was real, and it was never real for her.

And now she is the one who gets to go home, and I am the one who has to leave the only country I have ever known.

A train leaving the day after tomorrow. Pack your things. Leave Crystal City. Not to Iowa. Not to an apartment in San Antonio. Not to any of those places after all.

I will be working on my grandparents' farm in a matter of months. I won't go to college.

She's going to college, and she doesn't even care about it. Her family loves each other. They will love each other and find a way to be happy in almost any place. My family can't be happy in Germany. I won't be. My mother won't be. My father thinks he will be, but he's wrong. He'll be relieved for a minute, and then he'll wonder what we're doing there, and by then it will be too late.

I am just trying to be rational. I'm just trying to take control of the situation. I'm trying to make everything fine.

I never should have let you think we were friends.

I wish she hadn't let me think that. Every part of me wishes that. My eyes are starting to sting again, and my brain won't stop replaying everything we said to each other.

I guess you did misunderstand.

"Do you have many things?" my father asks again.

"Just the trunk, Vati."

"I have a present for you. Books the library was going to discard; they're only missing covers. Be sure to pack those, too; we can study them together on the train."

"Study them for what?" *Just let me leave. Just let me get out of here.*

"We'll talk later," my father says. "We are lucky to get to go so soon."

I leave the house, as my father asks me to. It will be the most profound thing that I do in my entire life.

TWENTY-FIVE

HARUKO

A MOTHER'S HELPER. I COULD GO BACK AND BE A MOTHER'S HELPER in Colorado, I tell myself. I could get on a train going in the opposite direction from the one I took here, one where the window shades get to be open the whole way. I can go home.

I'm telling myself this because I have been in our hut for over an hour, and distracting myself is the only way I have been able to not do what I want to do, which is go to Margot's house. Tell her, *Let's run away, right now*—take whatever food is in her kitchen, use up our cardboard tokens to buy the rest; the tokens won't do us any good in the outside world anyway. Dig a tunnel, or climb a fence, or petition the United States to recognize Margot as an adult, so that she can make her own decisions and not get on her own train.

"Will you write me letters from home?" Toshiko asks. Our parents must have told her about the plan while I was in the icehouse.

"I'm not leaving quite yet."

"At least twice a week. And send me pictures, and have my friends write me. I wish I could come with you." My sister throws her arms around me, and I know it's partly because my parents told her I'm leaving and partly because she can tell I'm sad.

"Oh, Toshi. I know you do. Me too."

When there is a knock at our door, my heart leaps because I know it is her, that she was able to see that my awful words were only masking fear.

But when I run to the door, it's not Margot.

It's Mr. Mercer, with his hat in his hands, standing in our doorway, almost as tall as the frame.

"Miss, ah, Tanaka? Are your parents home?"

He must have come to talk to my mother about the drownings. That's what he's supposed to be doing. Interviewing everyone who was there. My mother can tell him things, probably, like how long it takes a person to drown and whether they did everything they could.

When my mother sees who is at the door, she smiles. "We told Haruko the good news," she says to him, nodding at me to translate. "She is very grateful to you for advocating on her behalf and working so quickly. Aren't you, Haruko?"

"I am very grateful to you for advocating on my behalf," I repeat back.

But instead of smiling or wishing me congratulations, Mr. Mercer has a pained expression on his face. "Maybe you should go get your father," he says to me. "This might be easier with him here for translations."

"I can translate. Toshiko and I both do it."

"Just the same. Sometimes it's easier to have parents translate things."

My mother is prodding me in the back, because she doesn't know yet what Mr. Mercer has said, and I can tell that what she wants is for me to be a good host. "Can I offer you a beverage? We have Coca-Colas in the icebox."

"I think you should get your father. Right now." His expression is serious, and it makes my blood cool. Mama is beginning to realize something is wrong, too—there have been too many exchanges between me and Mr. Mercer that have not been translated back to her.

"What's going on?" Toshiko asks, emerging from our bedroom.

"Papa is out back. Go get him now."

Mama, driven by politeness made even sharper by fear, insists I get Mr. Mercer a Coca-Cola even though he doesn't want it and it's the last one in the icebox. I hand it to him in the glass bottle and he holds it awkwardly between his big hands while the rest of us line up in a row on the other side of the table.

"This is a bit of an awkward situation we have here," he says. He has red creeping up his neck, sweat dampening his collar. "And I'm not going to lie, it's not a pleasant one, and it's not one I want to be having."

"What is it?" my father demands. "Is it Kenichi? Just tell us."

"What? No. Your boy is fine, as far as I've heard. It's that—" He looks down at the soda bottle sweating in his hand, and decides at last to take a sip, and the sip seems to take an excruciatingly long time. "It's that, ah, you've been approved for repatriation in a few days. I've approved you. Myself. Today."

Repatriation. Back to Japan, where I have never been.

My family sits in stunned silence, and my father is the one to break it, in a voice tinged with relief. "There is a mistake," he explains. "We didn't apply for repatriation. When the war is over, we plan to go back to our home in Colorado."

Mr. Mercer looks pained. "I know you didn't apply for this. This was an administrative decision. Based on information that I received today, we have decided it is better for the safety of the camp if you leave."

Administrative decision. The phrase floats above my head. When the FBI came to our apartment months ago, this was the sort of thing they expected me to translate. *Tell your mother it is an administrative decision. Does she understand?*

"I know it's an awkward situation," Mr. Mercer repeats.

"An *awkward situa*—" I start, but before I can continue, my father puts his hand firmly on my shoulder.

"Can you give us any more information?" he asks. "Can you tell us any more about what brought this about?"

"Like I said," Mr. Mercer repeats. "I know it's an awkward situation."

My father's hand on my shoulder increases in pressure. "It is not an *awkward situation*," he says. "It is not a matter of you accidentally having our luggage sent to the wrong bungalow. You are trying to send us from our home."

My stomach is in knots. It's happening again, almost exactly like last time: an official man who has random power telling us that we will be forced to leave, and me wanting to know why, what is the evidence, what is the nature of these allegations.

My father said *home*, and I don't even know what that refers to anymore. What is our home? Denver, where we no longer have an apartment? Crystal City, a place that a few months ago I swore I would always hate?

"I think it wouldn't be appropriate for me to share where the information came from," Mr. Mercer says. "Only that it was a reliable source, and it has to do with a—with a plot. Against the camp."

"This is ridiculous," my father says. "A plot? There is no plot. Talk to my wife or my daughters. None of us are guilty."

"Perhaps you would like to discuss this away from your girls?" Mr. Mercer asks.

"Why? I have nothing to hide from them. When would I have time for this plot? You know where I am at all times. I am here. I am standing for roll call. Or I am working in your spinach fields under armed guard."

His voice is icy and he's saying everything I wanted him to say months ago. He is my father again, in control and unafraid, as Mr. Mercer plays with the cola bottle in his hands. "The plot had to do with explosive materials that were discovered in a place that we know you had access to, Mr. Tanaka."

"Explosives?" my father asks, confused. "I have no idea what you're talking about. Search the house, there are no *explosive materials* here."

"Like a bomb?" I interrupt. "Is that what you're trying to say? Materials to build a bomb?"

Mr. Mercer looks uncomfortable. "Yes."

Oh God. Oh God, Oh God. I know what the explosive materials are. I know they're not explosive materials. *I know they're not explosive materials.* I know they're pieces to make a distillery, a stupid distillery that will probably blow up, but not on purpose, and definitely not because my father put them there.

I know who would have told Mr. Mercer something like that. I know the only person who could have told him something like that.

How could you.

How could you.

Because she was angry I had the chance to leave? She would ruin my family because she didn't want to be left here alone? Margot went into Mr. Mercer's office and told him it was my father who needed to be locked up, not hers.

Because I broke her heart.

"It's a lie," I choke out, interrupting the adults who I now realize are still talking. "The person who told you that was lying."

My father stops mid-sentence and looks at me. "How do you know that?" he asks.

"It is a lie, isn't it?" I say. "You didn't do what he is saying you did."

"But do you have evidence?" he asks.

"Evidence, like proof? How can I have evidence against something that is not true?"

"An explanation, then?" Mr. Mercer offers. "Do you have an explanation?"

How can I explain it in a way that makes sense? Images and fragments swim in front of me. *A dust storm. An icehouse. Cold lips, a terrible fight, my heart hurting.* "Someone—if someone were angry with us. Or with me," I start. "If someone were angry with me, and they wanted to get back at our family, then this is what they'd do. They'd invent a story that would hurt me. They'd—"

I know that the way I'm phrasing this is confusing, and everything is made even more confusing by the fact that my father is translating for my mother, and Mr. Mercer keeps interrupting to ask questions.

"Haru-chan, I appreciate that you are wanting to help the family," my father says. "But these creative stories only confuse the issue." He turns back to Mr. Mercer. "What you need to do is interview every man I work with. Ask any of them if I could have done what you say I did. Ask any of them whether they ever noticed me doing anything with these— these explosives you speak about."

"We did," Mr. Mercer says, twisting the soda bottle. "A man named Wilhelm Boehner says he saw you with the materials."

Wilhelm Boehner. I have never heard of this person, but he must be a German man covering for whatever German prisoner is really at fault.

"They're not stories!" I break in again. "I'm not talking about a hypothetical situation, I am talking about someone doing something to our family."

"The person who made this report—" Mr. Mercer clears his throat. He looks at me meaningfully, I think, but my parents don't seem to notice. "The person who made this report is not connected to someone who could have placed these explosive materials where they were ultimately found."

"How do you know there's no connection? Maybe you didn't check hard enough!" My sister is sobbing in the background, and I have lost all of my ability to act serene or polite. "What is *wrong* with you; why aren't you listening to me?"

This was what my father was talking about when I confronted him about why he didn't fight harder to let us stay in

Denver. What could he have done? They are about to take him again on charges I know are lies.

So even as I'm trying to continue, my voice is weakening and I don't know what I'm trying to say because I don't know how to articulate what happened. Why Margot would have done something like this. How we ever had enough feelings to turn into this much anger. I'm continuing to babble but my words don't make sense even to me.

"This is outrageous," my father says. "We have done everything you ever asked. This is completely outrageous. We're not leaving. My son is fighting for America. He is coming back to this country. We're not leaving."

"Does it have to be so soon?" my mother asks. "These are serious allegations. Can't you take a few weeks to investigate them?"

Mr. Mercer looks pained again. "These trains and ships are not on a regular schedule. It takes months of coordination to find the right window. It has to be now."

"Months of coordination from your end," my father says. "But a minute's notice for us. Is that how it works?"

"Don't raise your voice to me, Mr. Tanaka."

Say something, I yell at myself inwardly, but I feel paralyzed; it feels like everything is happening out of my body, out of my control.

Say something, I yell at myself again, but then before I know it, the door is opening and Mr. Mercer is walking out, his back darkening the doorway, and starting down the path.

"Wait," I call out, finally finding my voice, as my mother pulls me back into the house.

"It will be all right," she says. "Everything will be all right."

But that's not the point, that was never the point. Everything might be all right in a new and different place, in a new and different time. But this current world has completely crumbled. My world is gone.

"We need to find the suitcases," my mother says quietly. "Everybody, wash your face, put yourself together, and start to pack."

MARGOT

That did happen. I need to be honest about that. This is not a time when Haruko was remembering things wrong. This is not a time where I can say it was a misunderstanding, or that Mr. Mercer misinterpreted something. Or that something slipped out before I had a chance to correct it. It is not like I had the information tortured out of me. I wish I'd had the information tortured out of me.

Mr. Mercer had his head on his desk when I came in. He told me to sit down anyway because I told him I had to talk to him about something that couldn't wait.

It is about the safety of the camp, I told him. I can give you information that will impact the safety of the entire camp, but before I tell you I need you to promise you'll help me.

This sounds serious, he said.

Some people are planning to escape, I told him. They are going to set off a bomb near a guard tower.

They are keeping supplies for the bomb in the supply shed near the spinach field. The organizer is Ichiro Tanaka. He is the foreman of the crew who is hired to work outside the fence. He has a key to the shed. You can check. I can wait here and you can check to see that the supplies really are there.

How do you know? he asked me.

I know because Haruko Tanaka told me.

Why should I trust you?

Because Haruko Tanaka is my best friend and it kills me to tell you this.

It's best for me to say what happened as closely as I can remember. Without emotions, without descriptions. Otherwise it could look like I am trying to make excuses. I am the one who knows what happened, and I have to be honest about it.

Why are you telling me this? he asked.

I am an American and I believe in America, I told him. People who would plan something like that are a danger to the rest of us. I know you have had to repatriate people for doing things like this. I think that is fair.

I stopped there. It would be better not to push him too much. But he liked that answer. He nodded at that answer.

If this is true, it is the most serious offense that has ever been committed in this camp, he said. We are trying. It's not easy. I don't even know if any of this is the right thing. He buried his head in his hands. He looked upset. He looked tired. He looked like he wished I had not come to him. I wasn't expecting him to talk so much; I must have caught him at the end of a long day. The funerals had just happened that morning. Everyone was angry. He must have felt like he didn't have anyone else to talk to.

I cannot repatriate the Tanaka family, at least not yet. I don't know if you realize it, but the next train is leaving in two days. Carrying both German and Japanese families. It goes to New York; the ships sail from there.

I know, I said. My family is supposed to be on that train.

There is no room on the train. It's already carrying volunteers for repatriation from other camps. I can't fit another family on the train.

Would it help if it were less full? I asked. Would it help if one German family wasn't going back after all?

Is that really why you came to me? he asked. A light seemed to go on in his head. Because you and your family have decided you want to stay here and not be repatriated?

I didn't say anything. I didn't say anything at all.

Is that why? he asked again. Did your father send you here because he changed his mind?

I said I had important information for you, and I said I needed your help. Check to see if I'm right, I said. If the materials aren't there, it doesn't matter anyway.

My secretary will see you out, he said. Would you mind closing the door behind you.

That was it. That was every single word that was spoken in that office. I've tried to remember them as best I could. I don't think I left many out.

If you are a person who thinks reasons matter and that there are usually extenuating circumstances, I could talk about other things. But if what you want to know is, did Haruko have it right when she assumed that I had betrayed her, then the answer is yes. I did. Everything she thought was true was true.

TWENTY-SIX

HARUKO

THIS TIME THE BUS IS RUNNING. BUSES, PLURAL. TWO OF THEM, lined up to collect us from the gate and take us to the train station. The train will come and there will already be people on it, prisoners from Seagoville and Kenedy, the two other camps in Texas. Then we go to New York, and then we get on a Swedish boat that ferries us halfway around the world and then it will return carrying Americans. Or people they think are more American than me, at least.

The other people waiting to board are excited. They've been waiting and planning for this; they signed up for this. People from school, the ones Chieko warned me to stay away from because they were only going to leave, keep coming up to tell me they didn't know I was going to be on this ship; why didn't I tell them earlier? I don't know what to tell them. I've been moving through the day like I'm sleepwalking.

The band is here, the same one that welcomed us. Missing its trumpet player. The trumpet player is coming with us on the bus, he and his wife and son. A lot of the camp is here, actually. Come to watch us leave, the way they came to watch us arrive, because it passes for entertainment. Chieko's here, talking on the other side of the rope to some people from school who are not getting on the bus. She hasn't made eye contact with me.

A camp guard, one I don't know, is trying to organize all of us into straight lines. Easier for the counting, to make sure everyone gets on the bus who is supposed to. Toshiko keeps trying to hold my hand. It's like last time, only this time I grab on, too. Everything is like last time, except reversed. And except for Margot.

She's not here sitting on the fence post like she was when we arrived, making notes in her little notebook. I don't blame her for not wanting to show her face.

I blame her for everything else.

"And I will show you where I went to school," my mother is saying to Toshiko. "We can get you a spot there, too. It's the best school for girls in the country. You will love the building; it is old and pretty."

"I'll be seeing it for the first time, too," my father adds. "Think of that: Your mother and I both came from Japan but we have never lived there together."

They have both said the same thing at least three times. It's beginning to make me think that they don't have very many stories about their childhoods to share, that they really can't remember much at all about living in Japan.

Technically, our repatriation is voluntary. This is one of the things that was apparently discussed yesterday when Mr. Mercer's words seemed to be floating above my head. If we leave now, voluntarily, then my sister and I will be eligible to come back to the United States sometime in the future. If we waited for an investigation to be carried out and they determined my father was guilty and forced us to leave, then we might never have that chance. That's what made my parents agree to go along with it.

So my mother and sister and I are not being deported, technically, just like, technically, we were never really arrested.

"Are you ready?" my father asks. The gates have been opened and our line is moving through the fence and toward our buses.

Our luggage has to be loaded into the storage compartment before we can board. I turn around and look one more time at the guard towers, the fence, the road leading to the swimming pool.

At Margot. Her blond hair has come loose from its braid as she fights her way through the crowds gathered to see us off. I watch her elbow past one woman and duck under another's armpit, her face red and sweaty. She scans the crowds, looking for me.

I could make it easier if I called out to her, if I said her name or waved my hand. But I can't bring myself to. All I can do is watch her, when it's like the first day, when I saw her taking notes and didn't know who she was or what she would become. I hate that a part of me is happy to see her, and that my heart leaps before it falls.

"Haruko?" Toshiko asks, because we need to keep walking but I still haven't moved my feet. Our parents are already ahead of us.

Margot finds me and our eyes lock, she on one side of the fence, I on the other.

"I'm right behind you," I tell Toshiko, dropping her hand. "Save our seats on the bus."

I don't know why I'm walking toward Margot, but when she sees me do it, her eyes melt with relief, or maybe remorse.

At the fence, her fingers curl around the chain links. I'm close enough to see the perspiration on her neck from running to find me, and to feel how her shaking hand is making the fence vibrate. She's holding something, a folded tube of paper, trying to pass it through.

I reach out to take it. The goodbye band is pulsing in my ears. My fingers brush against hers, through the fence, and hers are as small and rough as they were the first time I ever felt them.

The contact makes my fingers spark with static electricity, and suddenly I can't take her letter. Whatever it says, I don't want to know; however she apologizes won't be enough.

I don't have a letter to give her. It's not fair for her to get to have the last words between us.

I drop my hand and pull away. *No*, she shakes her head. I can't bear to look at her face anymore, so I turn and walk back toward the bus, trying to ignore the sound of my name and the words that I imagine I hear her yelling above the band.

Margot stands at the fence while I board. I know her gaze doesn't leave me the whole time, because when I find my seat next to Toshiko, and when I lean my forehead against the pane for one last look at this place I hated—when I do all of that, I see her eyes are still on me. She's followed me exactly to my seat, still holding the letter in her hand.

Forgive me, her eyes are saying, and the only thing my eyes are saying in return is *Never*.

TWENTY-SEVEN

MARGOT

THE BUS PULLS AWAY. IT'S HARD TO BELIEVE IT'S OVER SO QUICKLY and so finally. Around me, the musicians from the band are packing up their instruments, the other people who had come to see the bus off are heading back to their houses or their jobs.

And I'm still standing there, with Ken's letter in my hand. I knew she wouldn't want to see me, or hear anything I had to say. But I still owed her Ken's letter, I thought, and I was a coward for not trying to take it to her yesterday. *In case I don't get a chance later* is what he said. I know this isn't what he meant. But what if he does never get a chance, because of me?

I slide my finger under the envelope flap. I shouldn't. It's none of my business. But what does it matter now? What does any of it matter? This letter that isn't even addressed to me is the only piece of evidence I will ever have that Haruko existed.

Like every letter Ken wrote while Haruko was in Crystal City, it's short, just a few lines on one page.

> *An enemy's big mouth is what brought you down south.*
>
> *What you asked me about Papa—you must stop wondering about that. Promise me, you will stop wondering and get on with your life. I didn't mean for any of this to turn out this way.*

An enemy's big mouth. It must be a private joke. He left her a joke, and an apology for everything that happened to her. I wish I had thought to do something like that.

I can't think about that. It's over. I have to get home to my family. I did what I did.

TWENTY-EIGHT

HARUKO

THIS USED TO BE A CRUISE SHIP ONCE, WHERE RICH PEOPLE TOOK rich vacations. Someone says that as we board. A cruise ship that was conscripted for war things after the war began.

But my family isn't in the rich-vacationer part of the ship. There are more than two thousand of us on board, the equivalent of a small floating city, and the place my mother and Toshiko and I have been assigned is on a lower deck. When we board what I think is the lowest deck, we still have to take another flight of stairs down. The hallways get narrower, and there's already a faint smell of vomit from someone not used to the rolling motion of the sea.

It took us nearly a week to get to New York by train. And then we had several weeks of waiting there before all of our paperwork was processed and our boat arrived. And then it was several days after that, on the boat, before I learned that if I buried my face in my pillow at night, nobody would know it was me crying. The decks are set up like dormitories with bunk beds. It's hard to tell exactly where noises come from.

I spend a lot of time walking, up and down the stairs, around the deck in endless laps. One night, snow is falling from the sky. It shocks me to realize how much time has passed, that it must be November.

On the walks I overhear conversations among passengers who have come from Crystal City, and passengers who have come from Seagoville and all the other godforsaken camps in all the other godforsaken places.

It turns out that I hate boats. It turns out that seasickness is worse than train-sickness.

It turns out I will walk anywhere, overhear any conversation, do anything I have to do in order to make sure what I'm not doing is thinking of Margot. How angry and guilty and hurt I am. Not thinking about how cold and small her hand felt when we stood in silence and watched the Nazi flag. Not thinking about the last things I said to her.

It turns out that it's possible to wish you were back in a place that you never wanted to go to begin with.

My father is a thin figure when I see him standing alone at the stern of the ship, leaning over the railing with a collar pulled up against the wind. It's just before curfew, and I haven't seen him since lunch the day before when we ate in the mess hall. Now the sky is dark and my father is looking into the gray smears that the clouds make against the sky.

"Helen." When he sees me, he unwraps his scarf, wrapping it around my neck instead.

"Haruko is fine," I say. There's no point in being Helen on this boat, or at any other time in my near future.

We are both silent for a minute.

"I think we will be there soon," he says. "I heard some crew talking. A few days at most."

"I'll tell Mama and Toshiko."

"Do you have everything you need on your deck?"

"Toshiko ate dinner tonight. I think her seasickness is getting better."

My father nods and looks out again into the black. He seems to be struggling with what to say.

"I hope you both know that I'm sorry that we are going back to Japan," he says. "I didn't want to. And I'm sorry for all of—" He struggles to find the words, to describe the vastness of what we're experiencing, eventually sweeping his hand out over the ocean. "For all of this. I have been meaning to tell you that."

"You don't need to." I shake my head.

"I do. I know you feel that I disappointed you."

"You weren't trying to build a bomb, Papa."

"Do you believe that?" He leans in closer to me. "I swear I wasn't, Haruko."

A sharp light cuts across our faces: a crew member carrying a lantern, making rounds. "Everything all right over there?" he calls. "Miss, is this man bothering you?"

Papa steps back, embarrassed. "I'm just talking with my father," I call to the crew member, who looks over his shoulder a few times while continuing his patrol.

But this small indignity, my father being accused of yet another thing for which he is blameless, fills me with anger. At the man with the lantern, at America, at myself.

"You and Toshiko shouldn't be having to pay like this," Papa says. "To be taken away, yet again, from your friends."

And the anger I feel toward myself twists into shame. My friend wasn't taken away. My friend sent me away. My whole family, because of me.

"Papa." I touch his coat sleeve. "I know you weren't trying to build a bomb. Because I know what happened. And it's my fault. It's my fault we are here."

"Of course it's not."

"It is, Papa. It really is; you have to listen to me."

He considers this. "Okay, Haruko, I'm listening."

"My friend Margot. You saw her once, she came to our house."

"What about her?" I see him trying to place her, and it

287

gives me time to think about whether I really want to tell him this. But I have to. I can't go to the new place the same way I came to Crystal City, carrying mistrust and confusion.

"It was Margot who told Mr. Mercer that lie about the escape. I'm almost positive. She was angry with me because I'd been mean to her." *Because I'd been more than mean to her.* "But I never thought she'd do something like she did." *And a part of me still can't believe it.* "I wish I could go back and never talk to her to begin with, Papa. I wish I could go back and never—never even look at her to begin with, and I'm so, so sorry."

It's only because my face feels cold that I realize I'm crying, that I'm crying and the wind is so bruising that the tears have frozen on my cheeks. It's sadness, and regret, and also loathing myself for still thinking about her when she has done something so unforgivable.

I wait for him to yell at me, or to walk away.

"Did you hear me, Papa? I'm sorry."

"We don't need to talk about it. It's done," he says. "It's behind us."

"Didn't you hear what I said? My friend is the one who went to Mr. Mercer. She did it because she was mad at me, and—"

"It's not your fault," he interrupts again. "It might not even be Margot's fault."

"It couldn't have been anyone else."

"It might have been Margot who went to Mr. Mercer. But if that's true, he shouldn't have believed the accusations of a teenager, without a more thorough investigation. And Margot might have had her own reasons. Even if you don't know what they are. Even if they are not good reasons. We have all done confusing things."

He's looking off into the distance, into something I can't see, and I don't know how he can possibly defend her after what she did to us.

When he speaks again his voice is so quiet I can barely hear him.

"Haruko, I am going to tell you something now. It is something I wondered if I should tell you before."

"What, Papa?"

The light of the lantern cuts across us again. The lantern man is on the second lap of his rounds. When the beam swings across my father's face, I see that it's covered in the same shiny ice tears that mine is.

And suddenly I know.

I know that the thing he is about to tell me is the thing he was thinking of telling me on the day that the FBI took him.

"What is it, Papa?"

He clutches the railing, looking back out into the sea that is so big and so black.

"I did it," Papa whispers.

"You did what?"

"I did what the government said I did. I did share state secrets."

My heart forms a cold, ropelike knot in my chest. I've

wanted an answer to my question, but I didn't want the answer to be this.

"Not like they said it happened, Haruko. Not on purpose. But I did."

The waves are loud. Beneath the collar of his coat, I can see that he's wearing an old shirt that he used to wear to work, that my mother used to iron and starch on Monday afternoons. Now the collar is dingy and the top button is broken in half, but I can still see him heading off to work, absentmindedly smoothing his lapels.

"A hotel guest?" My voice comes out in a choke. "That's what they said happened, that hotel guests were using you to pass information to Japan. Wait, what do you mean, not on purpose?"

I am picturing information scribbled on a sheet of paper, a businessman telling my father that he has to rush off somewhere, but could my father pop this letter in an envelope and mail it? That's the kind of way he could accidentally transmit information.

He is already shaking his head. Not a hotel guest. Not the scenario I'm imagining.

"A general," he says. "I told a general who used to come into the hotel restaurant. He was a nice, friendly man who had traveled all over the world. I'd taught him a few Japanese phrases and he asked for me whenever he came for dinner so we could chat."

"You told a general *what*, Papa?"

"Asked him. Actually. I asked him a question about a unit

of soldiers, and the information I had was information that I shouldn't have had. I asked the general whether he knew anything about Camp Patrick Henry and whether the soldiers were treated well there. Especially the soldiers who were scheduled to ship out on April twenty-seventh."

"How did you have any of that informa—" I begin. The lantern light warms my face. The crew member's footsteps get louder, pounding the ship's deck while he circles again on his third round. I lower my voice. "How did you have that information?"

"As soon as I asked him that question, the general became a different person. He wanted to know why I was asking. Why I cared about a United States military base. Mostly he wanted to know what you did—how I had come upon that information. He asked that again and again. But I wouldn't tell him. Because he'd already decided I was not to be trusted, and so I knew I couldn't trust him."

"Papa, tell me what happened," I beg my father. "It's too late for any of it to matter anyway. Whether it was a mistake, or a misunderstanding, or something else. Start at the beginning and tell me what happened."

Papa looks around to make sure nobody else is on the deck. He slowly lowers to the ground, bending one knee. He unlaces his shoe, working his heel out of the brown leather and searching for something between his foot and the sole. He removes a folded piece of paper, soft and crumpled, and, still kneeling, lifts it above his head until I take it.

War and Navy Departments, it says. *V-Mail Service.*

It's a letter from Ken. I'm confused at first, that my father managed to get to one of Ken's letters before I did, but then I realize I have seen this letter before. In the dark I can barely make out the address on the envelope, but it isn't Crystal City, it's our apartment in Denver. This is the first letter Ken ever sent us.

"I don't—"

"Open it," my father says quietly. "You will."

My father follows me as I walk away from the stern, closer to an entrance with a light. Inside the envelope is Ken's precise block print, and when I see it I remember when we first received this letter. Papa read it out loud to the whole family. We were all so proud. We were all so together.

Crazy family, the letter starts.

> *Alas, you were hoping this would be a letter from some other dashing soldier, but it's only a letter from Me. Perhaps you can show it around a little, and the neighbors will be impressed by your son? Probably not—and I wish I could tell you where I was, but they say that's not allowed. A real big no-no. Though what I can tell you is I have a commanding officer who looks just like the pigeon that used to beg for scraps outside the soda fountain. Remember him—his rear end used to waggle like he was a beauty contestant? I swear, my commanding officer*

has the same walk. Can't look at him and not picture him as a bird, Klomping all over the park.

Hey, did you have a chance to see if you could track me down a book of crossword puzzles? Easy ones, even. Not too difficult for you to imagine, I'm sure, that I'd love to have something to occupy my brain a little bit.

Really, it's not so bad, except for all these infernal bivouacs they keep making us go on, which they say are to prepare us, but frankly I think I'd vote for the version where they prepare us by letting us stuff our faces and sleep on really soft mattresses. Yet here I am, learning to be an excellent soldier.

All I wish is that People here were a little less excited about going overseas. Rudimentarily, I understand it's going to happen and that, In fact, it's why we all signed up. Let me be honest, it's a little scary, which I can tell you even if I can't admit it to the others—and at least the food is good, though my pants are going to increase from a size 27 to a size 29.

Love, Kenichi/Ken

"Do you see it?" my father asks quietly.

"See what? What am I looking at?"

"It's probably harder to see when you don't know men's clothing sizes," my father says. "A size 27 waist is very small. Ken hadn't been a size 27 since he was twelve years old."

"He put the wrong trousers size?" I ask. "He was joking around?"

"He wasn't joking. He always liked puzzles."

"Yes, and we sent him some puzzles, didn't we? We sent him some crosswords?" After we got this letter, I had put a book of acrostics in a package along with a Bit-O-Honey and a Pearson's nut roll. I used my weekly sugar ration; I still remember making sure Ken knew I'd used my sugar ration. This letter sounds like Ken, the real Ken, the one I knew from before the war started and the one who had disappeared by the time he came to visit us in Crystal City.

"The first letters," Papa says finally. "The capitals."

Crazy: C. Alas: *A*.

And only then, when I'm combing through the letter word by word do I finally see it—the odd capitalizations of *Me*, and *Klomping*. The sentences beginning with *Yet* and *Rudimentarily*, which seem odd and stilted. All the oddly capitalized letters.

C.A.M.P. P.A.T.R.I.C.K. H.E.N.R.Y. A.P.R.I.L 27–29.

"Ken was the one who told you about Camp Patrick Henry."

"It's in Virginia." My father's voice is flat. "I actually didn't know for certain where it was until they brought me in and questioned me. Until they asked how I knew that there was a group of soldiers leaving for the Western Front on April twenty-seventh from Camp Patrick Henry in Virginia."

The ship hits a rough wave. I pitch forward and grab the door frame. I want to vomit.

Is this why we are here? Because my brave American war

hero brother was also a good son and didn't want his family to worry about where he was, so he devised a silly little way to tell us? Because he didn't think it would be a big deal, and because my father happened to mention it to the wrong man? Is this why we got on the train?

"I didn't know that they would say it was a state secret," Papa says. "I thought Ken was just giving us a game to play, to see if we could figure it out."

This is what my father wanted to tell me in our apartment the day he was taken away. This is what I didn't understand.

"Ken's letter is the reason why they came and took us."

I'd wondered, once, when I read one of his cursive letters with Margot, whether he was writing in cursive because he was trying to send a message to me. Really, it was because he knew he'd already sent a damaging message in the one my father could read.

"I couldn't tell you. I thought it would be better for only me to know."

"But…it *wasn't* a state secret, was it? It couldn't have been."

Even as my mind is trying to work through what he's telling me, it doesn't make sense. A whole army base that thousands of soldiers move through isn't a secret. The people who live in Virginia would *notice* truckloads of soldiers coming in and out. It's not a secret, especially not to a general.

"He kept asking me where I'd gotten my information," my father says. "How I knew. How many people I'd told. I couldn't tell him."

"But if you were a spy, that doesn't make sense. He thought you had learned information that was valuable to the United States government, and he thought the first thing you did was to share it with an official of the United States government? If you were a spy, you would have been an incompetent one."

"In a different time, I think that would have mattered. He might have been able to think things through more carefully. But people are not themselves right now."

I am so tired of this excuse. Of hearing that we have to excuse people for acting the way they act because they are scared. That I should excuse Margot because she was scared. That we should have excused her father because he was scared. That I should excuse a general because he was scared. *I am scared. Ken was scared. We are all scared.*

"People are exactly themselves," I say wearily. "People are exactly who they have always wanted to be; it's that now they have an excuse for it. Now they can pretend that they care about the country's security. Did you try to explain? Did you try to tell them it was just your son, sending you a puzzle in code?"

"I could never. I could never let him know it was Ken. I was afraid that they would do something to him. That they would send him to—to—"

"To a place like Crystal City?" I finish. "To a place like they sent all of us?"

"To someplace even worse," my father says. "Haru-chan, can you imagine the punishment if they thought Ken had enlisted in the army as a spy? It didn't matter to me if I was punished.

Do you see?" He sounds anguished. "I would have gone there alone. It never occurred to me that they would send women there, too, and children. I didn't know your mother would want all of you to come. I was only trying to do what was right."

I don't know what to say to him. He looks so sorry and I feel so wrung out. I reach down and take my father's hand, the least and most that I can do.

The guard is coming around with his lantern again. And ahead of us, far in the distance over choppy water, I see a dark purplish shape and I can't tell if it's land, or if it's shadows cast on the water, from the moonlight shining through a cloudy sky. My father and I look out together.

"A crew member told me we're arriving tomorrow, if the weather is good. The next day if it's not," Papa says.

"You said that."

After a while, he puts his other hand on my shoulder. "Curfew," he says softly. "It's time for bed."

"You go. I'll go soon." He pauses like he wants to make sure I'll go, but thinks better of it.

After he leaves, I watch the purple grow closer. The wind is cold and my borrowed coat is not warm enough, and I stand until I am numb. I stare ahead, because there is no other place to stare, because our ship is moving in one direction and my heart is moving in another, and the only way forward is forward. I watch until I'm sure what I'm seeing is land.

TWENTY-NINE

MARGOT

May 15, 1945
Number of prisoners left in Crystal City: 1,494
Number of Germans: 512
Number of Germans in my family: 3, always 3, never
    more

IT DOESN'T MATTER WHY PEOPLE DO THINGS. IT DOESN'T MATTER
because sometimes things are wrong, completely wrong, no
matter why they were done or what justifications people try
to give.

The war ended in Europe. V-E Day. A day of Victory. The
camp employees were weeping with joy. Some of the detainees, too. Some of them because they assume the whole war

will be over soon. Some of them because they assume Germany must have won, that the newsreel played before the last movie was just propaganda. The camp employees' tears look joyful, but some people can only imagine that Germany must have won. Two boys get in an argument about it in school. One said that Germany would return to its former glory now. The other said, *How stupid are you?*

It doesn't matter because I do not have a brother after all. I do know it would have been a brother. I know that much. It got far enough along that I know it would have been a brother. I don't want to talk any more about that.

It doesn't matter because my mother is a ghost again. I don't want to talk any more about that.

It doesn't matter because nobody has rebooked us on another ship to Germany. I don't know if that will happen, or if the prisoner exchanges are over.

But while I'm waiting to find out, I review a lot of things in my mind, and most of them have to do with Haruko, and the things we said and did to each other on that last day.

Frederick Kruse is in my house. Frederick Kruse, the man I have been thinking about in one way or another since I first heard about him in my father's letters almost a year ago. Only now he looks smaller than I could ever imagine a human man looking. Shriveled, like his life has been sucked out of him through his eye sockets.

Which it was. The second he saw Heidi on the deck of the pool. The one piece of humanity I was always sure about in Mr. Kruse was how much he loved his daughter.

He's sitting between my father and Mr. Mueller now, slumped in a way that makes me think it is only the back of the chair helping him stay upright. If it weren't for that, he would be on the floor.

"Mr. Kruse," I say automatically, as my heart finds an even deeper level of hurt, thinking of Heidi. "I'm so sorry for your loss."

My father glances up at me and his eyes dart to the door. He wants me to leave. "I didn't mean to disturb you," I mumble, backing toward the exit.

I do leave. I walk out the door. But I don't go anywhere. I don't know where else to go. The swimming pool is closed. I'm not a student at the federal school anymore. Haruko does not want to see me. She is going to leave and go back to her home.

So when I go, I go only as far as the front door, and then I lean against the bowed wooden sides of the house. I sink down lower, until I am sitting in dirt.

And while I am there, I can still hear everything that is happening inside. Because our walls are so thin, and because the outsides bow, and because curves amplify sound. My father taught me that on the farm.

So I can hear the soft *thumps* of mugs on the table. Mr. Kruse crying.

"The lifeguard is going to be replaced," my father is saying. "I don't think you'll see him working here for a while. People were too angry. You could see. The camp doesn't want to deal with that. He'll just be quietly reassigned, somewhere outside of camp."

"Both of them," the blond man agrees. "Both the lifeguard and that blond kid who tried to defend him. We're not going to be seeing them ever again. So there's nothing we can do about him, unfortunately."

The last sentence changes things. Until that sentence, I had thought my father and the blond man were trying to console Mr. Kruse by telling him he need not worry about encountering the people he associates with his daughter's death. But that's not what Mr. Mueller was doing. He was trying to figure out how to punish the men he thinks are responsible.

"Nothing you can do about them," my father says. "Best to put them out of your mind entirely."

Then all three of them are quiet, and I am filled with the smallest measure of relief. Thank God there is still reason in my father. Even if his brain is poisoned, thank God there is reason, too. Don't they see how terrible it would be, for them and for everyone in the camp, if something happened to a guard? It would solve nothing. It would mean punishment or restrictions on all of us. And then riots, probably, by the people who are already furious about the deaths of Heidi and Ruriko.

"What about the doctor?" Mr. Mueller asks now.

"The doctor?" Mr. Kruse says, his voice bleary.

"It was the lady doctor, the Jap lady doctor, who was supposed to be saving Heidi—" he says.

"Both of them were supposed to be saving both of them," my father interrupts. "Not just her."

"But she was the one who was supposed to be in charge of things," Mr. Mueller insists. "She was giving the orders, and she was the one who said to stop trying."

"She was," Mr. Kruse agrees. His voice is wobbly. He is the saddest man I have ever heard. "She stopped too soon. We have to do something about her."

"It was her fault," Mr. Mueller says.

This is crazy. What I am listening to is such pure, undiluted crazy. It is not Dr. Tanaka's fault that Heidi is gone. Only a man whose mind was warped by grief could think this.

"She walks home alone at night," Mr. Mueller is saying. "She works nights and then walks home alone."

"Or we could get kerosene," Mr. Kruse said. "It might take a few days to get enough, but then all it would take would be a match."

"I don't know that this is a good idea," my father says. "I think we should talk more when we're a little more calm."

"Calm?" Mr. Kruse's voice breaks. "Let's see how calm you would be if someone took—if someone took away your little girl."

"Frederick, I can't even imagine how much your family is hurting."

"Jakob, you can't expect us to do nothing," Mr. Mueller says.

As I perch lower in the dirt, my heart races.

I need to do something. I need to tell Haruko what these men are talking about.

But would she believe me, right now, minutes after we've just said we never want to see each other again? Or would she think I was inventing something to hurt her? *Am* I inventing something? Do they even mean what they're saying?

"We should act quickly," Mr. Mueller is saying. "Next week."

Mr. Mercer, I decide. *I can tell Mr. Mercer that Haruko's family is in danger.*

I'm standing to do this when I realize that I don't have any proof. I have something I overheard, a discussion between three men. And if I repeat it, at least two of them will swear that I misunderstood and the discussion never happened. I would like to think my father would back me up, but I don't know. I wish I did know. I can't be sure of what my father will swear to anymore.

So not that. Something else. I need to do something that will get Frederick Kruse far away from the Tanaka family. Something I can prove.

I can prove he has been building illegal alcohol distilleries. That one of them already exploded, that he is a danger to the camp. I can prove that because there are the pieces to build another one in the supply shed by the spinach fields.

Except that Frederick Kruse has never been in the supply shed by the spinach fields. He doesn't have a job outside the fence. There is nothing to connect Mr. Kruse to the distillery.

The door opens. Mr. Kruse and Mr. Mueller are leaving. My father stands behind them, seeing them off.

He looks down at where I am still crouching in the dust, and his face reddens. He knows what I've overheard.

"Are they going to do it?" I ask. He doesn't say anything. "Vati, are they?"

"I don't know what he is capable of doing right now, Margot."

"You have to stop him. We have to report him. They'll send him away."

My father leans his forehead against the door frame and rolls it back and forth. "Would they send all of them away?" he asks. "Come inside and pack."

All of them. I didn't even think of that. Frederick Kruse has spent months gathering a trail of followers, and they will still be here even if he's gone, and I can't report them all.

"I'll be inside in a minute."

I need to tell Haruko to run, but there is nowhere for her family to run, because we are all prisoners within a fence. I need to tell them to hide, but we are counted twice a day. I need to tell them to go backward in time and never come here, but none of us had a choice.

I need to do something that will make Haruko safe. I need to do it soon and it needs to be permanent.

304

I need to even though that same thing will make her hate me forever.

Are these my real reasons? Are these reasons or just excuses? Am I doing this because I want to protect her? Am I doing this because I am devastated she is leaving? Am I doing this because I want to stay in the United States, and because Haruko said terrible things to me? Am I doing this because I don't know what else to do?

There isn't enough time for me to think about my reasons.

There are no good choices here, here where I'm surrounded only by spinach fields and the wide expanse of my defeated heart.

I did love her. I think she loved me, too.

A NOTE ON
HISTORICAL ACCURACY

On the first weekend that I visited the town of Crystal City, Texas, it was late September in the middle of a heat wave, and the local high school was having a football game. I walked through an overflow parking lot to a section of land where the grass grew hip-high, and realized I was standing on the site of what used to be the Crystal City (Family) Internment Camp's swimming pool. A little farther away was the site of Federal High School, and beyond that, on what now appeared to be practice fields, was the entrance to the camp through which 4,751 prisoners of Japanese, German, and Italian descent were held captive in its five years of operation.

Much of it was grown over. A flyer said there were eight placards scattered throughout the former site of the camp, but after several hours of exploring I could find only six: museum-quality signs depicting photographs of women and children getting off trains, submitting themselves for imprisonment in a place most of them had never been, for a duration nobody could begin to predict. The other two placards must have been victims of my bad map-reading, or been removed for repair, or otherwise gone missing. I asked one woman, a mother of a student, if she knew where the other signs were, and she said, surprised, that she hadn't even known we were standing on the site of a former internment camp.

This book is for those two missing placards. For all the kinds of stories that get lost. For all the things that get overgrown by weeds, or overgrown by layers of history.

During World War II, in one of the darkest periods of American history, approximately 120,000 people of Japanese ancestry were forcibly removed from their homes and incarcerated at camps around the country. Two-thirds of them were American citizens. US government officials used panic, fear, and xenophobia to justify their actions, claiming they were necessary for the safety of the country.

The vast majority of prisoners were sent to camps run by the War Relocation Authority. Their only crime: They were West Coast residents, and President Franklin Delano Roosevelt had issued an executive order giving the military permission to "relocate" all residents of Japanese ancestry away from the West Coast. These camps often provided poor nutrition, cramped living quarters, and shabby barracks that left residents exposed to harsh weather conditions. Children in the camps attended schools praising American freedoms— all while behind barbed wire and under armed guard.

Crystal City was a different, less well-known kind of camp. It was the only camp to house both Japanese and German families. It was not built for the mass-evacuated West Coast Japanese Americans, but for so-called "enemy aliens," of both Japanese and German ancestry, who the US government had accused of being spies. Crystal City was run not by the WRA but by the Department of Justice's Immigration and Naturalization Services division. The INS, in an effort to broadcast to the world that it was treating its incarcerated "enemies" fairly, and that it was following international protocols, offered its prisoners better living conditions and morale-boosting activities. Prisoners there could take classes in accounting, or plant gardens, or go swimming. But they were all still behind barbed wire. They all still lived in a place where floodlights swept their windows and guards monitored their movement. They were there on flimsy or nonexistent charges and none of them could leave.

I spent several days at the National Archives in Washington, DC, gathering carts of materials from Record Group 85, the files pertaining to Immigration and Naturalization Services during World War II. The Crystal City records contained camp maps, diagrams of living quarters, correspondence about the swimming pool's construction, logs of which movies were being shown for movie night. There were official reports illustrating both the deep and the banal ways imprisonment was felt and cultures clashed: Japanese representatives engaged in an ongoing and unsuccessful campaign to request kettles be provided so that they could boil water for tea. Management responded that there was nothing a kettle could do that a saucepan couldn't, and since they had already provided the latter, the request was denied.

Some of the most moving files in the National Archives were the school records: mimeographed copies of the Federal High School student newspaper, which reported on sporting events and favorite teachers—a testament to how hard students worked to have a normal high school experience in the most abnormal of circumstances. There were also piles of correspondence between camp staff and the schools from which their imprisoned students had come. One letter was written by a schoolteacher in California about a prized pupil who, the teacher worried, would fall behind because she wouldn't be able to properly keep up her science studies. The teacher had written to supply physics experiments that the girl, Eva, could complete on her own, using a hairbrush, a flashlight, a fountain pen, and a piece of sealing wax. "I am very happy Eva is being permitted in this way to complete her course," the teacher wrote. "She is a very deserving and earnest student."

Some Japanese American students described the camp as a happy place where, for the first time in their lives, they were not in the minority population. A German student described it feeling like "summer camp." Real lives were lived inside that fence, with all the love, hate, hope, boredom, and pettiness that real life entails.

Some things in this book that are real:

The 442nd Regimental Combat Team, an all–Japanese American unit that fought in Europe, and that won seven

Distinguished Unit Citations. If those soldiers fighting for the United States had any leave, they could have spent it as Ken did—visiting family members at camps around the country, imprisoned by the same government that the soldiers were fighting to protect.

V-mail existed. Soldiers trying to skirt their secrecy instructions did, indeed, sometimes try to reveal their whereabouts by writing their letters in code. Sometimes they were successful, sometimes they weren't.

The "repatriation" of German and Japanese prisoners happened, even the ones who were not actually German or Japanese, but American-born. Hundreds of Americans of German and Japanese ancestry were sent across the ocean in Swedish ocean liners, commissioned expressly for that purpose. I didn't follow faithfully the timetable of deployments in this book (in real life the final Japanese exchange happened in 1943) but the prisoner exchanges did occur.

The Manzanar riot really happened, resulting in the death of two inmates.

The horrifying drowning of two Crystal City girls happened, in 1944, and grief-stricken citizens sent letters pleading that the pool bottom be painted a lighter color and that other safety precautions be undertaken in order to prevent such a tragedy from happening again. In real life, both of the girls were Japanese. I couldn't find detailed first-person accounts of what the reactions were like at the scene; I tried to envision the horror and sadness and anger of such a moment. There were no recorded riots or escape attempts in Crystal City's history.

The Popeye statue is real: It is still standing in Crystal City today, marking the place as the unofficial spinach capital of the world. The tofu factory—also real, and received with great joy by prisoners who were tired of having people with an American palate in charge of their diet and menu. There really was a female detainee doctor, a detail that I never would have thought to make up for a fictional character, but which added such unexpected depth to my understanding of women of the time. Homemade distilleries were real: One did explode, and the inmates did, in fact, tell guards they had been trying to make marmalade, which the guards believed, or pretended to. Cardboard money tokens, field trips outside the fence, crickets in the latrine, Nazi parades with swastikas—all real. The idea for the character of Frederick Kruse is loosely based on Fritz Kuhn, the leader of the German-American Bund, who headlined the thousands-strong Nazi rally in Madison Square Garden. Nationwide, the Bund officially dissolved in 1941. Kuhn was later sent to Crystal City, where he was elected leader of the German detainee association.

When I first started my research, I expected this would be a book just about the experiences of a German American internee—something that many Americans today don't realize existed at all, and that I only became aware of while researching a previous book, *Girl in the Blue Coat*. A few books helped with my early research: *The Prison Called Hohenasperg* by Arthur D. Jacobs; *America's Invisible Gulag* by Stephen Fox; *Shattered Lives, Shattered Dreams* by Russell W. Estlack; *Undue Process* by Arnold Krammer; *We Were Not the Enemy* by Heidi Donald; and *Nazis and Good Neighbors* by Max Paul Friedman. The documentary *Children of Internment* was also deeply helpful.

It became clear, though, that telling a story set in Crystal City would require many characters representing the people most affected by American internment in the war: the Japanese immigrant community—Nikkei—including first-generation Issei and their second-generation Nisei children. *Colorado's Japanese Americans from 1886 to the Present* by Bill Hosokawa was a wonderful starting point in helping me understand the Japanese community in World War II Denver. The locations and institutions that I cite, like the California Street church and the *Rafu Shimpo* newspaper, a California newspaper with more national distribution, were all real. *City Girls: The Nisei Social World in Los Angeles 1920–1950* by Valerie J. Matsumoto is a fascinating and meticulous examination of what it meant to be a Japanese American teenager at the time. *Letters from the 442nd* by Minoru Masuda is a moving collection of correspondence written by a Japanese American medic in the 442nd division.

Other must-read memoirs of individual Japanese families in internment include: *Farewell to Manzanar* by Jeanne

Wakatsuki Houston and James D. Houston; *Silver Like Dust* by Kimi Cunningham Grant; and *Looking Like the Enemy* by Mary Matsuda Gruenewald.

It would be horribly negligent to not mention, also, two books in particular about Crystal City. *The Train to Crystal City* is Jan Jarboe Russell's comprehensive nonfiction account of Crystal City's lifespan, and of the political machinations that made its existence possible. On several occasions in the National Archives, archivists mentioned, "Oh, another researcher was looking for this document a few years ago; let me think..." and they were invariably talking about Jarboe Russell's work. *Schools Behind Barbed Wire* by Karen L. Riley is specifically about the camp's three schools—federal, German, and Japanese—and provided insights into the unique experiences of teenagers in the camp.

There is nothing more important than hearing about history directly from the people who lived it. William McWhorter at the Texas Historical Commission provided oral history interviews and transcripts of several former Crystal City prisoners. In addition, the oral histories available at the nonprofit website Telling Their Stories, and at Densho, an organization dedicated specifically to preserving history related to the Japanese internment, are priceless resources.

A few particularly moving accounts from Densho: Kay Uno Kaneko, a Crystal City internee, who talked about being proud of her brother for enlisting in the US Army, but worrying about what would happen to him if her family was repatriated to Japan. Ernest Uno, Kay's brother, who talked about what it was like to come to visit his family in Crystal City after fighting for the 442nd Regiment, interacting with the family he hadn't seen in months in the administrative "visitors' cottage," under guard. Irene Najima, who talked about watching her father, under the strain of confinement, become a person she struggled to recognize, accusing her mother of having affairs.

The German American Internee Coalition has its own moving repository of family histories: Rose Marie Neupert wrote about the appalling living conditions on Ellis Island, where her family was held before being transferred to Crystal City. John Schmitz wrote about the FBI knocking on his family's door because neighbors had heard his father listening to German music on the record player.

Every one of the above accounts and resources is more important than anything fictitious I could ever write.

None of the specific personal stories in them ended up directly in *The War Outside*, which is a work of fiction. Haruko's and Margot's stories were completely made-up. But they became very real to me.

By the end of Haruko and Margot's journey, they are seeing the same act in two very different ways. Did Margot do an unforgivable thing, as Haruko thinks she did? Or is the terrible thing justified, as Margot believes it is, because she feels that the only way to ensure the safety of Haruko's family is to end their lives as they know it?

I kept asking myself that during my months of writing and thinking and research. I am still asking myself that now.

ACKNOWLEDGMENTS

I am deeply grateful to the editorial and publicity team at Little, Brown Books for Young Readers, in particular Lisa Yoskowitz, who constantly amazes me with her curiosity, tenacity, and gentleness, and Jessica Shoffel, for whom the word *unflappable* was surely invented. These women, along with my husband, Robert Cox, and my agent, Ginger Clark, are the people I would choose to have with me in any foxhole, any emergency, or any celebration.

Librarians have been my longtime heroes; with this book I add archivists to that list, especially the ones in Texas and at DC's National Archives, who helped unearth the primary sources without which *The War Outside* would have been impossible.

I also offer a special debt of gratitude to a few of the book's early readers: Kimi, who shared her Nisei family member's American nicknames, and who explained the nuances of Japanese terms of endearment; Joseph, who shared thoughts on Haruko's relationship with her father; Saho, who offered perspectives on displays of affection in Japanese families and who, along with another reader, Maiko, parsed the difference between the concepts of *shitsuke* and *oyakoko*.

ACKNOWLEDGMENTS

My deepest thanks go to curator and historian Brian Niiya, whose notes on an early draft's accuracy were as thoughtful as they were thorough: Did I have proper sourcing on what the Crystal City latrines looked like? Should I place a fictional article in the Denver-local *Rocky Shimpo* newsletter, or would the larger national *Rafu Shimpo* be a more likely place for the article to have appeared? If I diverted from historical timeline or historical fact, did I have a good enough reason for it, beyond making my authorial life easier?

Brian's mother was incarcerated in Crystal City in her youth. His notes were a constant reminder that in historical fiction, you owe accuracy and truth to future readers, but you owe it to past survivors even more.

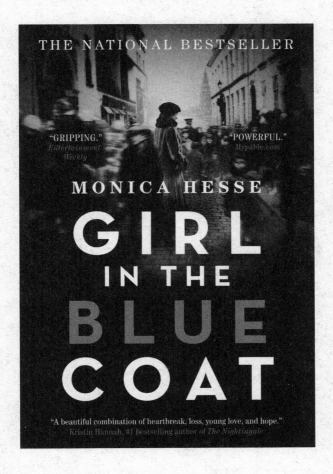

A long time before Bas died, we had a pretend argument about whose fault it was that he'd fallen in love with me. *It's your fault,* he told me. *Because you're lovable.* I told him he was wrong. That it was lazy to blame his falling in love on me. Irresponsible, really.

I remember everything about this conversation. It was in his parents' sitting room, and we were listening to the family's new radio while I quizzed him for a geometry exam neither of us thought was important. The American singer Judy Garland was singing "You Made Me Love You." That was how the conversation began. Bas said I'd made him love me. I made fun of him because I didn't want him to know how fast my heart was pounding to hear him say the words *love* and *you* in the same sentence.

Then he said it was my fault, also, that he wanted to kiss me.

Then I said it was his fault if I let him. Then his older brother walked in the room and said it was both of our faults if he got sick to his stomach listening to us.

It was only later that day, when I was walking home—back when I could walk home without worrying about being stopped by soldiers or missing curfew or being arrested—that I realized I'd never said it back. The first time he said he loved me, and I forgot to say it back.

I should have. If I'd known what would happen and what I would find out about love and war, I would have made sure to say it then.

That's my fault.

ONE

Tuesday

*H*allo, sweetheart. What do you have there? Something for me?"

I stop because the soldier's face is young and pretty, and because his voice has a wink in it, and because I bet he would make me laugh during an afternoon at the movies.

That's a lie.

I stop because the soldier might be a good contact, because he might be able to get the things that we can't get anymore, because his dresser drawers are probably filled with row after row of chocolate bars and socks that don't have holes in the toes.

That's also not really the truth.

But sometimes I ignore the whole truth, because it's easier to pretend I'm making decisions for rational reasons. It's easier to pretend I have a choice.

I stop because the soldier's uniform is green. That's the only reason I stop. Because his uniform is green, and that means I have no choice at all.

"That's a lot of packages for a pretty girl."

His Dutch is slightly accented, but I'm surprised he speaks it so well. Some Green Police don't speak it at all, and they're annoyed when we're not fluent in German, as if we should have been preparing our entire lives for the day when they invaded our country.

I park my bicycle but don't dismount. "It's exactly the right number of packages, I think."

"What have you got in them?" He leans over my handlebars, one hand grazing into the basket attached to the front.

"Wouldn't you like to see? Wouldn't you like to open *all* my packages?" I giggle, and then lower my eyelashes so he won't see how practiced this line is. With the way I'm standing, my dress has risen above my knee, and the soldier notices. It's navy, already tighter than it should be, frayed at the hem and several years old, from before the war. I shift my weight a little so the hemline rides even higher, now halfway up my goose-bumped thigh.

This interaction would feel worse if he were older, if he were wrinkled, if he had stained teeth or a sagging belly. It would be worse, but I would flirt the same anyway. I have a dozen times before.

He leans in closer. The Herengracht is murky and fish-stinking behind him, and I could push him into this canal and ride halfway home on my disgrace of a secondhand bicycle before he paddled himself out. It's a game I like to play with every Green Police who stops me. *How could I punish you, and how far would I get before you caught me?*

"This is a book I'm bringing home to my mother." I point to the first parcel wrapped in paper. "And these are the potatoes for our supper. And this is the sweater I've just picked up from mending."

"*Hoe heet je?*" he asks. He wants to know my name, and he's asked it in the informal, casual way, how a confident boy would ask a bucktoothed girl her name at a party, and this is good news because I'd much rather he be interested in me than the packages in my basket.

"Hanneke Bakker." I would lie, but there's no point now that we all carry mandatory identification papers. "What's *your* name, soldier?"

He puffs out his chest when I call him *soldier*. The young ones are still in love with their uniforms. When he moves, I see a flash of gold around his neck. "And what's in your locket?" I ask.

His grin falters as his hand flies to the pendant now dangling just below his collar. The locket is gold, shaped like a heart, probably containing a photograph of an apple-faced German girl who has promised to remain faithful back in Berlin. It was a gamble to ask about it, but one that always turns out well if I'm right.

"Is it a photograph of your mother? She must love you a *lot* to give you such a pretty necklace."

His face flushes pink as he tucks the chain back under his starched collar.

"Is it of your sister?" I press on. "Your little pet dog?" It's a difficult balance, to sound the right amount of naive. My words need to have enough innocence in them that he can't justify getting angry with me, but enough sharpness that he'd rather get rid of me than keep me here and interrogate me about what I'm carrying. "I haven't seen you before," I say. "Are you stationed on this street every day?"

"I don't have time for silly girls like you. Go home, Hanneke."

When I pedal away, my handlebars only barely shake. I was mostly telling him the truth about the packages. The first three do hold a book, a sweater, and a few potatoes. But underneath the potatoes are four coupons' worth of sausages, bought with a dead man's rations, and underneath those are lipsticks and lotions, bought with another dead man's rations, and underneath those are cigarettes and alcohol, bought with money that Mr. Kreuk, my boss, handed me this morning for just that purpose. None of it belongs to me.

Most people would say I trade in the black market, the illicit underground exchange of goods. I prefer to think of myself as a finder. I find things. I find extra potatoes, meat, and lard. In the beginning I could find sugar and chocolate, but those things have been harder recently, and I can only get them sometimes. I find tea. I find bacon. The wealthy people of Amsterdam stay plump because of me. I find the things we have been made to do without, unless you know where to look.

My last question to the soldier, about whether this street is his new post—I wish he'd answered that one. Because if he's stationed on the corner every day now, I'll have to either consider being friendly to him or change my route.

My first delivery this morning is Miss Akkerman, who lives with her grandparents in one of the old buildings down by the museums. Miss Akkerman is the lotions and lipstick. Last week it was perfume. She's one of the few women I've met who still care so much about these things, but she told me once that she's hoping her boyfriend will propose before her next birthday, and people have spent money for stranger reasons.

She answers the door with her wet hair in pins. She must have a date with Theo tonight.

"Hanneke! Come in while I get my purse." She always finds an excuse to invite me in. I think she gets bored here during the day, alone with her grandparents, who talk too loudly and smell like cabbage.

Inside the house is stuffy and dim. Miss Akkerman's grandfather sits at the breakfast table through the kitchen doorway. "Who's at the door?" he yells.

"It's a delivery, Grandpa," Miss Akkerman calls over her shoulder.

"It's who?"

"It's *for me*." She turns back to me and lowers her voice. "Hanneke, you have to help me. Theo is coming over tonight to ask my grandparents if I can move into his apartment. I need to figure out what to wear. Stay right here; I'll show you my options."

I can't think of any dress that would make her grandparents approve of her living with her boyfriend before marriage, though I know this wouldn't be the first time this war made a young couple reject tradition.

When Miss Akkerman comes back to the foyer, I pretend to consider the two dresses she's brought, but really I'm watching the wall clock. I don't have time for socializing. After telling her to wear the gray one, I motion for her to take the packages I've been holding since I arrived. "These are yours. Would you like to make sure everything's all right?"

"I'm sure they're fine. Stay for coffee?"

I don't bother to ask if it's real. The only way she would have real coffee is if I'd brought it to her, and I hadn't, so when she says she has coffee, she means she has ground acorns or twigs. Ersatz coffee.

The other reason I don't stay is the same reason why I don't accept Miss Akkerman's repeated offer to call her Irene. Because I don't want her to confuse this relationship with friendship. Because I don't want her to think that if one day she can't pay, it doesn't matter.

"I can't. I still have another delivery before lunch."

"Are you sure? You could have lunch here—I'm already going to make it—and then we could figure out just what to do with my hair for tonight."

It's a strange relationship I have with my clients. They think we're comrades. They think we're bound by the secret that we're doing something illegal together. "I always have lunch at home with my parents," I say.

"Of course, Hanneke." She's embarrassed for having pushed too far. "I'll see you later, then."

Outside, it's cloudy and overcast, Amsterdam winter, as I ride my bicycle down our narrow, haphazard streets. Amsterdam was built on canals. The country of Holland is low, lower even than the ocean, and the farmers who mucked it out centuries ago created an elaborate system of waterways, just to keep citizens from drowning in the North Sea. An old history teacher of mine used to accompany that piece of our past with a popular saying: "God made the world, but the Dutch made the Netherlands." He said it like a point of pride, but to me, the saying was also a warning: "Don't rely on anything coming to save us. We're all alone down here."

Seventy-five kilometers to the south, at the start of the occupation two and a half years ago, the German planes bombed Rotterdam, killing nine hundred civilians and much of the city's architecture. Two days later, the Germans arrived in Amsterdam by foot. We now have to put up with their presence, but we got to keep our buildings. It's a bad trade-off. It's all bad trade-offs these days, unless, like me, you know how to mostly end up on the profitable side of things.

My next customer, Mrs. Janssen, is just a short ride away in a large blue house where she used to live with her husband and three sons, until one son moved to London, one son moved to America, and one son, the baby of the family, moved to the Dutch front lines, where two thousand Dutch servicemen were killed when they tried but failed to protect our borders as the country fell in five days' time. We don't speak much of Jan anymore.

I wonder if he was near Bas, though, during the invasion.

I wonder this about everything now, trying to piece together the last minutes of the boy I loved. Was he with Bas, or did Bas die alone?

Mrs. Janssen's husband disappeared last month, just before she became a customer, and I've never asked any more about that. He could have been an illegal worker with the resistance, or he could have just been in the wrong place at a bad time, or he could be not dead after all and instead having high tea in England with his oldest son, but in any case it's none of my business. I've only delivered a few things to Mrs. Janssen. I knew her son Jan a little bit. He was a surprise baby, born two decades after his brothers, when the Janssens were already stooped and gray. Jan was a nice boy.

Here, today, I decide Jan might have been near Bas when the Germans stormed our country. Here, today, I'll believe that Bas didn't die alone. It's a more optimistic thought than I usually allow myself to have.

Mrs. Janssen is waiting at the door for me, which makes me irritated because if you were a German soldier assigned to look for suspicious things, what would you think of an old woman waiting for a strange girl on a bicycle?

"Good morning, Mrs. Janssen. You didn't have to stand out here for me. How are you?"

"I'm fine!" she shouts, like she's reading lines in a play, nervously touching the white curls escaping from her bun. Her hair is always in a bun, and her glasses are always slipping down her nose; her clothes always remind me of a curtain or a sofa. "Won't you come in?"

"I couldn't get as much sausage as you wanted, but I do have some," I tell her once I've parked my bicycle and the door is closed behind us. She moves slowly; she walks with a cane now and rarely leaves the house anymore. She told me she got the cane when Jan died. I don't know if there's something physically wrong with her or if grief just broke her and made her lame.

Inside, her front room looks more spacious than normal, and it takes me a moment to figure out why. Normally, between the china cabinet and the armchair, there is an opklapbed, a small bed that looks like a bookcase but can be folded out for sleeping when guests visit. I assume Mr. Janssen made it, like he made all the things in their house. Mama and I used to walk past his furniture store to admire the window displays, but we never could have afforded anything in it. I can't imagine where the opklapbed has gone. If Mrs. Janssen sold it so soon after her husband's disappearance, she must already be struggling with money, which I won't allow to be my concern unless it means she can't pay me.

"Coffee, Hanneke?" In front of me, Mrs. Janssen disappears into the kitchen, so I follow. I plan to decline her coffee offer, but she's laid out two cups and her good china, blue and white, the famous style from the city of Delft. The table is heavy and maple.

"I have the sausage here if you want to—"

"Later," she interrupts. "Later. First, we'll have coffee, and a stroopwafel, and we'll talk."

Next to her sits a dust-covered canister that smells like the earth. Real coffee beans. I wonder how long she's been saving them. The stroopwafels, too. People don't use their bakery rations for fancy pastries; they use them for bread. Then again, they don't use them to feed black market delivery girls, either, but here is Mrs. Janssen, pouring my coffee into a porcelain cup and placing a stroopwafel on top so that the waffle sandwich softens in the steam and the sugary syrup inside oozes around the edges.

"Sit, Hanneke."

"I'm not hungry," I say, even as my stomach betrays me with a growl.

I *am* hungry, but something makes me nervous with these stroopwafels, and with how eager Mrs. Janssen is to have me sit, and with the irregularity of the whole situation. Has she called the Green Police and promised to deliver them a black market worker? A woman desperate enough to sell her husband's opklapbed might do such a thing.

"Just for a minute?"

"I'm sorry, but I have a million other things to do today."

She stares down at her beautifully set table. "My youngest. Jan. These were his favorite. I used to have them waiting when he came home from school. You were his friend?" She smiles at me hopefully.

I sigh. She's not dangerous; she's just lonely. She misses her son, and she wants to feed one of his old classmates his after-school snack. This goes against all my rules, and the pleading in her voice makes me uncomfortable. But it's cold outside, and the coffee is real, and despite what I just told Mrs. Janssen about my millions of tasks, I actually have an hour before my parents expect me for lunch. So I set the parcel with sausage on the table, smooth down my hair, and try to remember how to be a polite guest on a social call. I knew how to do this once. Bas's mother used to pour me hot chocolate in her kitchen while Bas and I studied, and then she would find excuses to keep checking in to make sure we weren't kissing.

"I haven't had a stroopwafel in a while," I say finally, trying out my rusted conversational skills. "My favorites were always banketstaaf."

"With the almond paste?"

"Mmm-hmm."

Mrs. Janssen's coffee is scalding and strong, a soothing anesthetic. It burns my throat, so I keep drinking it and don't even realize how much I've had until the cup is back on its saucer and it's half empty. Mrs. Janssen immediately fills it to the top.

"The coffee's good," I tell her.

"I need your help."

Ah.

So the purpose of the coffee becomes clear. She's given me a present. Now she wants a favor. Too bad she didn't realize I don't need to be buttered up. I work for money, not kindness.

"I need your help finding something," she says.

"What do you need? More meat? Kerosene?"

"I need your help finding a person."

The cup freezes halfway to my lips, and for a second I can't remember whether I was picking it up or putting it down.

"I need your help finding a person," she says again, because I still haven't responded.

"I don't understand."

"Someone special to me." She looks over my shoulder, and I follow her line of vision to where her eyes are fixed on a portrait of her family, hanging next to the pantry door.

"Mrs. Janssen." I try to think of the right and polite way to respond. *Your husband is gone,* is what I should tell her. *Your son is dead. Your other sons are not coming back.* I cannot find ghosts. I don't have any ration coupons for a replacement dead child.

"Mrs. Janssen, I don't find people. I find things. Food. Clothing."

"I need you to find—"

"A person. You said. But if you want to find a person, you need to call the police. Those are the kinds of finders you want."

"*You.*" She leans over the table. "Not the police. I need *you.* I don't know who else to ask."

In the distance, the Westerkerk clock strikes; it's half past eleven. Now is when I should leave. "I have to go." I push my chair back from the table. "My mother will have cooked lunch. Did you want to pay now for the sausage, or have Mr. Kreuk add it to your account?"

She rises, too, but instead of seeing me to the door, she grabs my hand. "Just look, Hanneke. Please. Just look before you go."

Because even I am not hardened enough to wrench my hand away from an old woman, I follow her toward the pantry and pause dutifully to look at the picture of her sons on the wall. They're in a row, three abreast, matching big ears and knobby necks. But Mrs. Janssen doesn't stop in front of the photograph. Instead, she swings open the pantry door. "This way." She gestures for me to follow her.

Verdorie. Damn it, she's crazier than I thought. We're going to sit in the darkness now, together among her canned pickles, to commune with her dead son. She probably keeps his clothes in here, packed in mothballs.

Inside, it's like any other pantry: a shallow room with a wall of spices and preserved goods, not as full as it would have been before the war.

"I'm sorry, Mrs. Janssen, but I don't know—"

"Wait." She reaches to the edge of the spice shelf and unlatches a small hook I hadn't noticed.

"What are you doing?"

"Just a minute." She fiddles with the latch. Suddenly, the whole set of shelves swings out, revealing a dark space behind the pantry, long and narrow, big enough to walk into, too dark to see much.

"What is this?" I whisper.

"Hendrik built it for me," she says. "When the children were small. This closet was inefficient—deep and sloping—so I asked if he would close off part of it for a pantry and have the other part for storage."

My eyes adjust to the dimness. We're standing in the space under the stairs. The ceiling grows lower, until, in the back, it's no more than a few feet off the ground. Toward the front, there's a shelf at eye level containing a half-burned candle, a comb, and a film magazine whose title I recognize. Most of the tiny room is taken up by Mrs. Janssen's missing opklapbed, unfolded as if waiting for a guest. A star-patterned quilt lies on top of it, and a single pillow. There are no windows. When the secret door is closed, only a slim crack of brightness would appear underneath.

"Do you see?" She takes my hand again. "This is why I cannot call the police. The police cannot find someone who is not supposed to exist."

"The missing person."

"The missing girl is Jewish," Mrs. Janssen says. "I need you to find her before the Nazis do."

ROBERT COX

MONICA HESSE

is the bestselling author of *Girl in the Blue Coat, American Fire*, and *The War Outside*, as well as a columnist at the *Washington Post*. She lives outside Washington, DC, with her husband and their dog. Monica invites you to visit her online at monicahesse.com and on Twitter @MonicaHesse.

HISTORICAL FICTION FROM
BESTSELLING AUTHOR
MONICA HESSE

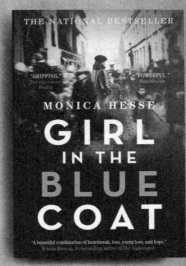

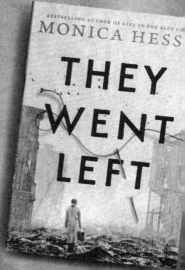

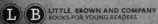